SILENT
RAIN

ALSO BY KARIN SALVALAGGIO

Walleye Junction

Burnt River

Bone Dust White

SILENT RAIN

Karin Salvalaggio

MINOTAUR BOOKS
NEW YORK

SILENT RAIN. Copyright © 2017 by Karin Salvalaggio Ltd. All rights reserved. Printed in the United States of America. For information, address St. Martin's Press, 175 Fifth Avenue, New York, N.Y. 10010.

www.minotaurbooks.com

LIBRARY OF CONGRESS CATALOGING-IN-PUBLICATION DATA

Names: Salvalaggio, Karin, author.
Title: Silent rain / Karin Salvalaggio.
Description: First Edition. | New York : Minotaur Books, 2017.
Identifiers: LCCN 2017002710| ISBN 9781250078933 (hardcover) | ISBN 9781466891487 (e-book)
Subjects: LCSH: Women detectives—Montana—Fiction. | Murder—Investigation—Fiction. | BISAC: FICTION / Mystery & Detective / Women Sleuths. | FICTION / Mystery & Detective / Police Procedural. | GSAFD: Mystery fiction.
Classification: LCC PR6119.A436 S55 2017 | DDC 823/.92—dc23
LC record available at https://lccn.loc.gov/2017002710

Our books may be purchased in bulk for promotional, educational, or business use. Please contact the Macmillan Corporate and Premium Sales Department at 1-800-221-7945, extension 5442, or by e-mail at MacmillanSpecialMarkets@macmillan.com.

First Edition: May 2017

10 9 8 7 6 5 4 3 2 1

To that man who dismissed my chances as a writer and

that friend who dismissed him as a chancer.

I needed both of you.

Acknowledgments

I'm fortunate to have not one, but two wonderful literary agents—Felicity Blunt and Kari Stuart, your continuing support means the world to me. Special thanks to Elizabeth Lacks and all the talented people at Minotaur Books and St. Martin's Press. I couldn't do this without you. Thank you, David Breck, Hayden Breck, Chelsea Kaderavek, and all the wonderful people at Bridger Brewing, Montana for feeding me beer, pizza, and inspiration—Bone Dust White Ale is divine! Police Officer Andrew Steinbrecher, our coffee morning was both enlightening and entertaining. I also learned a great deal sitting down with roller derby queen and jewelry designer Rjika Weis. Rebecca Hearst, our evening exploring Bozeman and continuing conversations online have provided valuable insight into day to day life in Montana. Many thanks to all of you for taking the time to speak to little old me! I'm forever grateful to Alison Lee and Lynn Noyce, two friends who are always available to answer questions about fine art and medicine—you continue to amaze me with all your accomplishments. I'm also indebted to the singularly gorgeous (and surprisingly daring) Amber Lindstrom for introducing me to Alex Van Nice, a crack shot who spent the day with Amber, Karen Breck, and me at the Matanuska Valley Sportmen's Range in Palmer, Alaska. It was a private tutorial I will never forget. And finally, my dear children, Matteo and Daniela—there are simply not enough ways to say how much your love and support means to me.

*"And this is the forbidden truth, the unspeakable taboo—
that evil is not always repellent but frequently attractive;
that it has the power to make of us not simply victims, as
nature and accident do, but active accomplices."*

—Joyce Carol Oates

SILENT RAIN

1

Halloween Night—Monday

The man standing shoulder to shoulder with Grace in the crowded Main Street bar took a sip of whiskey and let out a wistful sigh.

"If only a woman could make me feel this good inside," he said.

Grace studied her own drink. The Long Island Iced Tea that sat before her was so vast and dark it appeared bottomless. She had a taste but did not sigh.

"You're expecting a lot from a beverage," she said.

The man's laugh twisted into a rattling cough that cut him someplace deep inside. He was teary-eyed when he spoke again.

"Actually, I'm expecting a lot from a woman."

Their reflections were visible in the mirror above the bar. The man's long face floated like an apparition among the shelves of bottled spirits while Grace's distorted image was nestled within the long-stemmed martini glasses. She didn't recognize herself at first glance, disguised as she was in a Halloween costume. She'd traded her short dark bob for a wig of long wavy blond hair topped with a glittering tiara she'd borrowed from a friend. Normally partial to vintage dresses not seen since the 1950s, she wore a long pink prom dress draped with a red sash. The man caught her eye in the mirror and winked.

"I bet you're prettier when you smile," he said.

"I'll take that under advisement," she deadpanned.

"You can take it however you like. My advice is free."

He whipped a comb out of a pocket of his leather jacket and slicked back his jet-black hair. The long fringes that hung from the sleeves danced in the air between them. A small trophy sat on the perfectly polished bar next to his drink. Grace touched the shiny metal statuette of Elvis with her fingertips. It wasn't cold like she expected. She tapped it with her fingernail. Definitely plastic.

Every year the K-Bar on Main Street held a themed costume party on Halloween night. This year you had to dress up like Elvis or Priscilla Presley if you wanted to be considered for the grand prize but they'd added a twist for Elvis impersonators. You not only had to look like the King, you had to dance like him too. The prize money had been set at $500. Grace and her friends had arrived in costume but too late to see the show.

"Did you win?" she asked.

"Wasn't difficult," he said, shrugging like it was nothing. "The competition here tonight was pretty amateurish."

Grace almost laughed but then corrected herself. Laughing would mean smiling and she wasn't in the mood. Besides, it sounded like he took pride in his achievements and there was nothing wrong with that.

"I'm curious," she said, drawing her words out more than she normally would because she was a little drunk. "Are you a professional Elvis impersonator?"

He placed a business card on the bar between them.

"Best gig in the world," he said.

His voice was honeyed with that unique Elvis baritone. Grace had to admit she found it attractive. She read the card. The man standing next to her wasn't just Elvis. He was also Conway Twitty, Neil Sedaka, and Neil Diamond. Among other things he was available for corporate events, weddings, birthday parties, and bar mitzvahs. He posted videos of his performances on his Web site.

"May I take this?" said Grace.

He nodded. "My number is on it. Call me anytime."

Grace slipped the card into a slim gold purse. She wouldn't be calling this particular Elvis but she might stalk him online for a bit. She had to admit that she was curious. He was an older man. She wondered how he still managed to swivel his hips like Elvis. He certainly had swagger and it was the first time she'd met someone, male or female, who could pull off wearing tight leather trousers.

"So, what do you say, little lady?" he persisted. "A little smile for the best Elvis impersonator in Bolton?"

Grace forced her lips into a grin of sorts.

"I suppose that's a start," he said, opening a wallet stuffed with bills. "Can I buy you a drink?"

Grace held up her twelve-ounce Long Island Iced Tea, her version of a trophy.

"Thank you, but I'm spoken for."

She made a point of glancing over her shoulder as if indicating that someone out there in the crowded barroom was eagerly awaiting her company.

"No worries," he said, picking up his drink and trophy and moving on. He tipped an imaginary hat. "Have a good evening."

Grace slid her drink a little farther along the bar where she settled onto an empty stool next to two guys dressed as priests. She didn't like when men told her to smile. Being pretty was all well and good but she wanted to be taken more seriously these days. Besides, she'd been groped far too many times over the course of the evening to be in the mood for smiling. The guys frequenting the bars on Main Street would no doubt hold up their hands and say it was an accident, but Grace and her girlfriends knew better. To be fair, it did always seem worse on Halloween night. People didn't consider themselves bound by the usual rules of decorum when they were dressed up as someone else. It didn't help that everyone was drunk, herself included. Lines were being crossed everywhere she looked.

Grace once again checked her reflection in the mirror above the bar. Her wig and tiara were slightly askew so she straightened them, tucking her black hair in where it was poking through. The tiara was on loan from her girlfriend Lara, and Grace was under strict instructions to look after it. Whether it was an actual prom-queen tiara was a matter of debate. For someone known for oversharing online, Lara was very cagey about her comfortably middle-class roots. Apparently, it was much cooler if a debut novelist's parents were blue collar or, better yet, unemployed and, above all else, Lara dreamed of becoming a novelist.

They'd gone shopping together at a secondhand store for the prom dress Grace was wearing. Lara had gone into hysterics every time Grace had emerged from the changing room. When the cashier asked Grace if it was for a special occasion, Grace didn't have the heart to tell her she was going home to pour fake blood all over it. So far the costume had been an utter failure. Everyone she'd come across had thought she'd dressed up as a murderess version of Priscilla Presley.

Grace saw someone's reflection in the mirror and nearly tipped over her drink as she swung around to have a better look. She scanned the crowd near the front doors, slipping down from the barstool when she realized who she'd seen. A man she knew only as Jordan was standing by himself near the entrance. At around five foot nine with light brown hair and a beard, there wasn't anything remarkable about him. Grace guessed he was at least thirty but may have been older. When he'd first started coming into the coffee shop where she worked she'd thought he was a lonely guy, but her opinion changed when she'd caught him taking her picture. She really should have confronted him or, better yet, called the police. Soon after, he started showing up for all her shifts. A week later she noticed he was tailing her as she drove through town, his dusty green Bronco filling her rearview mirror every time she checked.

Jordan was no more determined than the others who'd managed to track her down, but this time she'd decided to wait a little longer before calling the police as she was hoping he'd eventually lose interest and leave town if she ignored him. Jordan was her fifth stalker in two years and she was pretty sure the local authorities were tired of hearing from her. The last police officer she'd spoken to had seemed impatient to take down the details and get her out of his office. Afterward, she'd spotted him speaking to a colleague. He'd nodded his head in her direction and laughed.

Now she was worried she'd left it too late. Jordan didn't seem as harmless as he was at the beginning, when he'd stammered through his coffee order and then blushed when she'd asked him his name so she could write it down on the takeaway cup. Instead of backing off, he now seemed emboldened. Grace was beginning to think he could be violent but that wasn't what concerned her most. She was more frightened that he might want to speak to her about the events that took place in Collier, a small town in northern Montana where she'd lived until she was eighteen. The case had been in the news for months and every detail of her life had been exposed, but that didn't stop people from wanting to know more. Grace had told her side of the story only once and she wouldn't be making that mistake again.

She headed into the crowd that had gathered near the doors leading out onto the back patio. She needed to find her friend Lara. One of the many hard-won lessons she'd learned growing up in Collier was that strange men like Jordan were to be avoided at all costs.

Grace heard Lara before she saw her. Lara was happiest when she had the full attention of the opposite sex, and at present she was smiling broadly as she stood next to a dark-eyed Elvis impersonator dressed in army fatigues. Her eyes were at half-mast and her long white arms waved about like fragile fairy wings. She raised her phone high and shushed the group surrounding her. Years of smoking had made her voice a husky mess.

"I'm going to get a photo of every Elvis in this shit hole tonight." Lara swung her camera in a slow arc, losing focus on her task when she caught sight of Grace.

"That drink better have my name on it," said Lara. She moved toward Grace, looking determined.

"It was a gift from a bartender who owes me for a free coffee," said Grace, a little unsteady on her feet. "I'm only too happy to share the spoils. Truthfully," she slurred. "I think I'm a little wasted."

Lara plucked the glass from Grace's hand and downed half of it in one go. Keeping to the bar's Elvis theme, Lara had dressed as Priscilla, the early years. Despite hours in costume she still looked fresh and alive. Grace, on the other hand, was wilting. She wanted to go home and was hoping Lara felt the same way.

Lara leaned in, eyes wide. She touched the tip of Grace's nose. "Perk up, babe."

Grace started to speak but Lara shushed her.

"What do you think of Hawaiian Elvis?" said Lara.

Lara pointed to a gathering of Elvis wannabes perched around some high tables. Grace had to admit that the odds were in Lara's favor. There wasn't a single Priscilla in sight.

Grace let Lara drag her across the room. Most people thought Lara was difficult company, but Grace was too grateful for their improbable friendship to take much notice. Lara had moved into Grace's spare bedroom eighteen months earlier. Grace hadn't grown up with girl-friends, shared secrets, and sleepovers, so she didn't really under-stand the dynamics as well as she should have at nearly twenty-one years of age. She'd learned to fake her way through most situations, but living in close quarters had proved to be a unique challenge. Thank-fully, Lara seemed oblivious to Grace's missteps. She introduced Grace to all her friends and even arranged a fake driver's license for Grace so they could go out together. Grace had never before felt so carefree. Grace returned the favor by overlooking Lara's worse excesses. There'd been a lot of men and a great deal of alcohol consumed since she moved in. There'd also been a lot of tears. When Lara was upset she drank and slept around. When Grace was upset she packed her bags and threatened to run home to Collier, a town where there were precisely zero people waiting for her. It had been Lara who'd convinced Grace to stay in Bolton when everything fell apart.

"Hawaiian Elvis does have a touch of the exotic about him," said Grace. She peered a little closer. "But that may be the fake tan talking."

The Vegas Elvis wore a white satin body suit, cape, and rhinestones, and the Hawaiian Elvis smelled like bronzer and cheap cologne. All product and no substance, the flower lei draped around his thin neck was looking as if it had gone through several seasons, but then again so did his face. He was a lot older than he'd initially appeared. Makeup powdered the deep lines that creased his eyes. There was something else that was odd about him that Grace couldn't quite place. He was a little too jumpy and kept making weird comments. Grace was wedged in tight between the two of them. Grace could tell Lara had already gone off Hawaiian Elvis, no doubt her attention already on some new opportunity. She was dithering with her phone's camera.

Grace was feeling more and more uncomfortable. Vegas Elvis was big, bordering on fat. He didn't so much as hold Grace tight but swallow her whole. He whispered in Grace's ear. He didn't smell of fake tan, he smelled of nylon and sweat.

"I think I might head home. Need a ride?"

Grace focused in on the camera, ignoring Lara's request that she smile.

"Lara, take the damn picture."

Lara stared at the screen on her phone with a barely-there look on her face.

"I got it," she said, waving one of her fairy arms into the air triumphantly. She reached for Grace's hand. "Come on, Grace, let's go find the others. Clare is over there somewhere." She smiled. "Made a little rhyme. Clever me."

Grace slid out from Vegas Elvis's embrace. His thick fingers lingered on her neck. She shuddered. As usual she'd managed to pull a couple of weirdos. Hawaiian Elvis pressed his hand to the small of her back and yanked her roughly to one side. Her heel was caught on the hem of the prom dress she was wearing. She nearly toppled over.

"Let her go," said Lara. "We're leaving."

Hawaiian Elvis didn't give up easily.

"What was all that noise you were making a few minutes ago when you were asking us to buy you a drink? Seemed like we were good enough then."

"Don't be an asshole," said Lara, cutting him off cold. "Grace, babe. We gotta go."

"What a couple of bitches," he said, giving Grace a hard shove.

Grace lost her balance and went down hard on a floor that was slick with spilled drinks. She tried to get up but her long dress was tangled around her legs. Lara grabbed her by the arm and pulled her to her feet. She had to shout in Grace's ear to be heard.

"This is shit," said Lara. "Let's get out of here."

Grace could barely stand up straight. She didn't feel right. Everything in her peripheral vision was blurred. Even Lara's voice was distorted. She felt her head. A bump was forming. Grace winced.

"I hit my head."

"Are you going to hurl?"

"Maybe."

"Time to move," said Lara. She raised her voice. "Out of my way, bitches. My girl is going to hurl." She laughed. "Another rhyme."

They huddled together on the wooden walkway in front of the bar. It was much cooler outside. Brittle autumn leaves skirted across the pavement and the American flag whipped around on its pole like a dancer. Their friend Clare's car wasn't parked across the street anymore.

"Damn, I'm freezing," said Lara.

"Where's Clare?" asked Grace. "Our coats are in her car."

"No idea. She was in a bit of a mood." Lara waved her cigarette in the air. "It may be something I said."

"Nothing new there."

"We should go back inside and wait for her."

"No, thanks. It's that time of night when everything gets a little weird."

Lara lit a cigarette and drew deeply. "Some guys get so agro when they drink. It's boring."

Grace felt unsteady. "Well, I'm through for the night. I can barely stand up straight."

"I hear you. All this drinking is getting me nowhere. I need to focus on my writing."

Grace held tight to the wooden walkway's railing. Their conversation had landed on familiar territory. Lara hadn't been able to work on her new novel for weeks. She'd sit for hours, declare it was all crap, and delete everything she'd written. All Grace had to do was say the same things she always did and it would be fine.

"Sounds good," said Grace. "Stop messing around so much and focus on what matters. Writing is what keeps you sane."

Lara pulled her hair back from her face. For someone with so much bravado she looked incredibly vulnerable.

"It's getting embarrassing. I made all that noise about getting published and nothing has happened." Cigarette ash flicked into the wind. "I think my agent is going to dump me if I don't get a contract soon."

"You're not going to get dumped. Aren't you their wunderkind? Tomorrow you can make a new start. "

"Tomorrow I'll be too hungover to do much of anything."

"Same here." Grace checked to see if Jordan was loitering nearby. Satisfied, she started to make a move. "I'm going home now. Do you want to come?"

"We really should find Clare first."

"Her car's gone so I bet she's gone too."

"We'll freeze without our coats," said Lara.

Grace adjusted her faux fur cape so it covered her shoulders.

"No one is freezing. Fifteen minutes and we're home."

Lara stubbed out her cigarette. "I'll go find Clare. She'll be pissed if she thinks we left without her. Are you really going to be okay on your own?"

"Better on my own than hanging out with fat Elvis," said Grace, thinking heels or not, she'd run all the way home if she had to.

A historic residential neighborhood separated Main Street and the small liberal arts college where Grace was majoring in art. The crowded bars were only a few blocks away, but here it seemed everyone had already gone to sleep. Mature trees arched gracefully over well-tended lawns and wide driveways. Streetlamps glowed at precise intervals and light pooled beneath deep front porches.

Grace ran with her arms spread wide and her high heels slapping the empty stretch of sidewalk, bursting into laugher every time she stumbled. Halfway home she bent over and clutched her side. She took a few deep breaths before continuing at a slower pace. The night air didn't feel as cold here among the houses and sheltering trees. The long hem of her prom dress dragged on the ground, picking up twigs, leaves, and candy wrappers. She occasionally stopped to admire the Halloween decorations draped from every house.

A bowl of candy had been left on the front steps of a particularly grand red brick home. Grace stopped to pick through the remains before settling back on the wide sloping front lawn. She worked her way through several miniature candy bars, tossing the wrappers over her shoulder one by one. She pulled off one of her shoes and held it up to the porch light. It was ruined, but then again so was her foot. The skin was creased and there was a blister the size of a quarter on her left heel. She slipped the other shoe off and laced the straps through her fingertips. It was only ten minutes further to her apartment building. It wouldn't be the first time she'd walked home barefoot.

The bump on the side of her head was tender to the touch. She couldn't figure out what she'd struck as she'd fallen to the floor but assumed it was someone's knee. She felt the top of her head. Lara's tiara was missing. Grace checked the lawn surrounding her before retracing her steps. She'd briefly become entangled in the low-lying branches of an elm tree as she ran down a particularly dark stretch of sidewalk. If the tiara was anywhere to be found, it would be there. She guessed that the tree was a couple of blocks away but she couldn't really be sure of anything except for the fact that she was still very drunk. She lay back on the lawn and flung her arms out to her sides.

Surrender.

She was actually feeling content. Now she just had to make that feeling last longer than the alcohol buzz. She closed her eyes and imagined the childhood home she'd left behind in Collier. She'd recently come across an article in the newspaper. The house on Summit Road had been vandalized. Someone had spray-painted a warning on the garage door. They'd wanted to be sure the world remembered what kind of monster her uncle was. They'd even been thoughtful enough to leave a postscript. Apparently they were hoping he'd *burn in hell*. Grace let her mind drift through the empty rooms they'd once occupied. Her uncle had taught her how to drive, fish, and fire a gun. He'd put a roof over her head when no one else wanted her. Not once did he touch her. Not once did he raise his hand in anger. Not once did Grace meet the monster.

An emergency vehicle's sirens woke Grace from a deep sleep. Her back was damp from lying on the grass and she was shaking from the cold. She fumbled with her phone but no amount of button pushing would bring the dead battery to life. She strained her ears and heard what might have been the dull roar of traffic and crowds along Main Street. She stumbled to her feet and headed toward her apartment, only to turn back a few seconds later. She still needed to find Lara's tiara. A few blocks ahead a fire engine raced through an intersection. Nearby a dog barked from the other side of a garden fence. She held her finger to her lips.

"No need for that," she said. "I won't hurt you, boy."

As Grace made her way along the darkened streets she did a quick tally of the number of drinks she'd consumed. The fact that she and her friends had been to three different bars was very clear in her mind. She'd drunk wine at the first one, but after that it got muddled. She started counting again and was surprised when she'd hit six drinks.

Grace was petite and prone to being underweight so one or two drinks was usually her limit. She couldn't believe she'd managed six. No wonder she'd passed out. She was more surprised that she'd managed to wake up.

The tiara glittered like a Christmas ornament in the low-lying branches of the suspected elm tree. Grace set it back down on her wig, being sure to dig the combs deep into the weave. The beams from a pair of headlights swept across the houses on the opposite side of the street as a car made a sharp right-hand turn and headed toward her. It was the guy that had been following her. Grace pressed her body up against the elm and watched as Jordan's late-model Bronco cruised along the block, its familiar engine rumbling out of tune. She stepped out into the open once he'd passed. One of the car's taillights was out and the other blinked like an eye. She couldn't make out the license plate. The Bronco stopped at the next intersection, but instead of going forward, it reversed at full speed.

Grace ducked through the nearest hedge and took off across a backyard in a sprint, stumbling on the hidden tree roots that snaked beneath the grass. She scrambled through an opening in a fence on the far side of the lawn and continued running across another property. Three more blocks of this and she'd nearly be home. In a break in the treetops she could just make up the dark outline of Pilot Hill, the highest point in the municipal park opposite her apartment building. She stopped running. It didn't matter if she made it home or not. Jordan had been following her around Bolton for two weeks. He would know where she lived by now. As usual she'd let things go for far too long. Now she really had no choice. She had to call the police.

The lights in the back of the next house were still on. She climbed the steps to the porch and stood at the back door. Music was playing inside. It would be okay. All she had to do was knock and ask for help. She leaned her forehead against the door. She didn't want to knock and she certainly didn't want to ask for help. The people who tracked her down were mostly harmless; they usually moved on after a few days. She imagined they had a long list of famous crimes and the people associated with them. Like bird watchers they ticked them off one by one. As far as they were concerned Grace Adams was just another name.

A window to her right swung open and a man leaned outside. He lit a joint and rested his elbows on the sill to smoke. A woman laughed as she put her arms around him. He shrugged her off. She tried holding him again and he raised his voice.

"You really need to stop smothering me," he said.

"Quit coming over if that's the way you feel."

A door slammed somewhere in the house. The man flicked some ash onto the porch and took another drag. Grace was only a few feet away from him. If he looked in her direction he'd see her standing there looking ridiculous in a soiled prom dress, her shoes missing. A wooden board creaked beneath her bare feet and the man's head snapped up.

"Who's there?"

Grace didn't answer. She was ready to run if she had to. By the time he made it outside, she'd be long gone.

"I see you." He struck another match and cupped the flame. "What are you doing hiding back here?"

"I was scared," said Grace.

He frowned. "You're all alone in the dark. It's not exactly surprising."

"I'll go now. I'm sorry for trespassing."

"Ain't my house so I don't give a shit. Want some?" he asked, holding up the joint. It was burned halfway down and looked like it had spent a long time in someone's back pocket.

Grace said a quiet no.

"Do you need to come in and call someone?" he asked.

"It's okay, I'm fine now. I just had a scare."

"It's Halloween. Isn't that what you signed up for? Come into the light. I want to see what you're wearing."

Grace shuffled past him with her head down. She had no interest in showing off her costume. She was embarrassed and wanted to go home.

"It's a lame costume," she said. "No one knew who I was."

"Let me have a guess."

Grace stopped and looked up at him. He was older, probably in his late thirties, but had long hair. He didn't look anything like Peter Pan but she could tell he was the type of man who never grew up.

"I know exactly who you are," he said.

Grace checked that her blond wig and tiara were still in place. Her disguise was intact. He couldn't know who she really was so she played along.

"I'll give you three guesses," she said.

"I don't need three guesses. It's obvious. You're Carrie. Great movie, by the way."

"You're the first person I've met tonight who's heard of it."

"You need to hang out with a better class of friends. Are you sure you're okay out there on your own?"

"Thank you but I'm fine. I just want to get home."

He held up his hands. "Suit yourself. I'm not going to ask again." He tilted his head. "Hear those sirens? There's fires all over town tonight. I saw it on the news. Apparently, there's a house on Madison . . ."

"Probably just kids." Grace started down the steps. "I should go. My friends will be worried."

"Don't let anyone give you any shit," he said. "As I recall, Carrie got her own back in that film."

"Thanks for that."

"No need to thank me. I didn't do anything."

He'd done more than he realized. Grace was no longer scared. Jordan was a coward. She'd been through too much in her life to let someone like him frighten her.

Grace took a shortcut through the narrow side yard and headed east, sticking to the long shadows thrown down by a fence bordering the sidewalk. She was on more familiar ground but that didn't ease her troubled mind as much as it should have. Peter and Hannah Granger's house was a short distance away. There was a time when Grace had felt like she was part of their family, but now she was careful to avoid Madison Road. Peter refused to speak to her since kicking her out of his writing workshop, and Hannah ignored Grace when they passed each other in the halls of the college's art department, where Hannah was a professor. Grace had not coped well with her sudden exile. There'd been nights she'd been so miserable that she'd wanted to give up on college and go back home to Collier. She was still in Bolton only because Lara had hidden her car keys when those feelings had become overwhelming.

A police car sped past with its emergency lights on, only slowing as it turned onto Madison Road. Several people were gathered on the corner. Some stood alone and silent while others spoke among themselves. Their faces glowed warm and bright in reflected light. Grace smelled smoke before she saw flames. She rounded the corner and nearly tripped into the road. For a few seconds she couldn't understand what she was seeing.

Two fire engines and several patrol cars were parked in front of what was left of Peter and Hannah's home. Plumes of thick black smoke rose into the night sky as the fire engulfed the upper and lower floors. Paramedics were treating a fireman for smoke inhalation. He sat on the back bumper of an ambulance with an oxygen mask pressed to his face. A police officer shouted a question in the fireman's ear and the fireman slowly shook his head. Grace made her way to the police barrier. Two officers stood with their backs to the growing crowd. She was about to tap the closest officer on the shoulder when Lara came rushing up. Her mascara had pooled in the hollows beneath her eyes. She grabbed hold of Grace with both hands and shook her hard.

"Oh my God, Grace. Where have you been?" Lara held up her phone as evidence. "I've been trying to call you."

Grace swallowed back the lump that was forming in her throat. She couldn't take her eyes off the house.

"My battery died," said Grace.

Lara twisted Grace around so they were facing each other.

"You scared the shit out of me."

Grace almost said something about Jordan, but now that she was sobering up he no longer seemed as threatening. She didn't trust herself not to have exaggerated what happened.

15

"I passed out on someone's front lawn," said Grace, hoping that would be enough of an explanation.

"You said you'd be okay."

"You probably shouldn't trust drunk people when they say they're going to be okay."

Grace focused on the small round window positioned above the Granger's front door. Backlit by fire, it glowed like an eye. It was as if Peter Granger was throwing her one last angry glance. She was tempted to throw one right back.

Grace had changed her surname from Adams to Larson before enrolling at Bolton College. For the most part it was easy to hide her past. It turned out that college was full of people who were trying to reinvent themselves, so Grace fit right in. The police only knew she lived in Bolton because she'd asked them for assistance on a few occasions. Jordan wasn't the first man to track her down and wouldn't be the last. She didn't know how these men found her. She'd never spoken to the press and had only used the name Grace Larson online.

Grace was pretty sure it was Lara who'd told Peter Granger her real name. It was just the type of thing Lara would have done to get his attention. Grace had thought of bringing it up but couldn't risk it. Flawed as she was, Lara was the closest thing Grace had to a real friend.

Peter had never really cared for Grace's writing. He'd only asked her to join his writing group because he wanted to write a book based on what had happened to her in Collier. He'd freaked out when she refused to give him permission. Grace had been sitting next to Lara on a sofa in his office when he'd grabbed hold of her shoulders. He shook her so hard her nose started to bleed.

God knows I didn't pick you to join this group because of your writing, which is shit by the way. For weeks you've wasted my time with schoolgirl fantasies. He'd dug his fingers into her shoulders and screamed. *You're Grace Adams for fuck sake. Quit hiding.*

That was the moment she'd told Peter Granger to fuck off.

"I'm trying to figure out why I still care what happens to Peter and Hannah," said Grace.

"You have every reason to hate them," said Lara.

Lara's continued loyalty to Peter had felt like another betrayal. Lara said she didn't have a choice. It was Peter who'd helped her find an agent and had been giving her feedback on her debut novel. He was a famous author. She needed his help to get published.

Grace caught something in Lara's eye.

"Have you finally seen Peter for the asshole he always was?" asked Grace.

"This isn't the time to discuss our issues with the Grangers," said Lara. She steered Grace away from the police officers. "We may have our reasons to hate them, but neither of us would ever wish them dead."

"Were they inside?"

"I don't know. The police won't tell me anything."

"Have you tried calling them?"

"They're not picking up." Lara's fingers flew over her phone's keys. Her voice was measured. "It doesn't mean anything. They could be away somewhere. They're always going on trips."

Grace's teeth were chattering. She needed to go home.

"Did you find Clare?" asked Grace.

"She's on her way. Not sure where Taylor has been all evening, but the fact that she's checked out of our lives again is hardly a surprise."

"Could you call Clare back and tell her to bring our coats?" Grace hesitated. "I've also lost my shoes."

Lara looked down at Grace's bare feet and frowned. "How on earth did you ever survive all these years without me?"

Sparks shot up into the sky as a large section of the roof collapsed and the fire crew scrambled for safer ground. A cloud of dust and ash rolled across the road and blanketed the onlookers. Grit coated Grace's bare skin. She could taste it on her tongue. It stung her eyes. This was all that remained of the home where Grace had once been so welcome. She'd drunk Peter and Hannah's wine, shared their meals, and slept in their spare bedrooms. It was the first time Grace had felt like she was part of a proper family.

She'd met them at a party they'd thrown a year earlier. They'd been very specific when they invited Lara. She was to bring her friend Grace. Grace had thought it was odd but Lara wouldn't let her say no, adding that Grace was her plus one. Grace had been so naive she'd had to ask what that meant. She'd been raised by a man who owned a trucking company and a woman whose life revolved around the church. Artists, authors, and intellectuals were outside her experience. She'd said that she wouldn't fit in but Lara reassured her.

Peter Granger likes you. That poem you read at poetry night at the café blew him away. And you already know Hannah.

I've never spoken to her. She doesn't know I exist.

Lara wasn't having it. *Don't be ridiculous. She thinks your work is fabulous.*

Grace had been taken aback at the way Lara had sauntered into the Granger's house like she owned the place. She was heavier then and favored vibrant, close-fitting dresses. She'd been so flustered after Peter's long hug she'd stumbled over her lines as she introduced Grace. Peter had taken Grace's hand and kissed her on both cheeks.

That was a brilliant little poem you read. We must talk. Be sure to find me later.

Hannah had taken Grace by the arm before she'd had a chance to respond. It had felt strange being singled out when there were so many other guests gathered in the downstairs rooms, each one with a drink and a smile for their hostess. A woman wearing a white shirt and black trousers had handed her a glass of champagne. Grace had felt as if she'd been transported onto a film set. Nothing seemed real. Hannah had led her through the house, introducing her to everyone they met as the rising star in the college's art department. Grace was only halfway through her sophomore year so she'd been surprised Hannah knew anything about her. Hannah was a well-known figure on campus. A retrospective of her paintings was on show at the campus art gallery and her graduate seminars were highly selective. She'd draped an arm around Grace's slim shoulders and squeezed.

Someday soon you'll be my student. She'd held Grace a little tighter. *That's when the fun will really begin. More champagne?*

Peter had been drunk when he'd caught hold of Grace as she was coming out of an upstairs bathroom. If not for the sudden appearance of another guest, Grace may not have been able to slip away unmolested. It was only later that she learned that he and Hannah adhered to a very loose interpretation of their marriage vows.

Grace wrapped her arms around Lara and all she felt were bones. Lara had lost more than twenty pounds in past six months. Her sole focus was getting her book published, but so far there'd been thirty-six rejection letters from publishers and her agent was gently suggesting that Lara start something new. Lara wasn't taking it well. Without anything more than a dream to sustain her, she was slowly wasting away.

Clare arrived at around half past one. She couldn't believe it when she saw what Grace was wearing. They were all the same age, but that didn't stop Clare from trying to mother her. After handing Grace her coat and some snow boots, she slipped her black leather gloves over Grace's blue fingers.

"You need to take better care of yourself," whispered Clare. "It can't be good for you to get so cold."

A man ran up and joined a group that was already gathered near them.

"Man, have you heard what happened at the K-Bar?" he asked. "Someone pulled a knife. It was mental."

Grace pictured the man who'd given her his business card. She hoped he was okay.

Lara sipped coffee from Clare's thermos. "Christ, did you hear that? It must have happened right after I left," she said.

"It was a weird crowd," said Grace. "Lots of guys from out of town."

"My mom is going to freak when she finds out about tonight," said Clare. "She only let me come to Bolton College because she thinks it's safe here."

2

Tuesday

Macy pointed to an empty chair at the kitchen table where her son's scrambled eggs were growing cold. "Luke, for the tenth time, sit down and finish your breakfast."

Luke ran through the living room with a Batman cape tied around his neck. His unruly dark hair stuck out at all angles and he was grinning from ear to ear. He was nearly naked under his cape. Macy was always trying to get more clothing on him but he seemed to run a few degrees hotter than everyone else. She found it came in handy during the cold winter nights when he climbed into her bed. It was like sleeping with a radiator.

Macy got up from the table and went into the kitchen so she could cut him off as he made his usual circumnavigation of the downstairs rooms. Her wet hair was wrapped up in a towel. Unlike Luke she was fully dressed and ready for work. Her suitcase and bag sat next to the door leading out to the garage. She'd only packed for a few days. She was hopeful that was enough.

Macy poked her head around the corner where she stood hidden and waiting for her son.

"Luke?"

Luke shrieked with laughter. Macy turned around and he waved at her from the kitchen table. He held up a spoon and smiled broadly.

"Mommy, sit down ten times!"

Macy was tempted to take her turn running through the downstairs rooms but thought better of it. She didn't have time for games. It took a little over an hour and a half to drive to Bolton from Helena and they were expecting her before lunch. She returned to her seat and made a point of putting on her napkin and sitting up properly. Luke mimicked her every move. She'd found this game of his a little disconcerting until her mother pointed out that it was the perfect way to get Luke to do exactly what you wanted. Macy took a bite of her eggs and so did Luke. She reached for her cup of coffee and Luke reached for his glass of orange juice.

The key turned in the front door and both Macy and Luke looked up. Luke was up and out of his chair like a shot when he heard his grandmother say good morning.

"Grandma is home!" he yelled.

Macy checked the clock above the stove and gave her mother a wry smile. She was tempted to ask Ellen what kind of time she called this but knew better than to make jokes about her mother's walk of shame. Situations like this required delicacy. It had been a little more than three years since Macy's father died of cancer, and Ellen had waited long enough to start dating again. Macy knew her mother had doubts about moving on and teasing her wouldn't help her confidence. But that same sensitivity didn't stop Macy from running a background check on her mother's new boyfriend. For Ellen it was enough to know that Jeff was a doctor. In Macy's eyes it was far more complicated. She'd never again take it for granted that someone was innocent based solely on his or her stature in the community. She'd seen too many cases where that simply wasn't the case.

Ellen picked up Luke and held him tight.

"There's more coffee. Would you like some?" asked Macy.

"No, thank you, Jeff took me out for breakfast at that new restaurant on Fourth."

"Oh, nice. I know the one. How was your evening?"

"Wonderful," said Ellen. She deposited her grandson in his chair and took a seat across from Macy. "We had a last-minute dinner invitation at the home of a couple he's known for years. Turns out I know them too."

"Hardly surprising," said Macy. "You've lived in Helena for nearly forty years. I doubt there are many people you haven't met."

"True," she said, glancing over at Macy's suitcase. "I got your message. Where are you off to this morning?"

"Bolton. There was a fire last night. Too early to say if it's arson, but it looks like a famous author may have died."

"Peter Granger," said Ellen. "I saw it on the news. Wasn't his wife in the house too? She's famous in her own right, you know. A well-known artist. Her work is highly prized."

"And controversial."

"Apparently, that's part of its charm."

"Anyway," said Macy. "All we know for sure is there are two bodies. Given the fire damage, we may have to wait for the state medical examiner to make a formal identification."

"Doesn't Bolton have its own detectives? You're usually farmed out to smaller communities."

"Six detectives on staff, to be exact." Macy wiped her mouth with her napkin and smiled when she noticed Luke was mimicking her again. "There were several fires last night and an incident at one of the bars in town."

"What sort of incident?"

"Drunken, most likely. Some place was holding an Elvis lookalike contest. Things got heated and one Elvis stabbed another Elvis. The victim is in critical condition and the perpetrator is on the run. The Bolton PD have been rounding up Elvis impersonators all night."

"If it wasn't so tragic it would make for great comedy. You can just imagine the line-ups. Doesn't explain why they need six detectives working the case, though."

"I spoke to the chief of police earlier. One of their detectives is taking some time off to deal with family issues and another is out due to illness. They're swamped. Given the fire may have been accidental, they thought it best to hand it over to the state so our crime-scene techs will handle everything, but we'll have a couple of local officers assigned to us and use other support services."

"You said an arsonist was setting fires all over town?"

"A couple of cars, a shed, and a Dumpster. This was the only house that went up in flames. It may not be related."

"I like Bolton. I've often thought it would be a better place to settle long term. There's a bit more going on there."

"You don't have to convince me. I loved living there when I was an undergraduate." Macy checked the time. "I need to scoot," she said. "I hope I haven't spoiled your plans by springing this trip on you last minute."

"Don't be ridiculous," said Ellen. "You have to go where they send you. It's been nice having you here for a few months straight though. We were feeling spoiled."

Macy took Luke's hand and led him into the living room. "I promised to finish the book I've been reading to Luke before I left, so I best get on it."

Ellen started to tidy up the dishes.

"Leave those, Mom. I'll deal with it," said Macy.

Ellen waved her daughter off. "You've got a long day ahead of you. It's the least I can do."

The cars on Main Street moved at a sluggish pace, eventually coming to a full stop in front of the K-Bar, where Bolton Police Department vehicles were parked two-deep. A length of sidewalk was cordoned off and pedestrians loitered at the barrier with their phone cameras held up high. A single reporter stood with a microphone and a camera on a tripod, trying to look appropriately serious. From the waist up he wore a suit and tie, but from the waist down jeans and tennis shoes.

Macy edged past the bar in her state-issue SUV. She could have gone around but had to admit she was as curious as everyone else who'd paused to gawk. This kind of thing didn't normally happen in Bolton where the police department, though pragmatic, had a solid reputation. As a special investigator working for the Montana Department of Justice, she was usually sent to towns where local police departments lacked manpower and facilities. Here in Bolton she would have to be diplomatic. They may have requested her assistance but that didn't mean they weren't territorial. If it turned out Peter Granger and his wife, Hannah, were murdered, it would be a very high-profile case. They might end up regretting their decision to hand it over to the state.

Macy took a right on Dukes Avenue and headed south toward an area famous for its historic homes. Halloween decorations were draped from almost every front porch and autumn leaves carpeted the lawns and sidewalks. Madison Road was blocked off to through traffic. A crime-scene tech van was parked in front of the Granger's residence next to a handful of construction vehicles and police cars. Macy pulled up to the house and checked her phone. There'd been several new messages, but nothing that needed her attention immediately.

It was possible to see straight through what had once been an imposing three-story home. Dark soot covered the sloping front lawn and sidewalk. A chain saw whined as a worker wearing protective gear lopped off dead branches from a badly burned oak tree overhanging the front porch. The neighbors had been lucky. The homes were far enough apart to avoid fire damage, though Macy doubted they'd be able to get the smell of smoke out of their homes for years. According to preliminary reports the fire had spread quickly and burned out of control for hours.

Macy spotted Ryan Marshall and went over to speak to him. Ryan was one of the state's top crime scene investigators and one of Macy's closest colleagues. It was always a relief when she found out they'd be working together. Aside from his protective suit, Ryan was wearing work gloves and a hardhat. His handlebar mustache had grown even more outrageous since she'd last seen him. It was only a matter of time before someone at the Helena office told him to rein it in.

"I'm a little surprised to see you," he said, holding up the crime scene tape for her. "I heard you were in Creek looking for a lost sheriff."

"He wasn't lost, he was dead."

"Any leads?"

"It was suicide. I was there and back in the same day."

Macy studied what was left of the once-grand home. There were lots of photos of the mansion on the Internet. It was considered one of the most historically significant homes in Montana. Following the Granger's extensive restoration, it was featured in a number of national magazines. They'd reportedly spent over a million dollars on the construction work. The amount they'd spent on the artwork and furnishings that packed its rooms was a matter of speculation. Macy was pretty sure the contents would have been insured for millions and the payout to the beneficiary would be enormous. If it turned out to be arson, that had to be looked at as a possible motive.

"So what do we have so far?" Macy asked.

"It's still early so not a great deal, but we've been interviewing the fire crews that were first on the scene. They've been pretty consistent. The fire started low at multiple points of origin and moved fast. The structure is wood framed, but the smoke was pitch-black, much like you expect in the presence of an accelerant like gasoline."

"Any fuel cans found on-site?"

"Not yet. They also noticed that interior doors had been propped open and there was some damage to the ceiling in the living room that didn't look fire related. Someone might have been punching holes and opening doors to create better ventilation. The more oxygen, the faster a fire spreads."

"Are we any closer to establishing a positive ID?" she asked.

"I managed to take a few preliminary photos before the structure was declared unsafe but I can't say much other than our victims are, in all likelihood, a man and a woman. Everything I've learned since then has come from peering through the windows." He pointed to the construction crew milling around a truck carrying heavy steel beams. "We're having to reinforce the building before we can start work. So far we have two bodies in the ground-floor living room lying in a four-poster bed. It's always possible we'll find more fatalities."

"Why is the bed in the middle of living room?"

"The master bedroom is directly over the living room. At some point the ceiling caved in," said Ryan.

"We need to confirm identification as soon as possible."

"That shouldn't be a problem once I have access."

"Who have you been liaising with from the Bolton PD?" asked Macy. "I don't want to put anyone out by not keeping them up to date on developments."

"Same officer who's heading up the Elvis homicide investigation, Detective Brad Hastings." He checked the time. "Should be dropping by soon."

"It's a homicide now? I hadn't realized the victim had died."

"Went into cardiac arrest on the operating table an hour ago. Never woke up. His father is one of the biggest political donors in this part of the state, which is probably why Bolton PD handed us this investigation. Peter and Hannah Granger are from California. Politics are way out in left field, so almost zero local interest from that standpoint."

"There's another way of looking at it. By all accounts the knife attack last night was vicious and unprovoked. Bolton isn't a town that sees that kind of violence. I don't think there's been a murder here in years. The guy is on the loose. There's more of a sense of urgency."

"I hate to break it to the good people of Bolton but, given what the firemen have told us, I think the body count around here is rising fast." He hesitated. "It's a shame. I'd like to think places like this still exist."

"You're showing a softer side this morning. What's up with that?"

"I have my reasons," he said.

Macy kept her voice low. "Did you meet someone?"

"Maybe. Just not willing to elaborate at this point."

"I know how to get you talking. I'll take you out for a drink tonight."

"I quit drinking."

She staggered back a step. "Excuse me?"

Ryan shrugged. "Don't look so shocked. It's only temporary. We decided to do it together. All bets are off come Christmas."

"So, there is someone," said Macy. "Who's the lucky guy?"

"Get this case wrapped up and I'll tell you everything."

"Somewhat out of my control, but I'll do my best."

Macy fell into step next to Ryan as they made their way across the Granger's sloping front lawn.

"Anyway, Mr. Softy, there's still a chance this was an accident," she said. "I had a look online. There are lots of photos of the home's interior. They liked to throw big parties and had a fondness for candlelight."

"I'll keep that in mind when I'm looking for the source of the fire."

"They were also both smokers. Could be as simple as falling asleep with a lit cigarette in that big four-poster bed."

"Couldn't have originated in a bedroom. There were multiple points of origin but they were all on the ground floor. That doesn't happen by accident."

The construction crews were busy erecting a temporary metal frame in the living room. An interior wall bowed precariously. Exposed ceiling beams were hanging down at odd angles.

"They're trying to reinforce what's left of the structure but there's a good chance they'll have to tear a few walls down before we can risk moving in to investigate the site."

"That will delay things a bit," said Macy.

"It will also compromise the crime scene."

Macy knelt down and studied a blackened book page. It crumbled to dust when she touched it. "The fire must have been intense to cause so much damage."

"Didn't help that the fire department was caught up with those other arson attacks that were happening all over town last night. There was a delay getting here." Ryan pointed to what was left of an upstairs window. Ribbons of black drapes fluttered in the breeze. "Given how rapidly the fire spread, I doubt Peter and Hannah Granger could have been saved, but it would be nice if we had a bit more evidence to work with."

"Have the neighbors been interviewed?"

"You'll have to ask Brad Hastings. When I arrived there were cops everywhere."

Macy left Ryan to get on with his work and walked back out into the middle of the road. Quite a few people had gathered next to a police cordon. Some were taking photos. Others were staring. A small group of young women stood apart from the others. They huddled together, clutching coffee cups to their chests like talismans. Given their ages, Macy guessed they could be students from the college. One was weeping on another's shoulder. Two were speaking in low voices. The last was studying her cell phone, a large black dog with a gray muzzle leaned against her legs.

A construction worker shouted out a warning and the crew scattered in all directions as an interior wall collapsed. Supporting timbers snapped under the weight of the upper floors. Several crashed down into the living room. The four-poster bed took a direct hit. In some places the upper floors were now sandwiched on top of one another. A solid oak staircase that was central to the house appeared to be the only thing propping up it up.

Ryan emerged from a cloud of dust.

"We're screwed. Half the ceiling just caved in on our bodies," he said.

"Will we be able to tell what damage is postmortem?"

"Difficult to say at this point. I'll let you know when my team is cleared for access."

"When you saw the victims earlier did you see any indication of foul play?"

"They actually looked as if they could have died in their sleep, which is quite an accomplishment considering they dropped through the ceiling and their bodies were badly burned. I'd show you the photos but I know how you feel about these things."

"I'm trying to grow thicker skin," said Macy.

"I like that you're squeamish. Shows you're human."

"I wish everyone at work saw it like that."

"So, how are we going to proceed?"

"I'm going to run with what the fire crews have told us. At this point they're our only witnesses. Until we know differently I'm going to assume it's arson and we have a murder investigation on our hands." She paused. "Let's keep that out of the press for now though."

A Bolton PD patrol car pulled up to the cordon and the onlookers cleared the way long enough for it to be let through.

"Have you met Hastings before?" asked Ryan.

"Not had the pleasure," she said.

"A bit dull but nice."

"The nice part is all that matters. I'm not expecting him to entertain me. That's your job."

Ryan went off to speak to the construction crew, leaving Macy to wait alone. Brad Hastings was taking his time stepping out into the sunshine. Macy checked the crowd gathered at the police cordon again. The group of young women she'd noticed earlier was walking away. Aside from one who trailed a few steps behind with her dog, they were all still huddled close together. There was something familiar about that last girl.

Macy looked up when her name was called. Detective Brad Hastings waved as he walked toward her. He was a couple inches taller than Macy and wore jeans and a blazer. She guessed him to be in his late thirties. She held out her hand and introduced herself.

"Detective Sergeant Brad Hastings," he said. "It's a pleasure to finally meet you, Detective Greeley."

"Likewise," said Macy. "I'm sorry to hear you've got a homicide investigation on your hands. Any progress?"

"I've been interviewing hungover Elvis impersonators for the past four hours. We've also got a team reviewing all the photos that have been posted online and chasing down anyone who was at the bar last night. Nothing yet." He looked over Macy's shoulder. "This house was quite something. It's a real shame to see it like this."

"Have you ever been inside?"

"A couple of times."

"In a professional capacity?"

Brad nodded. "In July a drunk student wandered in and passed out on their sofa. I happened to be nearby so I took the call. Mr. Granger was pretty angry but the houseguest who found the student asleep on the sofa thought it was funny. No charges were filed. I did warn him to lock the doors in the future."

"Do people often wake up to find drunks sleeping it off on their sofas?"

"It is a surprisingly regular occurrence in Bolton. This neighborhood is between Main Street and the university campus. Students drink too much and when they can't make it home, they decide to try their luck on someone else's couch."

"I was an undergraduate here. I don't remember that."

"Might have to do with the company you kept. It's a dangerous game if you ask me. A lot of people around here keep firearms in their homes. They'd be in their rights to shoot first and call us later."

"What was the house like inside?"

"Quite something . . . a bit like a nice hotel. I'd never seen so many books outside of a library. Lots of paintings on the walls. Knickknacks everywhere. It was a little too cluttered for my taste. I also imagine it was completely out of my budget."

"Did either of them smoke inside the house?"

"The wife wasn't there so I can't say, but the husband definitely smoked inside. He must have gone through half a dozen while I interviewed the girl. He seemed to be highly strung."

"I'm surprised a girl would risk walking into a stranger's house."

"I doubt she was thinking straight. I got the impression she was still drunk when I interviewed her. She seemed very confused."

"You said you've been inside on two occasions."

Brad nodded. "Two months ago there was a restraining order issued against a college student named Pippa Lomax. At the time Peter described her as an overly zealous fan of his novels."

"I'll need her details," said Macy.

"I've already checked on her whereabouts," said Brad. "Given she was in Wisconsin last night there's no way she could have been involved in the fire. According to her father, the girl is on a cocktail of antidepressants and is barely able to use the toilet on her own."

"That's tough. How old is she?"

"Twenty-one." Brad glanced up at the house. "She was part of Peter

Granger's writer's workshop for almost a year. She had a nervous break-down and was institutionalized for two weeks in late September."

"I thought it was his wife who taught at the college?"

"She does. He doesn't. Mr. Granger held a creative writing workshop at his offices at the Bridger Cultural Center."

"Have you interviewed the neighbors?" she asked.

"I sent some officers out late last night and early this morning. No one reported seeing anything unusual."

"Do the Grangers have family in Bolton?"

"No, but they share a personal assistant here in town. She's helping us with our inquiries."

"I should speak to her as soon as possible."

"I'll send you her details. She said she'd be willing to come to the station. Really broken up about what's happened but seems eager to help."

"The house nearly collapsed a few minutes ago, so it might be awhile before we can confirm identity. Any word on the Granger's cell phone usage over the past few days?"

"Hannah Granger's phone has been completely out of action since Saturday morning, when she called a work colleague named Jessica Reynolds. Peter Granger texted his wife's number twenty-three times over the past three days. As far as we can tell she never answered. Last text was sent at around half past three yesterday. We'll get all the records by the end of the day."

"Anyone seen him out and about recently?"

"He cancelled some plans he had on Sunday so he's not been seen since Friday, when he and Hannah had dinner with some friends." Brad handed Macy an envelope. "Warrants to search their offices. Hannah has one on campus and Peter's office is at the Bridger Cultural Center."

"What about their cars? Have they been accounted for?"

"The cars they usually drive are both in the garage, but the four-by-four Tundra they share hasn't been accounted for. There's a BOLO out on it."

. . .

Macy counted three sets of French doors that opened onto the Granger's wraparound porch. There was also what looked like a cellar entrance set into the base of the building's foundation, but the area was covered with heavy debris so Macy couldn't get close enough to have a proper look. The hawthorn hedges that enclosed the back garden were more for privacy than security and the gated fence wasn't locked. It would have been possible to access the backyard without any of the neighbors noticing.

Macy stood as close to the rear windows as she dared. The vast, dimly lit living room stretched from the back to the front of the house. The four-poster bed had made a hole in the ceiling the size of a wading pool when it crashed through from the upper floors. The bed was built from carved wooden posts as thick as tree trunks. Two of the four posts had snapped in half when the crossbeams fell earlier. All Macy could see of the bodies was what looked like a hand. It poked like a crow's foot from the burned black bedding. From a distance it was impossible to tell whether it belonged to a woman or a man. She turned her attention to the remaining interior walls. The paintings that were still hanging were heavily damaged. It didn't look as if anything could be salvaged. Some sections of the walls were bare aside from the vague outlines of paintings that had once hung there. There were thick piles of debris on the floor. It was impossible to tell whether or not the paintings had fallen during the fire.

Macy stood in the middle of the backyard and stared up at the house. It might have been her imagination, but it did appear to be leaning a little more to the right than it had been earlier. A middle-aged woman, wearing garden gloves and holding a pair of pruning shears peeked over the hedge from a neighboring backyard. She started snipping at the nearest bit of greenery when she realized Macy had spotted her.

"Excuse me," said Macy, pulling out her badge and identifying herself. "I'd like a word."

The woman put her basket down and peeled off her gloves. Her fingernails were decorated with pumpkins. Macy had noticed the front of her house as she drove up. The owners had spared no expense on Halloween decorations. Macy suspected they were equally zealous at Christmas, Easter, and the Fourth of July.

The woman held out her hand and introduced herself.

"Julia Dixon," she said, being careful to spell it out so Macy could write it down properly in her notebook. "It's been a horrible shock for all of us in the neighborhood."

"Did you know the Grangers?"

"Only as neighbors. They had their own set of friends. Someone was always coming and going in that house."

"So, you didn't socialize with them?"

"They invited us to a couple of Hannah's shows, and when Peter did events in town they were always kind enough to put an invitation through the door. I didn't really get Hannah's art but I loved Peter's novels." Her eyes widened a fraction. "Have you read them?"

"I'm afraid not," said Macy.

"I've been a fan for years. You can imagine my excitement when I found out he was moving in next door." She paused. "I spoke to a police officer yesterday evening. I didn't see anything last night."

"Your upper rooms overlook their backyard. Are you absolutely sure you didn't see anyone coming or going through the back of the house?"

"Not a thing. The house was quiet." Julia pressed her forefinger to her chin. "In fact, it was unusual for them to not participate. As a rule the houses around here make an effort on Halloween, but their house was dark all evening. Not so much as a pumpkin."

"What about lights in the back or in the upper rooms?"

Julia made a face. "I guess I really can't say for sure. I was out front answering the door most of the evening. There were a lot of people on the streets. Parents, kids, the odd college student trying their luck." She stared at the burned-out shell that was once Hannah and Peter's home. Her voice caught. "It's been kind of quiet the past few days. I thought they were out of town."

Macy handed Julia her business card. "I want you to call me if you think of anything."

"Do you think this was arson? I hear someone was setting a lot of fires around town last night."

The woman shrunk back into her garden. Macy knew what she was thinking. We pay our taxes, we go to church, we love our families and our fellow man, and yet there was this incremental chance that we'll fall afoul of fairness, that someday tragedy could visit us and no amount of firearms, fire alarms, security, or dead bolts will make a difference. Macy threw her a lifeline.

"We have to consider all possibilities at this stage. There's still a good chance this was an accident."

Julia gazed up at her own house. It was a humbler sibling to the burned-out ruins that sat next to it. A child's bicycle was parked next to the back steps. A blond head pressed against the window.

"That's my daughter," said Julia. "I should go."

Macy went to the far end of the Granger's property, where a shed stood among the trees. There was a bench butted up against it. She sat down and watched the workmen move cautiously in and out of the skeletal rooms. Her phone buzzed. It was a message from Brad Hastings. He'd sent her the Grangers' personal assistant's contact details.

Cornelia Hart was older than Macy expected. Heavyset with thinning hair, she had soft doughlike features. She was working hard at trying not to cry. At times her face seemed to cave in on itself and she spoke in a low, restrained manner. They met at the main police station in Bolton, where Macy had been allocated an office and a few members of staff, including a young officer named Alisa Montgomery, who'd only recently joined the force. She'd had one of Peter Granger's books in her hands.

"I can't believe you've not read any of his books. For a male author he had amazing insight into a woman's mind," Alisa had said. "His death is a huge loss for all of us."

Macy had felt the need to caution Alisa. The bodies found at the house on Madison Road had yet to be identified, so there was still a chance Peter and Hannah Granger were very much alive. Alisa trailed alongside Macy. For someone so sturdily built, she was surprisingly light on her feet. She had dark hair and dark eyes and was probably in her mid-twenties.

Macy had stopped at a vending machine as she made her way down the unfamiliar corridors of Bolton's vast police department. The thought of a Snickers bar with a Diet Coke chaser was all that was keeping her sane at the moment. She'd been digging loose change from her pocket when Alisa stepped in front of the machine and splayed her arms like a suffragette. Macy had once again felt the need to caution Alisa.

Alisa had stood her ground. "I'll get you something for lunch at the Co-op" Macy had tried to reach around her but Alisa was firm. "I minored in sports nutrition in college. The quality of the food consumed here at the Bolton PD is appalling. I don't see how anyone has the energy to do their jobs."

Macy had smiled because the alternative would have involved doing Alisa bodily harm. She'd even managed to thank Alisa before sending her off to buy her something appropriately healthy for lunch. Seconds after she'd gone, Macy dropped her coins in the machine and punched in the necessary codes. Consuming a Snickers bar was now a matter of principal.

Cornelia Hart was waiting for Macy in a conference room. Someone had brought her a cup of coffee. She looked up at Macy with watery eyes.

"You didn't have to come into the office," said Macy. "I would have been happy to visit you at your home."

Cornelia stared at Macy for a long moment. "I only know one way to cope when I'm upset, and that's to work . . . to stay busy. Hannah and Peter were like family." A fresh tissue came out. "I owe it to them to see this through." She pulled a stack of files out from a bag and slid it toward Macy. "I wasn't sure what you needed from me."

"What's all this?" said Macy.

"Insurance papers, names of their lawyers, their next of kin. They were both only children and childless so I'm afraid there's not much in the way of family. Peter's father died two years ago and his mother is in a home. Hannah cut off all ties with her parents more than thirty years ago and they've since died." Cornelia took a moment. "I understand the victims haven't been formally identified."

"That is correct. Is it possible that Peter or Hannah Granger had gone out of town?"

"There was nothing in their schedules. Besides, it's the middle of term. Hannah wouldn't have taken time off. She had a class to teach today."

"I spoke to their neighbor, a Mrs. Julia Dixon. She said the house had been very quiet the last couple of days. She thought that they might have been away."

Cornelia bristled but said nothing.

"Do you have some issue with Mrs. Dixon?" asked Macy.

"She's a nuisance . . . a busybody. They couldn't so much as trim a hedge and she'd be over like a shot trying to direct their every move. Peter and Hannah were always polite but I knew they couldn't stand her."

"She said the Grangers sometimes invited her to events."

Cornelia sniffed. "That's because she'd make them pay for it if she wasn't included. Check with the city. That woman lodged noise complaints on a regular basis, contested every time they did so much as pick up a screw driver, and wasn't afraid to bully everyone else on the street into signing petitions. The entire neighborhood lives in fear of her clipboard."

Macy took a few notes.

"Were there any disputes that turned particularly nasty?" asked Macy.

"No, Peter was a regular snake charmer when it came to Julia. He'd go over with a bottle of wine and an invitation to something or another. Julia was so in love with him it worked."

"What about Hannah?"

Cornelia shook her head. "Hannah refused to play those kinds of games. She couldn't stand Julia so she let Peter deal with her. They were quite a team, Peter and Hannah. So different and yet so perfectly matched." She pressed a fresh tissue to her eyes. "I can't believe someone would be so cruel . . . to murder them in their own bed. Do you think they suffered?"

"Ms. Hart, we may not know for some time whether this is a homicide investigation. The building needs to be secured before we can access the scene."

Cornelia picked at the frayed cuff of her jacket. "I thought it was arson."

"Your confusion is understandable. There were several fires last night. All of them arson—but that was a car, a shed, and a Dumpster. This was a house. It could have been a candle, a cigarette, a gas leak. We can't rule anything out yet."

Cornelia dug around in her bag again, this time coming up with a bundle of papers bound by a thick green rubber band. Many of the pages were marked with different colored Post-it notes. It only took her a few seconds to find the page she was looking for. She slid the whole pile toward Macy and pressed her finger to a few paragraphs of marked up text.

"This is Peter's latest manuscript," she said. "One of his central characters is a writer. In the final chapter he dies in a fire at home in his bed. I just read this part last night. I can't believe it's a coincidence."

"May I," said Macy, her eyes quickly scanning the page.

The novel's main character was a writer who lived in a sprawling ranch house located on a ridge of land overlooking the Gallatin Valley. The night sky was so clear, the fire was seen from airplanes passing overhead at 30,000 feet.

"Other than being a writer, is this character similar to Peter Granger in any other ways?" asked Macy.

Cornelia dabbed her eyes with the tail end of a tissue.

"Their appearance is very different but I felt Peter was writing about himself. Peter was at a crossroads in his career. Like the character in the book, Peter was constantly fighting to stay relevant and then hating himself for caring."

"Why did you have access to his manuscript?"

Cornelia looped the rubber band around her wrist. "It's true that I normally only handled his and Hannah's personal affairs as they related to work. Booking flights, paying bills, handling arrangements for the dinners and parties they often held at home. His writing life was kept very separate. I guess you could say this was the one exception. Peter trusts me with his work. He's always given me a copy of his manuscript before passing it on to his editor."

Macy pointed out the comments that had been made in the margins. "Is this your handwriting?"

"Yes, I've been editing his work for years now."

Macy flipped through the manuscript. Cornelia's notes were extensive. She'd circled, underlined, and written out lines of text on the backs of some of the pages. Her handwriting was small and precise. From what Macy could tell, the style of the passages seemed to reflect what Peter Granger had written.

"It looks like you've made a lot of notes. It must have taken a great deal of time."

"It was a privilege to work with Peter. I think I've come to know his writing better than anyone." Cornelia neatened the pages so they lined up properly. "I've been a huge fan for years."

"Is that why he employed you?"

Cornelia's expression brightened.

"I suppose it helped. Over the years I'd met him at various events back when he still did book tours. When he and his wife advertised a position for a personal assistant, I applied."

Cornelia bundled up the manuscript and slipped it back into her bag. She sighed.

"I'm sorry if I wasted your time with this," Cornelia said. "I suppose you need to figure out whether a crime has been committed in the first place."

"That's generally how things happen, but given it may be some time before I have solid information on that front, I'll continue interviewing anyone who was close to the Grangers. It would be very helpful if you could compile a list. I'd also like to know if they've had any recent disputes. The manuscript may yet become relevant." Macy took a quick look at her notes. "Do you have keys to his offices at the Bridger Cultural Center?"

"No, but the administrative office in the lobby is open during business hours. I'll speak to them on your behalf if you like. It shouldn't be a problem getting a spare key."

Macy had never before met someone who was so eager to smooth the way for the police.

"Thank you," said Macy. "That's very thoughtful, but I'm sure we can handle making the proper arrangements."

"Really, it's no trouble. One phone call to let them know you're coming will make all the difference."

Macy thought about it for a second. It really wouldn't make a difference if Cornelia made the call. Macy thanked her again for her help, but went on to caution her. She didn't want Cornelia talking about the case.

Cornelia sat up a little taller. "Don't worry," she promised. "I won't say a word."

"What were things like inside the Granger's home? Did they have a fixed routine?" asked Macy.

"For the most part they led very solitary lives."

"That's surprising. Everyone else is saying that there was a constant stream of guests and they liked to entertain."

"Oh, they did, but they only socialized a couple of evenings a week and on the weekends. During the day they were completely focused on their work. When she wasn't at the college Hannah spent a lot of time in her studio at the house, but she was too disorganized for Peter's taste. Her music was always playing too loud and she'd not bother with anything remotely domestic when she was working. It drove Peter nuts, which is why he rented an office."

"Was there any tension between them?"

"They argued all the time but they seemed to enjoy it."

"What did they argue about?"

"Authors, artists, creativity . . . nothing that touched on the every-day."

"That was your job."

"Pardon?"

Macy made some notes. "You took care of their everyday lives so they didn't have to argue about it."

"I guess I did shield them a bit, but they needed that freedom so they could create. I think they would have been a little lost without me around to run things."

"Have you always been a personal assistant?"

"No, I worked as a nurse practitioner in a critical-care unit for years. My ex-husband was the main partner in a corporate law firm in New York. It was only after the marriage broke down that I realized I was never more than his executive assistant. He'd even joked about hiring me after the divorce papers were signed." She shrugged. "He was try-ing to be funny, but it gave me an idea. I was burned out from nursing and I needed to make a change. I started working for friends but slowly took on other clients. This was my first full-time job. Hannah and Peter wanted the arrangement to be exclusive."

"What will you do now?"

"I really haven't thought about it. It will take some time to settle their affairs. I'm hoping the lawyers will want me on board to see it through to the end. I feel I owe so much to them for the past ten years. Then I'll move back to New York. Montana is nice but it's not my home."

"Tell me about the parties they held. Were they well attended?"

"Very. In summer the crowds spilled out onto the back garden. There were always a lot of students and faculty from the university. Famous authors, actors, and artists would come to stay. Hannah and Peter were very generous. The wine, champagne, and catering were always of the best quality. I sometimes questioned the expense, but they didn't seem to worry."

"Were there money problems?"

Cornelia hesitated for the first time. "It feels wrong to discuss their finances," she said.

"I really need to know if there were problems."

"It wasn't just the parties," offered Cornelia. "It was also dinners out, the clothes, and the travel. They weren't the type of people who believed in flying economy."

"Do you think that's what they should have been doing?"

"Yes, but flying first class isn't what killed them. A fire did. I'm not sure why it's relevant."

Macy put her hand on the stack of files Cornelia had brought with her.

"Do you know who stands to benefit in the event they both died?"

"Their will was reviewed about six months ago. Peter and Hannah were planning to leave the bulk of their estate to various arts foundations. As far as I know there were no changes made. I've included the name of the executor in my list of contacts. He should be able to help you."

"I'm sorry, this may seem indelicate, but it's routine in an investigation to ask all those closest to the victims about their whereabouts at the time of the incident."

Cornelia started crying again. "There's no need to apologize. I volunteer at the Norwood Pines Home for the Elderly. As a former nurse, they rely on my help. I sometimes stay late if a patient is feeling unwell or lonely. It's a big facility so they don't always have staff to spare."

"You were there all evening?"

"From six in the evening onward. I finally went home at around three in the morning. There's a sheet at the reception desk where we sign in and out."

"Thank you, Cornelia. I appreciate how hard this is for you. I will do my best to keep you up to date." Macy handed her a card. "You've been very helpful."

3

Tuesday

Grace stood next to the window with a blanket wrapped around her shoulders. She tucked her jet-black hair behind her ears and took another sip of tea. Her warm breath steamed over the glass. She rubbed it away with her pale fingers so she could watch the sparrows dart through the trees in the park across the street. Overhead, dark clouds lumbered across a fading sky. Weather warnings ran in a constant ribbon beneath the news reports about the town's recent crime wave. Snow was falling heavily in the surrounding mountains. It was only a matter of time before Bolton suffered the same fate. Grace tilted her face up as a lost ray of sunshine slipped through the clouds. For a few seconds it was as bright as summer. It was the first time she'd felt warm all day.

Her third-floor apartment overlooked the full length of Spruce Street, the road that ran in front of the building. At the moment it was empty save for a woman jogging alongside a yellow Labrador, but Grace had caught sight of Clare's car a few minutes earlier as she circled the block looking for a parking space. Grace turned away from the window. Lara was sprawled out on the sofa staring at her cell phone, a position she'd held since they'd returned to the apartment two hours earlier.

"Any word from Taylor?" asked Grace. "I'm really worried about what she's going to do when she hears what's happened."

"No one has heard from her since Thursday. Bet she's with her boyfriend," said Lara.

"You'd think she'd call."

"Do you remember his name?"

"Nope, but then again I didn't get the impression that he wanted to know who we were either."

"That's because we were behaving like a bunch of degenerates."

Grace's dog, Jack, was stretched out on a rug in front of the television. The black mongrel lifted his wide head a fraction and tracked Grace's progress across the living room. In the past few months his muzzle had gone gray. Grace had adopted him from the shelter so had no idea how old he was, and that bothered her. In the past few years she'd grown attached. Grace bent down and scratched him behind his ears.

"Don't worry, Jack. I know things are a little weird right now but everything is going to be okay."

Lara mumbled something Grace didn't catch.

"Pardon," said Grace.

"It's not going to be okay," said Lara.

"You don't know that."

"There's no way you can put a positive spin on what's happened, so please stop trying."

Jack let out a low growl as the front door swung open. Clare stepped inside the two-bedroom apartment, smelling of cigarette smoke. She set two bags of groceries on the kitchen counter before peeling off her scarf and jacket. The hat stayed on. She was out of breath from climbing the stairs.

"Sorry I took so long. I stopped by my place to change clothes and take a shower," said Clare.

Grace leaned against the counter where the stack of unopened mail was six inches high. Clare didn't live with Lara and Grace, but that didn't stop her from taking over their kitchen anytime she was given the chance.

"You guys owe me eighteen dollars each for food." Clare tilted her head toward Lara. "I take it you'll be giving me another IOU."

"I'll pay Lara's share," said Grace.

Clare kept her voice low. "You need to stop doing that."

Grace changed the subject. "We were just talking about Taylor."

"I went by her house," said Clare. "No one came to the door so I let myself in. Taylor's room was as tidy as ever, so there's no way of knowing whether she's slept there recently."

"Is she still seeing that grad student?" asked Grace. "We could call him."

Clare shrugged. "I don't know his name or anything about him."

"Taylor's housemates will know," said Lara.

"I would have asked but they weren't home." Clare opened the refrigerator and frowned. The leftovers from the last meal she'd prepared were still on the shelf. "Don't you guys ever eat at home?"

"Only when you cook," answered Lara.

"I'm worried about Taylor," said Grace. "She's close to Hannah and Peter. We really should be with her when she hears the news."

"Grace, you need to stop rewriting history. It was always Peter she was close to, or rather dreamed of being close to. Hannah never really figured into her fantasies." Clare put a pot full of water on the stove. "I'm making some pasta. Do you guys want any?"

Lara rolled over so her face was buried in the back of the sofa. "Not hungry," she said.

Grace didn't agree but she didn't have the energy to argue with Clare and Lara. They'd both been bitching about Taylor ever since Peter declared that she was his most gifted student a few months earlier. Grace no longer attended the Tuesday evening sessions, so she got to hear about Taylor's ascension to the throne when Lara came home in a particularly nasty mood. Clare and Lara had ganged up on Taylor the last time they'd gone out together. Grace had tried to defend Taylor but the argument had escalated too quickly. Once Clare, Lara, and Taylor started shouting at each other, Grace had no chance of being heard. Now that Grace had a little distance from the situation, she saw Peter Granger for who he really was.

One by one, he'd used them all. As an added bonus, he'd broken up their friendships.

"Thank you. Pasta sounds great," said Grace.

Clare's face was flushed pink from the heat. The blue beanie she wore was pulled down tight enough to cover what little remained of her hair. When it first started falling out her parents were convinced there was a medical explanation. One visit to a doctor eliminated that as a possibility. He instead referred Clare to a therapist. Sometimes Clare pulled her hair so hard it made her scalp bleed. She wasn't even safe while she was sleeping. In the morning there were always clumps of hair on her pillow. Her therapist had prescribed Xanax and told her to buy a nice hat. The blue beanie was part of a growing collection.

"Has your hair started to grow back?" asked Grace.

"The therapist told me it was just a matter of time. I'm trying not to worry, as that's what got me into this mess in the first place."

"You can take your hat off when you're here. We're not going to judge you."

"It doesn't matter if you judge me or not. I'm doing that all on my own."

Grace rubbed her eyes so Clare couldn't see how frustrated she felt. Discussions with Clare were often like this. For all of Clare's supposedly high emotional intelligence, she couldn't tell the difference between empathy and pity. Grace changed the subject. It was getting late and she still had a lot of schoolwork to do.

"I've got to get back in the studio and finish up a few more paintings," said Grace.

"When does the student exhibition open?"

"Next week."

"You could do a few hours this evening."

"I thought of that but I'm too tired. I'll go up to campus tomorrow

45

and stay the whole day. The head of the art department sent all the students an e-mail. Classes are cancelled until Monday next week, so there should be plenty of time."

"Why were classes cancelled?"

"I suppose it has to do with Hannah. I imagine everyone in the art department is freaking out as much as we are."

"That would take a lot of freaking out. Sometimes I think we're all seconds away from losing it completely," said Clare.

"We're doing okay."

Clare spoke sharply. "Grace, we are not doing okay. Lara doesn't eat, when Taylor is self-harming she goes off the radar for days at a time, Pippa is back in her childhood home eating happy pills, and I've pulled out most of my hair."

"You left me out."

Clare smiled as she dumped a jar of pasta sauce into a small pot. "That's because I wouldn't know where to start."

"Maybe our therapists should compare case notes."

"Bolton is a small town. It would surprise me if they didn't."

Lara fished the remote control out from between the couch cushions and pointed it at the television. The punchy theme music of a local newscast filled the room.

"They're talking about the fire on the news," said Lara.

A female reporter stared into the camera with a suitably grim expression but then stumbled over her lines when she introduced herself and the news channel she was representing. She said something under her breath that might have been a swear word. She took a second to compose herself before speaking again.

News has just come in from the Bolton Police Department. I can now confirm that they've requested assistance from the Montana Department of Justice. Special Investigator Detective Macy Greeley has taken charge of the ongoing investigation into a suspicious fire here on Madison Road that left the historic home behind me in ruins. Detective Greeley arrived in Bolton this morning to confer with crime scene investigators. I spoke to her briefly.

They'd interviewed Macy Greeley with the wreckage of the Granger's home in the background. Her red hair hung down to her shoulders. She took time to correct the young reporter on several occasions. They'd not identified the fatalities, and as of yet there was no definitive proof that the fire was the result of arson.

I understand that this is a very stressful time for Peter and Hannah Granger's friends and family and we wish to apologize for the delay in getting answers to those parties who most need them. Macy Greeley pointed to the house. *Part of the upper floors and a supporting wall have collapsed, so authorities have had only limited access to the property so far, but we have a team working flat out to secure the building so the victims can be removed for proper identification.*

We're making a direct appeal to the Bolton community. The fire occurred on Halloween night. There were a lot of people out on the streets. If you witnessed any suspicious activity in and around Madison Road we need to hear from you. The Bolton PD has set up an information hotline. I can personally assure you that everything you tell us is confidential. We would greatly appreciate your help.

The interview ended as abruptly as it began. The cameras followed the detective as she made her way back to what remained of the Granger's home. Grace took the remote control off the coffee table and hit reverse. She paused at a close-up of Macy Greeley's face.

Macy Greeley had changed over the past three years and it wasn't just the faint lines around her eyes. She'd been pregnant when they met so Grace remembered her having a fuller face and an open, almost mischievous expression. Now she was all angles and cheekbones. She also had a barely veiled air of impatience. It wasn't just her appearance that had changed. Grace sensed that Macy Greeley wasn't the same person who'd come to Collier to investigate her mother's murder. The sharp edge in Macy's voice was new.

"She's that cop we saw earlier at the house," said Lara.

Grace didn't answer. She turned around. Clare was heading for the door with an unlit cigarette in her hand.

"I'm going out for a few minutes," she said.

Lara's hair was sticking out at odd angles. She brushed it away but static sent it shooting up in the air again. For a few seconds she looked like a child but then she spoke. Her voice was too hoarse to belong to someone so young.

"Grace, is that the cop you were telling me about? The one who was in Collier when your mother was killed?"

"Yep, it's her."

"You should have talked to her this afternoon. She may have told you what's going on with the investigation."

"I haven't spoken to her for a long time. I wouldn't know what to say."

Grace, Lara, and Clare had held a vigil in front of the Granger's house until three in the morning and then returned at noon carrying coffee cups and bouquets of flowers to leave at a makeshift shrine that a neighbor had organized. They weren't the only people standing at the police cordon. Several Bolton College faculty members and at least a dozen students Grace recognized from the art department were also there. Jessica Reynolds was Hannah's closest friend and worked the art department's administration offices. She'd kept apart from the others, her eyes never leaving the house.

Grace had already been anxious, and seeing Macy Greeley again had done nothing to calm her nerves. She'd had to make a real effort to not openly stare at the detective. They'd first met when Macy came to interview Grace in the hospital where she was recovering from hypothermia following her mother's murder. Macy had jotted down everything Grace said in a black notebook. It was the same sort of book she'd held in the crook of her arm as she moved among the team investigating the fire. Much had happened to Grace since their first meeting, a lot of it painful.

Lara asked Grace if she was okay.

Grace didn't want to talk about Collier. She picked up her cell phone. The number of messages in her in-box had been growing steadily since dawn. Everyone was talking about Peter, Hannah, and what had happened at K-Bar. At least three people had died last night. This was a small town where people rarely locked their doors. Grace knew what it was like to live in a place where people didn't trust their neighbors. She didn't want Bolton to change.

"Does she know you live here?" asked Lara.

"I don't see how she would. I've moved since the last time I saw her. I am on Peter's class list though."

"You've been going by Grace Larson. She won't know it's you."

Grace shrugged. "She knows Larson is my father's surname. It's only a matter of time before she makes the connection."

"Why would the writing workshop interest her anyway?"

"Everything interests her. She's kind of scary that way."

"It doesn't matter. You didn't do anything wrong," said Lara.

"You were all there. I threatened to kill him the night he kicked me out."

"That may be so, but we're not going to say anything."

"What are you guys talking about?" asked Clare. She pointed to the frozen image of Macy Greeley on the television screen. "Grace, do you know that woman?"

Clare stood in the open door. Neither Grace nor Lara had heard her come back inside. Grace was suddenly worried what Clare may have overheard.

Lara didn't give Grace a chance to respond. "Grace, maybe Peter was right about what happened back in Collier. Maybe it's time you quit hiding from the truth."

"Lara, you're the last person who should talk about the truth," said Clare.

"What do you mean by that?" asked Lara.

Grace tried to say something but Clare wouldn't let her. "It wasn't just Taylor that was in love with Peter, it was all of us. He'd play us off each other. It's how he got his kicks and you fell for it every time."

Lara turned off the television. "That's total bullshit."

"Well, maybe it wasn't love, but you would have done anything for him if you thought it would help you get your book published. He used you just like he used the rest of us," said Clare.

It was unusual for Clare to confront anyone directly. Passive aggression was more her style. Grace kept a wary eye on Lara. There was nothing passive about her aggression. When she was cornered she liked to throw things.

"You were always his favorite until you weren't anymore," said Clare. "Admit it, Lara. You freaked out when he started paying Grace more attention than you. Must have been particularly galling since you're the one who introduced them."

"*I* freaked out?" said Lara. "Look in the mirror, Clare. I'm not the freak, *you* are."

Clare pulled off her hat and threw it at Lara. It was worse than Grace had imagined. Clare was practically bald.

"Congratulations," said Clare. "Pick on the girl who's lost her hair. I didn't think it was possible, but you've sunk to a new low."

Lara jumped up from the sofa and grabbed her coat. "I'm going for a drive." She addressed Grace. "Call me when Clare is gone."

Grace quietly shut her bedroom door behind her and turned on the desk lamp. Her sketchbook was open to a drawing she'd done the day before. Bent over by the driving wind, a man struggled to stand upright on an ice-crusted river. She'd filled a sketchbook with drawings of this same scene but was nowhere near to getting it right. She turned to a blank page but, instead of picking up a pencil, she picked up her cell phone.

Grace dialed Pippa's number in Wisconsin and waited patiently as a phone rang a thousand miles away. Although she'd known them socially, Grace hadn't become close friends with Pippa, Taylor, and Clare until after she'd been invited to attend Peter Granger's writing workshop. Grace had never really felt like she belonged there. Where Grace only managed a few paragraphs of scrappy prose, the others churned out whole chapters and complete short stories on a weekly basis. Every Tuesday evening Peter Granger would sit in his leather chair, a cigarette in one hand and their fate in the other. If he was in a particularly foul mood he'd pick their work apart one sentence at a time. He'd make them account for every sentence, every word. If it didn't bring some depth to the prose it was superfluous. If it didn't draw from their lives it wasn't real. If he didn't see truth in their writing he'd dismiss it as mediocre. He'd praised Grace's work even though it was clearly shit. There was always someone who was his favorite and apparently it had been Grace's turn. Grace had lasted eight whole weeks in the top spot before Peter lost his temper and admitted the only thing he'd ever been interested in was her past.

Pippa's father answered the phone. Grace had last seen Pippa's parents when they'd come to collect their daughter at the hospital where she'd spent two weeks recuperating after having a nervous breakdown. They'd not dealt well with their daughter's sudden decline.

"Hello, Mr. Lomax. It's Grace Larson, Pippa's friend. I wondered if I could speak to her."

"Grace, thanks for calling, but I'm not sure that's a good idea."

Grace's voice broke. "How is she?"

Mr. Lomax sighed. "Hard to say. She's still pretty heavily medicated. She's in therapy twice a week."

"I'm sorry," said Grace. "I miss her."

"So do we. She's not the same girl we dropped off at the dorms three years ago."

"Has she talked at all about what happened?"

"Some." He paused. "The police called earlier. We know about the fire. I suppose they thought she may have been involved."

Grace remembered the day the judge had issued a restraining order against Pippa. She'd been stalking Peter for weeks. If she wasn't camped out in a car in front of his house she was calling him hundreds of times a day. It all came to head one night in late September. Peter claimed she'd become violent when he'd threatened to call the police.

"I wasn't going to say anything to her about that," said Grace. "It's just brought it all back. I wanted to know that she was okay."

"I know my daughter, or at least I thought I did until she developed this crazy obsession with Peter Granger. People tell me he's charismatic but I just don't see it. I can't believe she'd have taken things so far without there being something in it. Grace, if you know something, please tell us."

"I'm sorry, Mr. Lomax, but she never said anything to me about it. Have you managed to get her to talk?"

"Her therapist thinks she's blocking out some traumatic experience."

"Maybe if I spoke to her."

"I'm sorry but that's not going to happen."

"Will you tell her I miss her?"

"Yes, of course."

Grace put her cell phone on her bedside table and covered her face with her hands. She knew Pippa was in the right place. She had a large and loving family. Grace had gone home with her at the end of August for a two-week visit. They'd shared a little apartment over the garage at a sprawling house her extended family had rented on Lake Winnebago. Long days were spent canoeing and swimming with Pippa's siblings and cousins and when the sun went down they'd spend hours talking. There were signs that Pippa's obsession with Peter Granger was already getting out of hand, but when Grace tried to make her see him for who he really was, Pippa wouldn't listen.

Lara was supposed to come on the trip, but Peter and Hannah had asked her to housesit for them at the last minute. Instead of spending time with her friends, Lara was stuck by herself for two weeks in the house on Madison Road.

4

Tuesday

Jessica Reynolds, an administrator who worked in the Bolton College art department, led Macy into Hannah Granger's office on the fourth floor. Macy wasn't sure whether Jessica was wearing black because she was in mourning or if it was how she normally dressed. Either way, it didn't suit her pale complexion. Macy had seen murder victims with more life in their eyes. Jessica guided Macy into Hannah's office and quietly shut the door behind them. There was a picture of Jessica and Hannah prominently displayed on the bookshelf. Hannah was petite, tan, and had straw-colored hair that hung past her shoulders. Jessica was a good six inches taller and looked uncomfortable wearing a dress, but had smiled broadly for the camera.

Jessica may have kept her arms locked around her body but her eyes touched on one object after another. "I can't believe this is happening."

"Did she give you any indication that she might be going out of town?" asked Macy.

"She would have asked me to find someone to cover her classes if that were the case."

"Did that happen often?"

"Not particularly." Jessica started to pick up a small sculpture on the desk but her fingers froze short of the mark. "I don't understand why you'd want to search her office."

"Her studio and much of the house were destroyed. Aside from her husband's office at the Bridger Cultural Center, this may be all we have to go on."

"Was all her work destroyed?"

"I doubt anything can be salvaged."

Jessica steadied her voice. "There's something you're bound to find out so I want to be the one to tell you. I don't want it to seem like I was hiding anything."

"I'm listening."

"Hannah and I were in a relationship. She'd recently decided to leave Peter."

"Up to this point, I've not heard anyone say there were problems in their marriage."

Jessica shrugged. "It wasn't something they talked about openly."

"Do you know if Hannah had spoken to Peter yet?"

"She'd been putting it off, but she'd promised to do it soon."

"You must have found that frustrating."

"I understood her reluctance. Peter and Hannah have been together a long time. There's also a business side. They're almost like a brand. It's hard to break free from that."

"Why did Hannah want to leave him? Was it just to be with you or was there something else going on?"

"Hannah wasn't wired to make rash decisions. She also wasn't prone to gossip. She would only say that she didn't trust Peter anymore, that he'd crossed some line. She didn't say what that line was."

"I need to ask where you were last night."

Jessica walked over to the big windows. The college's football stadium glowed in the distance. "I was home. I live alone."

"Were you on your own all evening?" asked Macy.

"Pretty much. Downtown Bolton tends to become a bit of a zoo on Halloween so I avoid going out."

"Did any children come to your door?"

"I forgot to buy candy so I kept the lights off and hid in my bedroom."

"Were you online?"

"For about an hour early evening, say around six to seven. Later I read and watched television. I only found out about the fire when one of my colleagues phoned me."

"What time was that?"

"A little after one. My cell phone was switched off so they called my house phone." She paused. "I thought it was my sister calling about our mother. She hasn't been well."

"When did you start seeing Hannah?"

"Two years ago. It was pretty soon after I started working here."

"That's a long time to be in limbo. It must have been difficult to keep it a secret. Did people know about it?"

"There were rumors. I can't say I went out of my way to stop them from spreading."

"Why's that?"

"I told Hannah I was happy to wait, but in truth I wanted it to all come out in the open. I was hoping she'd finally leave Peter when it did."

"A risky strategy. When was the last time you spoke to Hannah?"

"She called me on Saturday morning but there hasn't been anything since then, which isn't unusual. She didn't have classes over the weekend so she wasn't around the university. I figured she was in her studio. She's very focused when she's working." Jessica studied the photo on the bookshelf. "I really can't accept that she might be gone."

"What is her schedule this week?"

"She doesn't have anything on Mondays but today she was scheduled to give a lecture and hold office hours."

"Has she ever missed a lecture?"

"No," she said. "This is the first time."

Macy rested her head on Hannah Granger's desk and closed her eyes for a couple of seconds. Outside, the football stadium's loudspeaker echoed across the floodlit pathways that crisscrossed the university. It was coming up on eight o'clock in the evening, but it felt more like midnight.

"Most of this is class notes and student evaluations," said Macy, waving a hand over the files she'd pulled from Hannah's desk drawers and cabinets. "Nothing stands out."

"I'm not finding anything either," said Ryan. He scanned the incoming messages on his phone. "What's our timeline thus far?"

"Hannah made her last phone call to Jessica Reynolds on Saturday morning. Up until noon that same day Peter's phone records indicate fairly normal activity, and then he isn't seen or heard from aside from twenty-three unanswered texts to his wife's number. The last text was sent at 3:00 P.M. Monday afternoon. Later that day the house burns to the ground. The neighbor also said the house was unusually quiet over the past three days. We need to figure out what the hell was going on in there."

"He may have gone postal when Hannah told him she was leaving him for another woman, and we have a murder-suicide on our hands. Wouldn't be the first time that scenario played out. If the trail of text messages are to be believed, that means she may have come home on the night of the fire."

"Until we've formally identified the victims it's all academic. Are the team at the house any closer to securing the building?"

"Have a little patience. We'll get access soon enough. We're just lucky that snowstorm that was supposed to hit here today stayed south of us."

"Three feet of fresh powder. Maybe we should go skiing."

"Stay focused, Greeley. Oh," said Ryan, raising his voice. "What in the hell is this?"

Ryan held up four Polaroids that he'd found in a manila envelope. He handed one to Macy. The subject was young, female, and nude. Her face was covered with a black mask. She was lying back on a bed with her arms flopped to her sides.

"Hannah Granger's work is known for being controversial, but this is unacceptable," said Macy.

Ryan handed Macy the remaining photos. There was more than one woman. Three were posed on the same upholstered chair. Only one was on the bed.

"Impossible to tell for sure from the photographs, but I think these women are fairly young," he said.

"Something about how they're slumped on the furniture makes them look like they're sleeping."

"Or dead."

Macy lifted an eyebrow. "Or drugged. Where did you find them?"

"Tucked beneath the files in the cabinet. I'll have a closer look at the images. We may be able to find some distinguishing marks that could help identify them. I can check any details against Missing Persons."

Macy dropped the photos into an evidence bag and handed them back to Ryan. Both their phones buzzed at the same time.

Ryan read the message out loud. "A homeowner found four fuel cans hidden on their property."

"How far away from the Granger's home?"

"Only two doors down, so close enough for it to be significant. I think I should head over and check this out firsthand. Do you need me here anymore?"

"I don't think I need me here anymore." Macy checked the time. A visit to Peter's office at the Bridger Cultural Center would have to wait until morning. "You go on," she said. "I'll finish up here."

"It may be wishful thinking, but should we try for dinner?"

"If I remember correctly there's a nice tapas place a couple of blocks from Main. It stays open late."

"Sounds good. I'll give you a shout if and when I'm finished."

Macy picked up the framed photo of Hannah Granger and Jessica Reynolds. They looked relaxed in each other's company. Hannah had one arm draped around Jessica's shoulders. They were caught mid-laugh. Their relationship complicated things. Macy would have to look more carefully at the Granger's marriage. Ryan was right. It could have been a murder-suicide. The timing certainly fit. The question was whether Peter Granger would have been distraught enough to kill his wife when he found out she wanted a divorce. Then again, Hannah may not have ever planned on telling Peter anything. She may have been stringing Jessica along. It was strange that Cornelia Hart hadn't mentioned it. Though she'd admitted that the pair fought, she'd gone out of her way to say how strong the relationship was. Perhaps she was also protecting the brand.

Macy scrolled through the messages on her phone. Her mother had sent her a couple of photos of Luke in his Halloween costume. He'd had his heart set on dressing like a lion, but at the last minute he'd insisted on going as a pirate because that's what all the other boys in his nursery school were doing. Thankfully Ellen was a master of improvisation. Macy leaned on the window as she keyed in her mother's phone number. The phone rang several times before Ellen answered. There were sounds of a restaurant in the background. Macy checked the time. It was half past eight.

"Mom, sorry to disturb you. I didn't realize you were going out for dinner tonight."

Ellen had to raise her voice to be heard.

"I completely forgot there was a Chamber of Commerce dinner this evening. Sarah is babysitting Luke. I was lucky to get her at short notice."

"That will be a treat for him. He loves Sarah."

"We're going to miss her when she starts college next fall. Is everything okay there?"

"It's fine. Just wanted to check in. We'll speak tomorrow."

Macy locked Hannah's office door and went in search of a women's bathroom. The dimly lit corridor was empty and as far as she could tell the offices on Hannah's end of the building had been vacated for the night. After she washed her hands, Macy studied her reflection in the bathroom mirror. There had been a lot of upheaval in her life over the past few years, but things had taken a decidedly positive turn over the past few months. It was still a little difficult to understand how she'd managed to pull off some semblance of happiness. She knew her relationship with Aiden had a lot to do with that. There were no head games. She realized that hope was something she'd been lacking for a very long time. Her son, Luke, may have gotten her out of bed in the morning and forced her to confront the day regardless of what was coming, but it was Aiden who made her feel loved. Her job wasn't easy. Knowing there was a safe place she could go when everything got to be too much made it bearable.

Macy turned away from the mirror. The door leading out into the corridor was ajar. It sounded like someone was running down the hallway. It wasn't yet nine o'clock, so it was perfectly feasible that other people were in the building. She slung her messenger bag over her shoulder and stepped outside. The light in Hannah Granger's office was on. Macy looked up in time to see the stairwell door at the far end of the building swing shut. She ran the length of the corridor. An alarm sounded as she started down the stairs. At the bottom of the stairwell the emergency exit door was hanging open. Outside the night air was cold and clear. Macy headed up a short set of steps and found herself on one of the main paths that cut across the campus. Lampposts dotted the grounds. The shadows were too numerous to count. She waited and watched, but aside from a couple strolling hand in hand, there was no sign of the person she'd seen at the top of the stairwell.

The only seats free at the tapas restaurant were at the bar. Ryan had given the menu a cursory glance before getting frustrated. He told Macy to order something for them to share. He had more luck with the wine. Within seconds of studying the list he picked out a bottle of Rioja.

"I have zero willpower," he said, handing the wine list back to the bartender before turning to Macy. "I am, of course, blaming you."

"I'll drink water before I let you pin this on me," she said.

Ryan pretended to be shocked. "Not on my watch you won't. Let's compromise and get a glass each. For me that's a major sacrifice."

"I'm sure the world will acknowledge your suffering."

"Your sarcasm is duly noted." He waved the bartender over. "Scratch the bottle and bring us two large glasses instead."

"Still a slippery slope," said Macy. "Are you sure you'll be able to stick to one glass?"

"I'm hoping you'll be my conscience."

Macy raised an eyebrow. "In that case we're in trouble. So, who's this guy you met anyway?"

"He's in my support group."

"Alcoholics Anonymous?"

Ryan lifted the glass of wine that the bartender set down in front of him and had a taste. He had a familiar look of glee in his eye. "I like my drink but I'm not that far gone. It's a support group for homosexual men."

"I had no idea you needed support."

"Being gay in Montana can be a very lonely existence. It's nice to be in a safe space where you're considered completely normal."

"I can see that."

"By the way, his name is Paul."

"And what does Paul do?" asked Macy.

A wicked grin. "Among other things, he has a law practice in Helena."

"Criminal?"

"Thank God, no. Family law."

"How long have you been seeing each other?"

"Only a couple of months, but we've known each other for years," said Ryan.

"Sounds promising."

"Best thing that's happened to me in a while. How are things with Aiden?"

"Drama free," said Macy. "He's been working loads. They're hoping to start construction on the resort in the spring. He's been coming down to Helena as often as possible."

"Must be cozy. How does your mom feel about having him staying at the house?"

"If I'm happy she's happy. When I come home from work I find them hanging out together in the kitchen. They take turns looking after Luke."

"Considering your relationship with Ray only ended a little over a year ago, that's quite a turnaround." Ryan raised his glass. "Here's to landing on your feet."

Macy tried not to let her reservations show. Her life seemed to be on course but she had to be vigilant. Aiden's predecessor had cast a dark shadow. It was time to steer the conversation back to the investigation.

"So," said Macy. "Did you find anything on those fuel cans that tied them to the fire at the Granger's house?"

"Nothing definite yet but, given the proximity and the timing, I'm certain they were used to set the fire."

"Makes me think we're dealing with an amateur. No serious arsonist would have left evidence like that so close to the scene."

"The fuel cans were well-hidden under a tarp in the side yard. The house has been under construction for months now. The homeowner only came to check on things because he was worried that the fire at the Granger's house may have done some damage. We're hoping for some prints, but at this point any physical evidence that puts those fuel cans at the Granger residence would be helpful. I'd like a little more than the fire crew's statements to prove this was arson."

"You do believe this was arson though?"

"I'm in no doubt. I just need a bit more evidence to prove it to everyone else."

"The arsonist had to have been familiar with the area to have known that the house where they stashed the fuel cans is unoccupied."

"That's my thinking as well. They may have ditched them there temporarily."

Macy lifted her glass to make room for their first few plates of food.

"There was someone in Hannah Granger's office besides us this evening," she said. "After I locked up I went to the bathrooms near the elevator. When I came out, the door to Hannah's office was wide open. Whoever was there escaped through the emergency exit at the base of the stairwell."

"Are you sure you locked the door?"

"That's the one thing I'm absolutely sure of."

"We should go back and check for prints," said Ryan.

"The campus police are dealing with it. I'm not hopeful, though. A lot of people move through that building."

"Was anything missing from the office?"

"No, but the file drawer where you found the Polaroids was open."

Ryan raised an eyebrow. "Anything else?"

"It looks like they'd gone through some of the papers on the desk as well."

"We need to find out who else has keys to that office."

"I'll chase that up tomorrow. When do you think you'll have a chance to look at those Polaroids?"

"They're on their way to Helena now. The forensics team promised to have a look first thing tomorrow morning. I'm hoping to get into the house as early as tomorrow afternoon. Meanwhile, I'll have a closer look at those fuel cans."

5

The café's employee entrance was propped open with a cinder block. It was a little before six thirty in the morning and Grace had not slept well. She'd been tempted to call in sick but changed her mind. Among other things, she needed the money. She stood in a small cramped area stacked with boxes and slowly unwound her scarf. Her manager, Steve, was the only one who ever arrived before she did. The lights in his office were on and she could hear him talking in a low voice over the telephone. Grace stepped into a break room that was located next to the employee entrance. Her locker was shut, but the padlock wasn't secured. She checked her locker. She'd never given much thought to what she'd thrown into it over the past couple of years—scraps of paper, receipts, and the odd photo. There was nothing of value.

Grace spun around at the sound of her name.

Steve stood in the doorway watching her.

"Sorry about that," he said. "I didn't mean to frighten you. We've got a delivery and you're the only one here. Do you mind bringing it in? I have to make a couple more phone calls."

Grace shoved her bag into her locker and swung the door shut. She must have forgotten to close it properly after her last shift. An apron with her name on it was hanging on a hook. She slipped it over her neck.

"It's out back on the loading bay," said Steve. "Don't know why the driver didn't bring it to the door like he usually does. Some of the boxes are heavy so you'll have to use the hand truck."

"Don't worry. I'll deal with it."

"I heard about the fire. Didn't you know the Grangers?"

Grace put her hand flat against the locker door. She'd written a scathing letter to Peter a few months earlier as a therapeutic exercise. Though she put it in an envelope with his name on it, it was never meant to be sent. She'd written most of it during a break she'd taken at work. Grace opened her locker again. Her hands were trembling. There'd been something of value in the locker after all. Steve moved closer.

"Grace, did you know them?"

"Yeah, I knew them." She pulled her bag out of the locker and started sifting through the pile of papers on the shelf. "Hannah taught in the art department, and I was in Peter's writing group."

The letter wasn't there. She went through the locker twice. Steve was so close Grace could smell the coffee on his breath. He was wearing cologne. That was different.

"Are you okay to work? If you're too upset, I'll find someone to cover your shift," he said.

Grace put her stuff back into her locker and closed the door. She was trying to remember exactly what she'd written. Vague phrases and entire passages came to mind. At times she'd been harsh. She'd definitely threatened Peter on occasion. Without context she'd sound unhinged, vindictive, and potentially violent. The café's employee entrance was only a few feet away from the break room and it was often unlocked. Anyone could have snuck in.

Steve put a hand on Grace's shoulder.

"Hey," he said. "I didn't mean to upset you."

Grace couldn't speak. It felt like a grapefruit was lodged in the back of her throat.

"I'll see if someone can take your shift," said Steve.

Grace found her voice. "It's okay. I want to be here." She paused. "You remember my friend Taylor?"

"Vaguely."

"Do you know the name of that grad student she was seeing?"

Steve frowned. "I'm not sure who you mean."

"I saw you talking to him when he came into the café. He's into cycling. Has red hair."

"Oh, that's Alex. He's South African."

"Do you know how I can reach him? I've been trying to call Taylor but she's not picking up."

Steve turned toward the front of the shop. The lights had come on.

"Vicky's here," he said. "I forgot I gave her keys to the front door. I'll need to get them back."

"It's important that I talk to Alex. I'm worried about Taylor."

"They broke up last week."

"I had no idea," she said.

"I got the impression it wasn't mutual."

"I'm sorry. Alex seemed nice."

Steve smiled. "It happens. You don't need to apologize."

"I'd like that number anyway. He still may know where she is."

Steve pulled out his phone and scrolled through his contacts. "I'm texting it to you now."

Grace felt her phone vibrate in the apron's pocket. "Thanks," she said.

Steve continued to hover.

"Look," he said. "This might not be the right time, but I think you could use a fun night out. Would you like to go to the Steve Earle concert with me? It's on Friday, so short notice." Steve's voice trailed off. "It's okay to say no."

At six foot three Steve towered over her. His dark hair and beard were cropped close. He had one eye that wandered ever so slightly. Steve cocked his head to the side. He looked hopeful.

"Was that a yes?" he asked.

Grace's face felt flushed. "This Friday?"

"I was just offered the tickets and thought of you."

"Thank you," she said. "I'd like to come."

"Great, I'll pick you up at your place. Are you still in the apartment on Spruce?"

Grace didn't have a chance to answer. Vicky bustled in the room, bringing her larger-than-life personality with her.

"Why are you two hovering back here?" Vicky said, throwing Steve a sly smile. "You're not harassing my favorite northern girl, are you?"

Steve retreated. "Vicky, could you give Grace a hand with the delivery boxes? They're stacked out back on the loading dock." He held out his hand. "Plus I'll be needing those keys back from you."

Vicky dropped a set of keys into his outstretched hand. "Changing the subject won't save you. I know Grace will tell me everything."

Vicky helped Grace load the boxes onto a hand truck. Vicky was almost as tall as Steve and outweighed Grace by at least sixty pounds. She played for the local roller derby team and was a bit of a celebrity around Bolton. She was often covered in bruises.

"Did Steve ask you out?" Vicky barely seemed to notice that she was manhandling a stack of boxes that looked as if they weighed as much as Grace. "He's been wanting to for ages."

Grace struggled to pick up a box from the pallet.

"God, Grace you have such skinny little chicken arms. I'll deal with the heavy stuff," said Vicky. "You grab the paper towels."

Grace trailed behind Vicky, feeling like a child.

"God knows what Steve was thinking, asking you to carry this stuff." Vicky laughed. "Maybe he wanted to be the one who came to your rescue."

She and Vicky made their way single file along the narrow walkway to the employee entrance.

"He did ask me out," said Grace.

"He's a nice guy. You should definitely say yes."

"I did."

"Good," said Vicky. "And don't listen to what Lara has to say about him. They don't get along. Never have."

"Lara thinks he's too old for me."

"Steve is only twenty-eight. That's not too old."

"Lara knew his last girlfriend. She said it didn't go well."

Vicky headed for the storage room. "Do you like him?"

"I think so."

"What do you mean you 'think so'? You've worked for him for two years."

"That's different."

"I suppose it is."

"I think someone broke into my locker," said Grace.

"Anything missing?"

"Some personal stuff."

"Did you tell Steve?"

"It's nothing of value. Doesn't seem right to bother him about it."

On their last trip out to the loading dock, Grace's phone vibrated in her pocket. She didn't recognize the number. She told Vicky she'd be inside in a minute.

"Hello," said Grace. "Who is this?"

"It's Jordan. We need to talk."

"I'm going to call the police if you don't quit following me."

"Why would you do that, when all I want to do is have a conversation with you?"

"You don't scare me."

"Then what do you have to lose by talking to me?"

"Please don't call me again," said Grace.

Grace hung up the phone and slipped it in her apron's front pocket. Aside from a couple of people quietly smoking their cigarettes behind the shop next door, she was alone. Jordan's Bronco wasn't parked anywhere along the road.

The stress of not knowing when Jordan would show his face again was taking its toll. Grace jumped every time the café's front door opened. She couldn't focus so she was messing up people's orders. Steve eventually told her to go bus tables, something she hadn't done in a long time. She spent her break on the loading dock with her phone pressed to her ear. When Taylor's ex-boyfriend Alex finally answered he sounded more angry than sad.

"She dumped me. Why should I care where she is?"

"We're all worried about her," said Grace. "She was very close to Peter and Hannah Granger."

"I know you mean well, but it's none of my business now."

"I'm going over to her house to have a look. Can you meet me there?" Alex hung up.

Grace went and asked Steve for the rest of the day off. He walked her to the employee entrance and gave her a long hug.

"I'd give you a ride home but I can't leave," he said.

Grace felt guilty. She couldn't look him in the eye.

"I'll be okay," she promised.

"Are you still up for Friday?"

"Yes, definitely. I'm really looking forward to it."

Grace ducked outside before he could say anything more. The hug he'd given her had gone on a little too long and there was a brief moment that she worried he might try to kiss her. She liked Steve well enough but no longer trusted her own judgment, given how many times she'd been wrong about men in the past. Grace checked that Jordan's Bronco wasn't parked nearby before making her way to a neighborhood north of Main Street.

Taylor's house was a sky blue bungalow situated on Black Avenue. There was a park across the street where Taylor spent a lot of time in the summer. A cold wind rattled the bare trees and lifted Grace's skirt. The park was empty save a large black dog and its pint-size owner.

Taylor's housemates were a couple of grad students who'd recently gotten married during a trip to India. Nobody believed the ceremony was legal but they liked to pretend they were newlyweds anyway. Taylor had always complained about how loud they were when they were having sex, but apparently the volume had increased tenfold since they'd returned from India. Grace rang the bell several times before calling Taylor's name through the mail slot. There was no answer so she let herself in. She stepped over a couple of long-haired cats that were laz-ing near the front door and made her way down the hallway. Taylor's room was the last one on the left.

The north-facing windows let in very little natural light. A dresser, a double bed, a desk, and a closet were squeezed into the small space. A doorway led into Taylor's one luxury, an en-suite bathroom. The bed was made and everything was in good order. Wherever Taylor had gone, it didn't appear that she'd been in a huge hurry to get there.

Grace started with the papers that were stacked on the desk. There were a couple of unopened credit-card applications, notes on scraps of paper, articles she'd printed out to read, and a handful of receipts. Un-like the other members in Peter's writing group, Taylor was no longer a student at Bolton College. She'd graduated a year early, but instead of leaving Bolton to take a job she'd been offered in Chicago, she'd stayed on because she'd become attached to Peter's writing group. She held down two waitressing jobs and worked as a private tutor to make enough money to support herself. While everyone else slept she was up half the night working. Grace checked the desk drawers and beneath the bed. Wherever Taylor was, she had her laptop with her.

Having found nothing on the desk, Grace moved to the chest of drawers. Grace felt around the back corners and beneath the carefully folded clothing before searching the bedside table where she found a small bag of weed, a couple of condoms, and some loose change. Grace went through the closet, pulling wadded-up receipts from coat pockets, tissues and the odd bit of change from a couple of pairs of jeans. If the number of empty hangars was any indication, it appeared that her clothes were all accounted for, including her winter coats.

Grace saved the en-suite bathroom for last. Taylor's toiletry kit sat open next to the sink. There was a single toothbrush in the cup. Her hairbrush was under the sink next to a blow dryer. Her cosmetics were in a clear box beneath the mirror. Grace shut the door so she could use the toilet. The seat was as cold as ice. The toilet paper had fallen off the holder and rolled behind the toilet. As she was reaching for it, some-thing in the trash can caught her eye. What looked like packaging for a pregnancy test poked out from a pile of wadded-up tissues. Grace flushed the toilet and pulled up her tights.

The white pregnancy-test wand was at the bottom of the trash can, a blue cross clearly visible in the little window. Taylor had been raised by devout Catholics. Giving up a child would not have been an option. If Taylor really was pregnant, she'd want to keep the baby. Grace wondered what her boyfriend, Alex, thought about having a child. They'd not been going out for that long. Maybe this was why they'd split up.

Alex opened Taylor's bedroom door just as Grace was leaving. He looked past Grace like he was expecting to see Taylor standing there with her.

"She's not here," said Grace, backing farther into the room.

Alex sat down on the edge of the bed. Like Grace, he was still wearing a jacket.

"I'm sorry I was such a dick on the phone," he said. "It's not your fault Taylor dumped me."

"When's the last time you spoke to her?"

"Thursday afternoon. She came by my place and told me it was over. I felt like an idiot. I knew things weren't perfect between us, but I didn't think it had gotten that bad."

"Did she give you a reason?"

He shrugged. "She said we wanted different things. I've been hoping she'd change her mind."

"Did she say if she was going away?"

"She went to see her parents."

"Her parents live in Denver," said Grace.

"Yeah, I know. It's like she couldn't get far enough away from me."

Grace studied Alex's profile. He was a big South African man with a full beard but he sat with his shoulders slumped. Taylor had said that he'd played rugby for the national team when he was younger. Grace couldn't imagine it. The man next to her seemed so diminished. She wanted to shake him. It was time for him to quit feeling sorry for himself.

"Aside from her laptop, most of her stuff is here. If she was going away you'd think she'd at least pack a toothbrush," said Grace.

"She was pretty upset. Maybe she just got in her car and drove."

"Why was she upset?"

"That's a good question. She was the one that was breaking it off with me, not the other way around. She swore there was no one else, but I'm not sure I believe her. She's been a little weird over the last couple of months." His voice trailed off. "We haven't been together as much as we used to. At first I thought it was sort of nice. Things couldn't stay as intense as they'd been, but then I started to worry. Did she say anything to you about it?"

"No, but then I'm not sure she would have. Taylor and I aren't as close as we used to be."

"I guess that's my fault."

"It had nothing to do with you. Things got a little weird between her, Clare, and Lara. I think she wanted to get away from them for a while and since we're always together that meant getting away from me too. Do you have her parent's phone number? I'd like to call them to make sure she's okay."

"No, but I know their address. It's logged into the navigation system in my car."

"Could I have it? I promise to let you know if I manage to speak to her."

He nodded. "I'd appreciate that, but don't tell her I was in her room. It would piss her off."

Grace thought about the pregnancy test. It was in the inside pocket of her backpack. She'd put it in a Ziploc bag she'd found in the kitchen. She wasn't sure why she was taking it with her, and she was pretty sure Taylor would be angry if she found out. She followed Alex down the hallway. His wide back filled the narrow space.

"Alex, have you spoken to Taylor's housemates? Have they seen her since Thursday?"

"No, but they've been putting a lot of hours in on campus, so they haven't really been paying attention."

6

Wednesday

Macy parked next to the wide walkway leading up to the Bridger Cultural Center, where Peter Granger rented office space. Surrounded by sloping lawns and shaded by mature trees, the two-story brick building took up an entire block of downtown Bolton. It had once been a school but now housed galleries, offices, a restaurant, and a theater. Ryan was waiting in front of one of the three arched door-ways. He wore dark sunglasses even though the sky was overcast. He handed a cup of coffee to Macy as a way of greeting.

"You took your time getting here this morning," he said, pushing his sunglasses back on his head. "I hope I didn't keep you awake too late yesterday evening."

"Breakfast meeting with my new assistant, Alisa. She should be join-ing us soon."

Macy tried one of the doors but it was locked.

"Doors open at ten," said Ryan. "Who is Alisa and why is she join-ing us?"

"She's the new recruit I was telling you about last night. She's refreshingly keen, so I'd appreciate it if you didn't spoil it for me." Macy held up a copy of Peter Granger's latest novel that she'd stashed in her bag. "She's also a big fan of Granger's work and has read all his books. As I've read none, I feel her insight will be invaluable."

"I heard that his star has been falling for some time. Apparently he was a bit sour about it."

"Then you already know more than I do. Any news on the fire?"

"They're confident I'll have access this afternoon, at the latest, which is good as it looks like it's going to snow tonight."

A patrol car pulled into a space behind Macy's SUV. Alisa practically skipped up the walkway. She pumped Ryan's outstretched hand as Macy introduced them.

"Is it morbid to say I'm excited to be in Peter Granger's office?" asked Alisa.

Ryan tried to open the door again. "I collect body parts for a living. From my point of view, nothing is particularly morbid. But I do draw the line at taking selfies at crime scenes. That goes ditto for autopsies."

Alisa held up a set of keys. "I picked up the keys to Peter Granger's office yesterday afternoon, so we're all set."

"That may be so, but they won't open these doors," said Ryan.

Macy peered into the darkened entryway. There was a tall woman with sloped shoulders moving around a small office that was off to one side. She didn't seem to be in any hurry to open the doors. Macy tapped on the window and watched as the woman approached them. She used three separate keys to undo the locks. She craned her long neck and blinked at the trio.

"Detective Greeley?" she asked, making a point to study each one of them in turn.

Macy held out her hand. "Mrs. Holland, I spoke to you on the phone very briefly yesterday. These are my colleagues, Officer Montgomery and Special Investigator Ryan Marshall."

The door was opened a little wider and they were ushered inside. Mrs. Holland was dressed in a bright blue pantsuit and spoke with a Southern accent.

"We're all heartbroken," she said. "We have a lot of talented writers in Montana, but to have someone of Peter's caliber living on your door-step is something else entirely."

"How often did he come in?" asked Macy.

"As far as I know he was here pretty much every day, but as we have no requirement for our tenants to sign in, I can't say much beyond that."

"Did he use the facility in the evenings as well?"

"Yes, but not as often."

"I understand he had a writing workshop that met here on Tuesday evenings."

"That is correct. I'm not normally here in the evenings, but I have caught sight of him and his group on occasions when I've had to be here to attend an event that was scheduled in the evening."

"Do you know a Ms. Cornelia Hart?"

"Of course; she made all the arrangements for Peter's office rental. She let me know that you'd be needing the spare keys."

"I noticed the keys don't open the main doors. Is there any way tenants can get in after hours?"

Mrs. Holland pursed her lips. "Peter would have had keys for the front door as well. The set of spares you've been given only has his office keys." She directed them to a set of stairs. "Mr. Granger's office is on the second floor."

"Is there an alarm?"

"No, ma'am. Bolton really isn't the type of place people need alarms."

Ryan held up his phone. "Sorry, Macy, I've just heard from the crew working over at the house. I'm needed, so you're going to have to get started without me."

Macy had expected shelves full of books, but there wasn't a single vol-ume in Peter Granger's office. A low cabinet that was a good fifteen feet wide sat beneath the west-facing windows and the only thing hanging on the opposite wall was a framed pencil drawing. Macy stood in front of the image for a few minutes. The man's pose was similar to depic-tions of the crucifixion, but instead of a cross, Jesus was entangled in the branches of a tree. Gray water swirled inches beneath his bare feet. There was no signature. Macy slipped on a pair of latex gloves and took the frame down from the wall. The artist's name wasn't on the back either.

"Find something interesting?" asked Alisa.

She was standing at Macy's shoulder. The light coming in the east-facing window settled on Alisa's throat. The skin was mottled and scarred from where it looked like she'd been badly burned. Alisa pulled up the collar of her shirt when she realized Macy had noticed.

"Sorry for staring," said Macy. "I'm so used to looking for evidence I sometimes forget myself."

"No worries. It happened a long time ago."

It was the first time since they'd met that Alisa had let her guard down. For a split second the smile was gone. The burns to her neck may have happened a long time ago, but Alisa wasn't fooling anyone. She hadn't gotten over it.

Macy placed the frame back on the wall. "I feel like I've seen this image before. Do you know who the artist is?"

"Way outside my field of expertise."

Macy stepped away. "Mine too."

Peter Granger's polished metal desk looked like it had been manufactured in the 1930s. It faced a white wall that was blank aside from a crude crucifix carved from a piece of driftwood. This time there was no mistaking the religious reference. On the far end of the room things were less austere. A comfortable-looking brown leather chair and three two-seater sofas surrounded a low wooden coffee table that looked like it had been made from a set of antique doors. Other than an ashtray crowded with half-smoked cigarettes and a few magazines, the table was empty. The Persian carpet was old and threadbare but it looked like it had been recently vacuumed. Macy knelt down to inspect a dark stain at the foot of one of the sofas. She rubbed it lightly with her gloved finger and it came up clean. She pulled the carpet up and checked underneath. Nothing had seeped through onto the wooden floors.

"Where shall I start?" asked Alisa.

Macy directed her to the cabinet beneath the window. "Start on the left and move to the right."

Alisa slipped on a pair of latex gloves before opening the first set of double doors.

"There's a lot of stuff stored in here," said Alisa. She had a little poke around. "Thankfully, it looks like it's well organized."

Macy knelt down next to her. "This might be his archive."

"He's written twenty-six books. This is probably only a fraction of his work. I hope the rest wasn't in the house."

"I know it sounds daunting but I'd like you to go through what's here. We're looking for any recent correspondence, journal entries etc. I'll start on his desk."

Macy pulled the chair back from the desk and got down on her hands and knees. She swept a flashlight across the bare wooden floor, but there was nothing more exciting than a paper clip. She checked the chair. It was an expensive model with multiple levers. A few long gray hairs were embedded in the fabric of the headrest and dust clung to a strip of sticky residue on one of the armrests. She swiveled the chair around and wheeled it into the light streaming through the window. There was a dark patch on the seat. She bent over and sniffed, recoiling at the smell of urine. Peter Granger was in his late fifties. That was a little young to be incontinent, but Macy guessed anything was possible. She studied the sticky residue on the arm of the chair. There was a sliver of what looked like packing tape. The chair looked new. It could have been from the packaging. She'd have Ryan take a closer look.

The desktop was bare aside from a stainless-steel lamp, wireless keyboard and twenty-four-inch screen. Macy switched on the lamp before stooping down so she was eye level with the polished metal surface. It appeared to be completely free of marks.

"Alisa, do we know if Peter has his office cleaned?"

"Someone would have come in today, but it was cancelled."

Macy checked the trash can. It was empty.

"I wonder if Peter Granger always keeps his office this tidy. There's not so much as a fingerprint on this desk."

The central desk drawer contained three identical pens, a book of stamps, a small stack of Peter's business cards, and other miscellaneous items, all arranged so they sat in their individual compartments. She found a roll of packing tape, envelopes, printer paper, and several blank notebooks in another drawer. The two file drawers were more chaotic. Macy flipped through the tabs, finding everything from contracts to correspondence with publishers to royalty statements. There was a letter dated three weeks earlier inside a file containing Granger's rental agreement for the Bridger Cultural Center. A handful of tenants and some of their clients had threatened to make an official complaint against Peter Granger, saying he'd been verbally abusive on a number of occasions. Macy wrote down the names of the people who'd signed the letter, recognizing a couple of them from a list of tenants she'd seen on the center's Web site. A second letter was from the center's management, thanking Peter Granger for a generous donation that he'd made following the complaint. They'd sought to reassure him that he was a valued addition to Bolton's cultural scene.

As Macy was setting a thick folder labeled WRITER'S WORKSHOP on the desk, a slim notebook fell onto the floor. She picked it up and turned it over in her hands. The cover had a brown circular stain that could have been from the bottom of a coffee cup and the pages were stiff. Macy pried the notebook open. In places the ink bled across the pages, making it too blurry to read. On other pages the quality of the penmanship was as varied as the pen. Everything else in Peter's desk was well organized so Macy assumed the notebook must have belonged to one of his students. Aside from rough sketches of everything from a dog to a bearded man there were bits of poetry, shopping lists, and fragmented lines of hastily written text that Macy had trouble reading. The corner of one of the pages was folded back. A circle had been drawn around the text with a highlighter. In the margins someone had written in a very clear hand—*Read this one at the poetry slam!* Macy skimmed through the short poem before putting the notebook to one side.

A class register listed all the writers who'd attended Granger's Tuesday evening sessions since they'd started. He held approximately ten workshops a quarter, which extended into the summer months. Macy flipped through four years of lists, noting that at times the names varied more than others. Some attendees' names stood out as they were enrolled in the group for two or three years. Other students had been crossed off the lists after one quarter, never to reappear. Pippa Lomax had lasted an entire year. Macy flipped through the file but could find no other mention of her name.

Macy was a little surprised that all of Peter's students seemed to be female and wondered if that was significant. She glanced over to see how Alisa was getting on with the storage cabinets. Alisa was gingerly removing the files and placing them on the cabinet top as if they were holy relics. It was clear that she worshipped Peter Granger. Macy took the book Alisa had bought from her bag and flipped it open to a page that was marked with a receipt from the Country Bookshelf. The hardcover doorstop had set the Montana Department of Justice back $22.

"Alisa," said Macy. "In your opinion, is Peter Granger's fan base male or female?"

"Definitely female. I don't think guys get him."

"Why's that?"

"Well, for starters, the women he portrays are often the characters that drive the narrative. They're never secondary to men. He's also not afraid to make his male characters vulnerable. I guess it's refreshing coming from a male writer of his caliber."

"You seem to have a bit of a crush on him."

"Only a mild one. I'm not that far gone."

"Do you think he inspired that kind of reaction from a lot of women?"

"I've gone to a few of his author events here in Bolton. He has a huge number of female fans who hang on his every word."

"I had no idea he had so much charisma."

"A talk he did a few years back is posted online. It's hard not to be impressed with how well he connects with the audience. I'll send you the link."

"That would be helpful."

"Did you find something interesting in the desk?" asked Alisa.

"Class lists from his writing workshop. All his students appear to be female. Have you ever been to something like that?"

"No, but I once read an article in the local arts magazine. If you wanted to get in you had to know your shit. I can't imagine he needed the money."

"His P.A. hinted at money troubles."

Alisa raised an eyebrow. "He's a bestselling author."

"Times are tough all over. His last three books didn't do very well."

"Might explain why he's been so standoffish in the press."

"Ryan said something about that. Care to elaborate?"

"He claimed he'd been misquoted too many times for him to trust the newspapers so he quit doing interviews."

"What kinds of things did he supposedly say?"

Alisa shrugged. "Apparently, he could come off as a bit of an elitist. He was always refusing to do any interviews with publications he didn't deem worthy."

"Not exactly on a charm offensive then. Did this happen recently?"

"I think so, but I'd have to check to be sure. It would be such a shame if it's really him in that house."

"Every hour that passes without hearing from him makes it more likely."

Alisa opened the next set of cabinets. "Detective Greeley, I'm still not sure I understand what I'm supposed to be looking for. This is mostly notes on manuscripts, early drafts, and folders containing research."

"I'm not entirely sure either. I'm hoping we'll know it when we see it."

Alisa held up a sheaf of papers bound with thick green rubber bands. "These are the copyedited notes from one of his bestsellers. I'm surprised he doesn't have this locked up in a vault." She flipped through the pages. "Do you have any idea how much this would be worth online? Take a look at these notes. He was so meticulous."

Macy studied the manuscript Alisa was holding. The rubber band was the same color green she'd seen on Cornelia's copy of Peter Granger's most recent and yet unpublished novel. The sheaf of papers was a few inches thick. Macy went over to where Alisa was sitting on the floor for a closer look. She recognized Cornelia Hart's handwriting immediately.

"This isn't Peter Granger's handwriting," said Macy. "Cornelia Hart made these notations. Are there any more manuscripts in there?"

Alisa pulled out a few more edited manuscripts and placed them on the floor. Macy and Alisa checked them over a few times to be sure.

"It looks like Cornelia Hart has been editing his manuscripts for the past ten years," said Alisa.

"Would you say that it's a little unusual for an author's personal assistant to give such detailed feedback on their work? Isn't that the publisher's job?" Macy took a moment to read through some of the notes. "This isn't just fixing a few typos. It looks like she's suggesting whole new plotlines."

Alisa read through some of the notations on the manuscript she'd pulled out first. "I've read this novel a couple of times so I know it pretty well. It would be interesting to see how many of her suggestions made it to the final draft."

"Have a look but don't get too caught up in it. I don't know what their working relationship was like. It might be that these suggestions actually evolved from conversations she was having with Peter. They may not all be her ideas."

There was a light knock and the door swung open. A tall man with gaunt features stepped into the room. The glare from the overhead lights bounced off his bald head.

"Oh, sorry," he said. "I heard people talking and I thought it might be Peter. So much for wishful thinking."

Macy pulled out her badge and introduced herself and Alisa. "How do you know Peter Granger?"

The man wasn't intimidated by the fact that they were police officers. He closed the door behind him and studied the stacks of Peter's edited manuscripts on the floor.

"I have an office two doors down. Peter and I are friends, or rather were friends. I keep hoping this is all a horrible mistake."

Macy took up her pen. "We're hoping to have some clarification later this afternoon. Could I have your name, please?"

He frowned. "Richard Nichols. As I said, I have an office down the hall."

"Mrs. Holland mentioned your name when I spoke to her yesterday. I understand you're a writer as well?" said Macy.

Richard pulled out a couple business cards and handed them to Alisa and Macy. Macy found herself looking down the barrel of a gun. The words LOCKED AND LOADED and AMAZON BEST-SELLING AUTHOR were emblazoned across the stark image. Macy flipped it over and studied the contact details. She'd never heard of Richard Nichols.

Alisa piped up. "Cool card. How many books have you written?"

"I'm working on my fourth. If you're interested you can download an e-book. Ninety-nine cents a title at the moment. You should check it out."

Macy tapped Richard's business card on the table. She didn't know anything about Richard or his relationship with Peter Granger, but it did strike her as callous that he was trying to make a sale while standing in the office of a man who may have been murdered. She'd read somewhere that authors were supposed to be more empathetic than the average person. She placed Richard's business card on the desk, gun barrel up.

"I'm not familiar with your name," said Macy.

"I'm self-published, strictly e-books."

"How well did you know Peter?"

"I'd stop by and we'd talk shop sometimes. Quite a thing to have someone of his reputation a few doors away."

Alisa's fingers had been flying over the keys on her phone since he'd introduced himself. "From what I can tell from your Web site, Peter Granger's novels are very different from yours. I've read many of his interviews. He was very negative about genre fiction, crime in particular," said Alisa. "Did that cause any friction between the two of you?"

Richard stiffened. "I'll admit we didn't always see eye to eye, but during a particularly heated discussion he admitted his last three books were commercial disasters. A couple of weeks later he told me he'd decided to give self-publishing a try."

"In a way that would make sense. He already has the name recognition," said Alisa.

"That's where we parted ways again. He would only use a pen name. I told him it wouldn't work but he was insistent."

"Why did you think it wouldn't work?" asked Macy.

"He'd decided to write a crime novel."

"That's crazy," said Alisa. "He wouldn't—"

"Wouldn't stoop to writing a crime novel? Is that what you were about to say?" asked Richard.

Macy cut in. "I'm trying to solve a real crime here so I really don't care what sort of fiction we're talking about. I just want to know what he was up to over the past few months."

"To tell you the truth I think he was doing a great deal of soul searching. He knew I was right about using his real name but he still insisted on anonymity."

"And what's to say he couldn't create a bestseller under a new name?" asked Macy. "He's clearly a gifted writer."

"Self-publishing is a crowded market so you've got to hustle for every sale. There's a great deal of self-promotion on social media. Peter finds the commercial side of writing distasteful. With that attitude I really didn't see how he'd manage but he wouldn't listen. He insisted the story was all that mattered and he had a good one."

"Did he elaborate?" asked Macy.

"No, but I imagine you'll find something here in his papers. I know he's been working on it."

"Did you ever socialize outside these offices?"

Richard walked over to the framed pencil sketch and stared at it.

"Peter was a bit of a snob. If he was afraid to let the world know he was writing a crime novel he certainly wasn't going to admit to knowing a crime writer," he said.

"That must have hurt."

"Not as much as you think. I've read a couple of Peter's books. I was bored senseless. As far as I could tell his characters were all navel-gazing narcissists."

"Did you ever tell him that?"

"That's not the type of thing you say to Peter Granger's face."

"Did he ever criticize your work?"

Richard almost laughed. "Peter never read my books but that didn't stop him from being critical. He dismissed anything that was mass-market as rubbish."

"And yet he was trying his hand at a crime novel," said Alisa. "He'd have been worried that the truth might come out."

"He actually swore me to secrecy, which is crazy. If anyone leaked that he was the author he would have gotten loads of free publicity. For a man who was supposedly so worldly he was incredibly naive."

"Can you tell me anything about Peter Granger's work habits?" asked Macy. "Did you ever witness anything that caused you concern?"

"Aside from me and the writing workshop students, Peter had very few visitors." He spread his arms. "This was his sanctuary. He had difficulty focusing on his work if there were any distractions, hence the almost bare white walls. When he was here he worked."

"It reminds me of a monk's cell," said Macy.

"That's exactly what Granger was going for," said Alisa. "He wrote his first book in a cell he rented from monks in some northern Italian village. It was a silent order. All he had was a desk and a small window looking out over a lake. It was so cold he had to wear gloves."

Richard smiled. "I've been to that same monastery. They now have Wi-Fi, espresso makers in the rooms, and central heating, but thankfully the view hasn't changed."

"What about his students? Did you ever see them hanging around the office?" asked Macy.

"Yes, there were always a half-dozen young women waiting outside his door on Tuesday evenings."

"Always women?"

Richard nodded. "Without exception. Given feminist bloggers have recently outed him as an overrated white male writer who'd had far too many privileges, he was surprisingly supportive of female authors."

"Were there any students who may have been closer to him than others?"

"Perhaps. To tell you the truth they all looked the same in my eyes— young, keen, and a little too highly strung. I'm not sure I'd be able to pick any of them out if I saw them on the street."

Macy handed Richard her business card. "I may contact you with further questions."

Richard turned the card over in his hands. As he read Macy's name he smiled. "Of course, Detective Greeley, anytime."

Macy put the file she'd been reading to one side.

"I don't know if this was a waste of time or not," said Macy. "Granger's laptop was probably destroyed in the fire. Without it we're going to be in the dark until the tech guys track down his recent activity online."

"I hope he was backing up his recent work on a remote server," said Alisa. "It would be a shame if it was lost."

"Cornelia Hart should know. I've given her details to the team in Helena. I'm sure they've been in touch."

"The tech guys should also be able to access his e-mails."

"Cornelia Hart hinted at money problems. If his last three books were flops he may have been getting desperate."

"You think this could have been an insurance job?" asked Alisa.

"Under normal circumstances I'd say yes, but given we've got two dead bodies that are most likely the homeowners, I seriously doubt it. The house and art collection were insured for over twenty million dollars. According to Cornelia Hart, a collection of foundations stood to benefit in the event of their deaths. If there was an individual benefactor I'd be far more suspicious."

Ryan Marshall poked his head in the door. "It's pretty Spartan in here."

"Should make your job easier," said Macy.

"This isn't even a crime scene, why are you bothering?" asked Alisa.

Ryan tilted his head in Macy's direction. "Between me and you, Special Investigator Greeley is a bit of a taskmaster. If she says jump, I generally say after you dear."

Macy looked up from the file she was reading. "Alisa, ignore him. He's bored because he's on hold until they give him access to the house. He begged me to give him something to do."

"The temperature is dropping outside. At least it's warm in here," said Ryan.

"Any news at the house?" asked Alisa.

"I need to be back there in a couple of hours to oversee the removal of the bodies. Thankfully, going over this office shouldn't take long." He pulled out a pair of latex gloves. "I see you are both appropriately gloved and booted. Where would you like me to start?"

"There's a stain on the carpet that may be worth looking at."

Ryan got on his hands and knees so he could have a better look at the Persian carpet. "You mean this one between the sofa and the coffee table?" he asked.

"Yep," said Macy. "I didn't look too carefully, so there may be more."

"Are you going to check if it's blood?" asked Alisa.

"Among other things," said Ryan.

Ryan told Alisa to close the blinds and shut off the lights. He sprayed the sofa and carpet with Luminal and checked with a UV light. A bright patch of blue fluoresced on the carpet. A couple of drops showed up on the sofa as well.

Alisa's voice went up an octave. "It's blood?"

Ryan lowered his voice so only Macy could hear him. "Where'd you find this girl? It's like working a crime scene with a cheerleader."

"Play nice, Ryan," said Macy. She asked Alisa to switch on the lights when Ryan was finished taking photos.

"I'm not sure this is significant. It's not a large quantity." He took out a flashlight and examined the stain more closely. "I would also say it's been there for a while. Hopefully it's not degraded. I'll take samples and send it off for analysis. Anything else you want me to look at?"

"Could you check his desk chair?" asked Macy. "It smells of urine and there's some sticky residue on one of the arm rests."

Ryan smiled. "Macy, are you suggesting that Peter Granger was incontinent?"

"When you alert the press leave my name out of it," said Macy. "The chair looks relatively new. The sticky residue could be from packing tape."

Ryan had a sniff. "You may be right on both counts. I'll take a swab but I'd say it's definitely urine."

Macy peeled off her gloves and set the office keys down on the desk. "We're going to leave you to it. We need to go back to the office and arrange some interviews."

Ryan pulled his camera out of one of his cases. "No worries. I'll let you know what I find."

7

Wednesday

Grace's uncle wasn't the first person to say, "a man without guts lives on his knees," but Grace was pretty sure he'd said it with a frequency and volume that left all pretenders in the dust. Not that it mattered. He was dead and so was her aunt, two people Grace couldn't help but love despite their transgressions. Over the years Grace had learned to live with what she called relative degrees of disappointment. She had to balance all that they'd done for her with all that they'd done wrong. Grace's childhood wasn't easy. Her mother was prone to drink and when she drank she was prone to forget she was a mother. Following years of neglect she abandoned Grace at the age of seven, leaving her locked in their mobile home for three days straight in the middle of a heat wave. If not for her aunt and uncle, Grace would have been put into foster care. Under their roof she'd felt safe for the first time in her life. Grace focused on that single factor when she looked back on the time she'd spent living with them. If she dwelled too long on the horror that came before and after she probably would have jumped off a bridge long ago.

Grace's aunt also peppered everyday conversation with her favorite sayings. Often lifted straight from the scriptures, her aunt's words were more than just lessons. She used them as a reminder of the great burden she carried in saving all of their souls. The woman prayed daily, attended church several times a week, and went to great lengths to help the less fortunate but, try as she might, it just wasn't possible for her to compensate for her husband's crimes. If there was a hell, Grace knew that both her aunt and uncle were there. That didn't stop Grace from loving them, and if loving them destined Grace to hell, so be it. If she wanted to be reunited with any of her family members in the afterlife it seemed that was the place she needed to be.

Grace pulled the art studio door shut behind her and switched on the lights. It was only a little after nine in the evening so she'd expected to run into some other students, but the room was empty. She unbuttoned her woolen coat and pulled off her red hat and mittens as she made her way to her work space. It was cold in the studio so she'd be leaving her scarf on. She removed her sketchbook from her shoulder bag and shut off her phone.

Several of Grace's drawings were tacked to the corkboard above the worktable alongside random images plucked from magazines, postcard racks, and Internet searches. There was also a growing list of her aunt and uncle's favorite sayings. Whenever she remembered a new one she'd write it down. She pulled off the sheet and quickly scanned it before making an addition.

Blessed are the meek, for they shall inherit the earth.

The best offense is a good defense.

Whoever keeps his mouth and his tongue keeps himself out of trouble.

Even a fish wouldn't get caught if he kept his mouth shut.

Owe nothing to anyone except to love one another.

It's easy to be generous with another man's money.

The name of the LORD is a fortified tower; the righteous run to it and are safe.

A man without guts lives on his knees.

Grace opened the locked cabinet where she stored her work and set a small canvas measuring 11 by 13 inches on an easel. She'd always been good at drawing, but it wasn't until she'd enrolled in school that she'd realized art could help her make sense of her past. It wasn't her fault that her past was a scary place.

The outline of four young women huddled in the back of an eighteen-wheeler's cavernous cargo bay was slowly emerging from the canvas. A single shaft of light cut through a thin gap in the container's metal siding. Only one of the girls directly engaged the viewer. The others were slumped together in a tangle of bare limbs that were so lifeless they could have been body parts. It was one of twelve paintings Grace was working on for a student show that was taking place the following week. The other paintings were already finished and stored safely in the cupboard. Together they formed a visual narrative of her past. If Grace was going to be forced to tell her story, she was going to do it on her terms. She'd already decided to sign the paintings with her real name. Peter Granger had been right about one thing—hiding wasn't a workable solution.

After Grace was invited to join Peter's writing workshop, he arranged to meet with her privately in his office a couple times a week. She'd thought it was for extra tuition but he had other ideas. It turned out that Peter wasn't just gifted at telling stories; he was also good at getting other people to tell theirs. He seemed to understand that Grace craved two things in life. She needed to feel safe and she needed to talk to someone about what had happened in Collier. Going to his office felt a bit like going to confession. She sensed they were growing closer. It was a bit like falling in love. For a few glorious weeks she felt loved.

Grace pried the lid from a plastic container and mixed the dark slurry with the butt end of a paintbrush, occasionally smearing a bit on a scrap piece of paper to see whether the tone and texture were right for what she wanted to achieve. She set it aside and opened a drawer containing dozens of jam jars. She picked out two. One was labeled red dust and the other, medium gray ash. She added a bit of each to the mixture and stirred it well. She checked the color again before adding a bit more red dust. It took several tries to get the shade she was after. This was her thing. She painted with dust and ash.

She dipped a thin brush in the paint and set to work. As the scene grew darker and gathered detail, everything aside from the canvas faded into the distance. Sometimes Grace was so focused she forgot to breathe. Numbness would creep into her bones. In winter it was always worse. Her fingertips would go lily white. If you broke the skin there would be no blood.

Grace had tried to find out more about the four girls in the painting but the newspaper articles only said they were young, Polish, and trafficked for the sex trade. After they died of heat exhaustion their bodies were dumped behind a toilet block at a popular picnic area along Route 93. Grace's only personal contact had been a whispering voice through a small air vent in the container. Grace had been seven years old but she still remembered the roughness of the girl's lips. They'd cracked like ice. She'd been too dehydrated to cry. Grace touched the paintbrush against the face of the girl who'd begged for help. Her name was Katya and she was just shy of sixteen when she died.

The studio's windows rattled as wind whipped around the building. Overhead the lights flickered. Flecks of fresh snow stuck to the glass and the ground glowed white under the glare of the lamps that dotted the campus pathways. It was half past two in the morning. Grace sat back in her chair and appraised the canvas in front of her. The image was certainly haunting. The girl's mouth was open wide and screaming. This time Grace wanted to make sure Katya was heard.

Grace reached over and opened the cabinet door. She needed to line up the paintings so she could look at them as a group. She placed the twelve canvases in a row along the base of a wall where the class gathered to critique each other's artwork. She was setting the last painting down at the end of the row when she heard someone shouting.

The door to the studio was still shut and as far as she could tell she was alone.

"Hello," she called. "Is anyone there?"

Receiving no answer, Grace went to the door. The hallway was also empty. She stood for a few minutes, listening, but aside from the wind gusting outside and the click and tick of the building's heating system it was silent. Grace headed toward the front entrance. Sometimes one of the security guards would hang out in a little seating area near the elevators. One of them often had homemade cookies and was always willing to share. Halfway along the corridor, Grace noticed the light was on in the staff break room. She stood outside the door for a few seconds and listened. Someone was crying. Grace knocked lightly and waited for a reply. The door swung open just as she was about to knock again.

Jessica Reynolds's face was flushed to the point of looking feverish. Her hair was a wild mass of dark curls. She tucked it behind her ears and seconds later it escaped again. Her eyes were raw from crying. She sniffed into a tissue.

"Grace, you're here late."

Grace tilted her head toward the studio. "I've been preparing for the student show." She hesitated. "Are you okay, Ms. Reynolds? I thought I heard someone shouting."

Jessica held open the door and indicated that Grace was to follow her inside.

"That was the sound of me being frustrated. It turns out paperwork doesn't respond well to neglect." Jessica waved a hand at several folders that sat open on a round table. A bottle of white wine stood among them, also open. "I thought it would help to get on top of things. There's all the scheduling for next term, new applicants. I'll have to find someone to cover Hannah's classes . . ." Jessica picked up the bottle and checked how much was left. "I'd offer you a glass, but it seems I've already finished most of it."

"That's okay," said Grace.

Jessica half smiled. "Another time then."

Everyone in the art department knew Jessica and Hannah were close. There had been rumors going around that they'd been having an affair for quite some time. Grace was hoping it was true—anything to put a giant female-size hole in Peter Granger's ego.

"Have you heard anything from the police?" asked Grace.

"Nothing definite, but every hour that goes by without any word from Hannah and Peter makes it more likely they were in the house."

"I am sorry. I know you and Hannah were close."

Jessica raised an eyebrow. "We were more than that."

"I know."

Jessica leaned against the counter.

"I was hoping she'd leave Peter." Her voice faded. "But it didn't seem to be in the cards."

"She would have been better off without him."

"I thought you were a fan."

Grace shrugged. "Apparently, I was a disappointment."

"Hannah was convinced you were sleeping with him."

"That didn't happen."

"I told Hannah that she was being a hypocrite. If she was having an affair there was no reason Peter shouldn't have his fun, regardless of how inappropriate it was."

"What made her think I was doing something inappropriate?"

"Hannah knew all about you girls. God knows how many of you slept with him."

"I never . . ."

Jessica poured the remaining drops of wine into a plastic cup. "Even I saw how you girls were with him. You'd hang on his every word. Personally, I don't understand what you could have seen in him. You're less than half his age."

Grace stammered. "This isn't right. I never did anything like that."

"Peter said that you were so obsessed with him that he had to cut you out of the writing group."

Grace felt the color rising in her cheeks. Her mouth was dry. She went to the sink and filled a glass she found in the drainer with tap water.

Jessica turned away. "Anyway, it doesn't matter anymore. They're both dead."

"It matters to me," said Grace. "I don't want to be accused of something I didn't do. Peter was angry because I wouldn't give him permission to use what I'd told him about my past in a book he was writing. He tried to get me to sign a release form but I wouldn't do it." She paused.

"You work in the administration office so you must know my real name. . . ."

Jessica's voice caught. She seemed to want to say one thing but then said another.

"Grace, for what it's worth, I believe you. Hannah told me things about Peter. The man was a pig."

Jessica nearly tripped on a table leg as she turned back toward the table. She was crying. She snatched a tissue from a box and pressed it to her face.

"I'll give you a ride home," said Grace. "Just give me a few minutes to put my stuff away."

Jessica closed her eyes for a few seconds. "This is so humiliating."

"I'm not going to tell anyone."

Jessica took a deep breath.

"Thank you, Grace. You're being very kind."

Grace resisted the urge to give Jessica a hug.

"Come find me in the studio when you're ready to go," said Grace.

Grace reshuffled the order of the finished canvases several times until she was satisfied. Two needed more work and one wasn't going to make the cut. She'd already decided to paint something else. She just wasn't sure what that would be. She was starting to put the paintings away when Jessica came in the studio.

Jessica looked far less vulnerable bundled up in her heavy coat and scarf.

"Grace, these look amazing. Are you pleased?" she asked.

"Two need some retouching and that one on the end isn't working at all. I'm going to trash it and try something else."

Grace was suddenly conscious that no one aside from her advisor had seen any of her work for quite some time. Part of her wanted to step between Jessica and the canvases, but she stood her ground. She needed someone to tell her that the work was good and Jessica seemed a safe bet. Jessica stopped in front of each painting for a few moments before moving on. For a long time she stared at the image of the man crucified in the limbs of a tree. At the bottom, Genesis 3:19 was scribbled in pencil next to Grace's very faint signature. That was something else that needed retouching. If Grace Adams was going to out herself she would have to be bold about it.

"What is Genesis 3:19?" asked Jessica.

"For dust thou art, and unto dust shalt thou return."

"My parents were lapsed Catholics so it's all lost on me. Were you raised in the church?"

"My aunt wouldn't have had it any other way."

"And your mother?"

Grace could only guess. "I'm pretty sure she was an atheist."

Jessica's voice was so soft Grace barely heard her. "Where does that phrase 'ashes to ashes, dust to dust' come from?"

"Funeral rites. 'We therefore commit his body to the ground; earth to earth, ashes to ashes, dust to dust.'"

Jessica smiled but she didn't look happy. "'Ashes to ashes, funk to funky. We know Major Tom's a junkie.'" She turned her back on the paintings. "I'm afraid that's the extent of my biblical knowledge."

"We should get going," said Grace. "Give me a few minutes to put these away."

Jessica's offer of help was declined. "I'm sorry about earlier," said Jessica. "I shouldn't have said that stuff to you. I don't want Hannah to be remembered as someone who was vindictive."

Grace carried the canvases back to the cupboard and locked them inside. She didn't think she could respond to Jessica's comment without sounding bitter, so she kept her mouth shut. Grace had lost all respect for Hannah. She couldn't understand how a woman she so admired could be married to a man who had absolutely zero integrity. Hannah wasn't liberated. She was weak. All Grace had ever been to Hannah was a potential threat to a marriage that was, for all intents and purposes, a complete sham. Hannah had no right to judge Grace or anyone else's behavior.

Grace found Jessica sound asleep on one of the sofas near the building's entrance. She had to shake her awake.

"Here," said Grace, taking her by the arm. "Let's get you home."

"I hope we don't get stuck in a ditch," said Jessica. "The roads will be a mess tonight."

"Don't worry. My truck can get through most anything."

It quickly became clear that Jessica was uncomfortable with silence. The more Grace withdrew the more she talked.

"Hannah and I met two years ago when I started working in the administrative offices," she said. "She'd come in to pick up her class schedule for the new term. It was so mundane and yet that was the moment that changed everything for me."

Jessica didn't wait for Grace to reply before detailing the circumstances of their first evening out together and how long it took to admit that they had feelings for each other.

Bundled up in their coats, gloves, and scarves, they pushed open the double doors and headed outside. Grace was beginning to wonder if Jessica had any friends she could talk to. Keeping her relationship with Hannah secret for two years would have been lonely and, now that Hannah was gone, it was about to get a lot worse. Grace locked arms with Jessica and together they ploughed through the northerly winds that were blasting across the parking lot.

"I'm not ready for winter," said Jessica. "I'm not ready for anything."

Jessica's side yard butted up against the railroad tracks that ran through the north end of town. The mournful whistle of a passing train was the first thing Grace heard upon opening the car door. The fallen snow was already turning soupy and the dark puddles trembled as the great lumbering locomotive passed like a shadow through the neighborhood. Grace regarded Jessica for a few moments. The woman had yet to make a move. She sat in the front seat of Grace's pickup truck staring at her house. Grace went around and pulled open the passenger-side door.

Jessica was like a child. Grace coaxed her out into the night and led her to the front door where she fumbled about looking for the keys, checking her coat pockets, backpack, and purse in turn.

"Always the last place you look," Jessica said, sliding the key into the lock and opening the door. "I could never get my head around leaving my door unlocked. People around here are too trusting."

Grace didn't mention her dog, the three dead bolts on her door, or the handgun that was hidden in her shoulder bag. After nearly two years of living without it, she'd started carrying it again. She no longer felt safe in Bolton.

"People around here don't always know what's best," said Grace.

Grace turned on the lights in the front room while Jessica stood watching her from the cramped entryway.

"Come and sit down." Grace helped Jessica out of her coat and led her into the living room. "I'll make us some tea."

The digital clock on the microwave put the time at twenty minutes to three in the morning. Grace went through the cupboards until she found some mugs and a couple packets of tea that looked vaguely herbal. She put the kettle on the electric stove and switched on the heat. She should have asked Jessica if there was anyone she could call before they left the campus. Now it felt like it was too late. She peeked out into the living room. Jessica still had her hat on. She was curled up under a blanket on the far end of the sofa.

"Here," said Grace. She handed Jessica a cup that had GO BEARS written on the side.

Jessica wrapped her hands around the warm mug and said a quiet thank-you.

"There's another blanket on the back of the chair if you want it," said Jessica.

Grace sat in an armchair and sipped her tea. "You have a nice house. Have you lived here a long time?"

Jessica didn't answer. She'd traded her mug for a small, carved figure of a bird. She turned it over in her hands several times before returning it to its place on the side table.

"Hannah carved this for me from a piece of wood she found when we were out hiking near Big Sky. Have you ever been so happy that it actually makes you fearful? Until I met Hannah, I never felt like I had anything to lose."

"The police haven't confirmed anything yet. There's still a chance it wasn't Hannah in the house the night of the fire."

Jessica kept her voice low. "Grace, I've been living on hope for far too long already. I can't do it anymore."

"Is there anyone I can call? I don't think you should be on your own."

"You can go if you like. I'll be fine."

Grace didn't believe that was the case, so she stayed put.

Jessica's chin dropped to her chest and some of the tea tipped out onto the blanket. Grace took the cup and Jessica mopped up the mess with a tissue.

"Grace, have you ever done anything you regret?" she asked.

"I suppose so, but I think it's a pretty common feeling."

"I did something stupid. I'm worried—"

Grace cut her off.

"You got drunk. Stop beating yourself up," said Grace.

"You misunderstand me."

Grace didn't want to hear any more. She was already more involved than she wanted to be. Besides, Jessica was too drunk to know what she was saying, and if she knew something about the fire at Peter and Hannah's house she could go speak to the police. Grace wasn't her confessor.

"You should try to sleep," said Grace.

Jessica took hold of the wooden bird again.

"Will you stay?" she asked.

"If it's okay with you I'll sleep on the sofa."

"Hannah was sorry. I think you should know that. She wanted to speak to you about what was going on with Peter and so many things. It was just a matter of time." Jessica's voice caught. "And now there is no time."

Grace led Jessica to the bathroom. "Let's get you ready for bed. My aunt always used to say 'God's mercies never end; they are new every morning.'"

"Do you actually believe that?" asked Jessica.

Grace studied Jessica's face and found someone who didn't need to hear the truth.

"There's always a reason to hope," said Grace. "Until you know for sure, you need to believe that anything is possible."

Thursday

Grace sat up on the sofa and looked around. She'd been sleeping heavily so it took her a few seconds to remember where she was. A car's headlights trailed across Jessica's living room wall. Grace checked her phone. It was coming up on six thirty in the morning, but it was still pitch-black outside. She'd been having a nightmare. Someone was pulling off her clothes. All she could do was watch. She had felt like she was trapped in her own body.

The hallway light was on. Grace kicked off the blankets and went to investigate. Jessica must have passed out on her way to the bathroom. She was halfway out her bedroom door, sprawled across the carpeted floor. Grace gave her a gentle shake.

"Jessica," she said. "Wake up. Let's get you back into bed."

Jessica's pulse was very weak and there was a pool of vomit beneath her head. Grace took hold of Jessica's shoulders with both hands and shook her hard. Jessica's head rocked back and forth but her eyes did not open. Grace went into the bedroom and switched on the light. There was an empty bottle of prescription medication on the nightstand next to the phone. Grace read the label while she waited to be connected to emergency services.

"I need an ambulance to come to 23 Copper Road," said Grace. "I think my friend has overdosed on Xanax."

8

Thursday

Macy's guilt multiplied along with the calories, but the triple stack of blueberry pancakes on the plate in front of her was calling her name. Working flat out had done nothing for her exercise routine. She went to the gym half as often as she used to, and the only running she seemed to do on a regular basis was chasing her son around the house. Full of good intentions, she'd carefully considered the daily special on the menu board, resigning herself to the poached eggs with spinach, but a waitress had walked by with a stack of blueberry pancakes for another customer and all of Macy's willpower evaporated. She dribbled a bit more maple syrup on the pancakes and wondered if she should order the eggs anyway. A little protein might soften the sugar high that was surely coming her way.

She scanned the front page of the local paper. A short article about the ongoing investigation into the fire featured a photo of an ambulance being driven away from the house. Snow was just starting to fall when they'd finally removed the remains at around nine the previous evening. Macy checked the time. Ryan was supposed to be meeting her for breakfast with news from the medical examiner in Helena. Without proper identification of the bodies, her investigation was going nowhere. She caught sight of Ryan speaking to the hostess and waved him over to her table.

He sat down in the chair opposite and ordered some coffee from a waitress who'd come to give him a menu.

"Large Americana, black please," he said.

"Would you like to order while I'm here?" The waitress pointed to the wall. "The specials are on the board."

Ryan gave Macy's pancakes a reproachful glance before ordering the poached eggs and spinach.

"What on earth are you trying to achieve, Detective Greeley?" he asked. "A hyperglycemic coma?"

Macy's mouth was full of an unholy trinity of blueberries, pancake, and maple syrup. She swallowed the pancakes along with her pride. "I have zero willpower."

"I hope Aiden likes women on the large side."

She sipped her coffee. "Please say you have news from the medical examiner."

He unfurled his napkin. "We have a positive ID on Peter Granger."

"And the other victim?"

"That ceiling beam did some serious damage. Shattered the skull, pelvis, and rib cage. Dental records won't do so they're having to look at other means of making a positive ID, such as DNA, which will take some time."

"But you're sure the body is a female."

"Absolutely."

"What's the ME's gut feeling?"

"You know Priscilla, she's being tight-lipped. Won't think of sharing her findings until all the facts are in."

"And do we have a cause of death on Peter Granger?"

"Given the state of the remains you'd think it was the fire that killed him, but that's not what happened."

Macy pierced a pile of pancakes with her fork. "Ryan, stop being so cagey and spill."

Ryan moved to one side as the waitress served him his coffee. He waited for her to leave before speaking again.

"There's evidence that he'd been tied up at some point . . . deep ligature marks on his wrists and ankles."

"How could you know that if the bodies were so badly burned?"

"Two things saved us from losing all the evidence in the fire. First and most important, the victims were lying under not only a duvet but also a polyester blanket, which is a decent flame retardant. Only the areas that were completely exposed were heavily charred. In Peter's case this was the entire left side of his body and his head. The female victim's legs and head were exposed, but her arms and torso were well protected. It also helped that she was wearing a sweatshirt that happened to be flame resistant. Have you heard of a clothing brand called Carhartt?"

"Vaguely."

"The company started off making clothing for workers in blue-collar industries, the railroads, the oil fields, that sort of thing. They might be considered trendy now, but a lot of their clothing is still produced at a high industry standard. Our victim probably wasn't even aware that she was wearing a sweatshirt that was NFPA 2112 compliant. It didn't prevent all the damage, but that in combination with the duvet and polyester blanket means we have something to work with."

"Any indication she was tied up?"

"Nope."

"Tell me about these ligature marks you found on Peter Granger."

"The ligatures were restrictive enough to lacerate the skin. We're thinking a thin-gauge wire was used. You can actually see where the skin separated. . . ."

Macy held up her hand. "That's enough detail at the breakfast table. Could it have been some sort of kinky sex act that went wrong?"

"Would have been some pretty aggressive foreplay."

"Any wire found at the scene?"

"Nothing so far, but we did find trace metal in the wounds. We're thinking he'd been tied up for some time, possibly days."

"Shit. So what actually killed him?"

"A severe skull fracture most likely caused hemorrhaging in the brain. Poor guy was dead before the fire started. Tox screen should tell us if he was otherwise impaired."

"So, your hunch that this was arson holds true."

"Looks that way. The fire was probably set to cover up a murder."

"Wouldn't be the first time. What about the house itself? Has it revealed any clues to what happened that night?"

"No, not yet. The weather moved in last night. It's too big a structure to protect it in full but they did what they could. You've got to admire the crew we've got over there. They've been working flat out to secure the crime scene. I'll head over there after breakfast and do what I can. Any suspects?"

Macy shook her head. "Nothing glaring."

"There was that incident at the university. Did they find any fingerprints in the office?"

"Only Hannah Granger's."

"Tell me what you have so far."

"So far I have a writer with money problems, a wife who was having an affair, an overly efficient PA who should feel resentful for not getting credit for writing Granger's novels, a woman who claims she was Hannah's lesbian lover, a missing crime novel that Granger was supposedly working on, a nosy neighbor who was prone to complain, and several colleagues at the Bridger Cultural Center who found Peter Granger's behavior offensive."

"What about stalkers? Apparently all these literary types have them."

"Pippa Lomax is the most likely candidate, and she's safely tucked away in her home in Wisconsin. There may be others. We're in touch with his publisher, as they get most of his fan mail. Plus we'll interview everyone who attended his workshops."

"Why would you do that?"

"Pippa Lomax was one of his students. It stands to reason there may be more like her out there."

"What about insurance fraud?"

"A possibility, but there is no single individual that stands to benefit and the art foundations listed as beneficiaries in the case of death aren't exactly hard up for the cash." She handed copies of the household's insured contents to Ryan. "The insurance company has provided us with a list of artwork that's supposed to be in the house. Let me know if something is missing. Arson may have been used to cover up theft and murder."

Ryan's phone rang. "Sorry," he said. "I've got to take this."

"Take your time," said Macy, holding up her hands. "I've somehow managed to get maple syrup all over me. I'll be back in a few minutes."

Macy had just finished drying her hands when her phone rang. Alisa was more excited than usual. Macy held the phone a few inches away from her ear.

"I'm right here, Alisa. No need to shout," said Macy.

Alisa apologized. "I've been on the phone with Bolton College. Jessica Reynolds was admitted to the hospital this morning. Attempted suicide."

Macy's heart sank. "Is she okay?"

"She's conscious but weak. They're assessing her."

"Are we sure it's a suicide attempt? Any reason to suspect foul play?"

"It seems pretty straightforward. She's admitted to taking the drugs. It was a prescription she's been taking for anxiety. Xanax, I think."

"As I recall from her statement, she lived alone. Who called it in?"

"I have no idea but I'll find out."

"Thank you, Alisa." Macy checked the time. It was just coming to nine. "I'm about to finish a meeting with Ryan. Let me know if you hear anything more."

"Have they identified the bodies yet?"

"The male was definitely Peter Granger. There were ligature marks on the wrists and ankles and the ME believes he died as a result of a skull fracture. Tox screen is pending. We're still waiting on clarification on the female. I was supposed to make a formal statement this afternoon but I think we should give the ME a bit more time."

"Don't worry. I'll take care of rescheduling. Is tomorrow afternoon okay?"

"That should be fine." Macy headed back into the restaurant. "I'll speak to you later."

Macy's plate had been cleared.

"Ryan," she said, slipping into her chair. "I hadn't finished my breakfast yet."

He pointed his fork at Macy. "Your mother may have told you to wear nice underwear in case you were in an accident, but I think there's a strong argument for taking it several steps further. Have you ever attended an autopsy of a person who's been living on a diet that's high in sugar, alcohol, and fat? It's revolting." He pushed a bowl of sugar cubes across the table. "But if you really want to continue down that path knock yourself out. By my calculations you had about a dozen more sugar cubes' worth of food sitting on your plate. Enjoy."

"You really are the most annoying man I know."

Macy waved the waitress down and ordered another cup of coffee.

"What took you so long in the bathroom, or am I not allowed to ask that anymore?" said Ryan.

Macy was tempted to stick her tongue out but decided it was best to keep things professional. A lot of reporters were in town covering Bolton's recent crime wave. The last thing she needed was a photo of her having a laugh with the state's leading forensics expert as she received confirmation that Peter Granger was one of the victims.

"Alisa called. Jessica Reynolds attempted suicide," said Macy.

"That's a little surprising. She seemed pretty frazzled when we met her at the college, but not desperate enough to kill herself. What's the prognosis?"

"She's awake but they're doing tests. Any news on those photos we found in Hannah Granger's office? My gut tells me that those women weren't aware of what was happening to them."

"Nothing specific on the photos. One of the girls has a tattoo that might help in making a positive identification. Another has some scarring on her arms . . . possibly self-harm. An intern had the rather brilliant idea of comparing the furniture in the photos with images posted online of parties held at the Granger residence, but we had no joy. I should remind you that we have no way of knowing whether the women in the photos are consenting adults. They look like they're unconscious, but with that mask covering their faces it's impossible to say for sure."

"You know I'm right."

"Yeah, I know. We just have to prove it."

"What about the fuel cans?"

Ryan had to finish chewing his food before he could answer. "No fingerprints and nothing on them that could be traced back to the Granger's house. I don't suppose it matters though," said Ryan. "The fractured skull and ligature marks are enough to confirm that someone probably set fire to that house to cover up two murders."

"Why would the arsonist hide the fuels cans nearby instead of driving off with them?"

"Maybe they didn't have a car."

"So, they were collecting cans one by one until they had enough to proceed and then on the night of the fire they took them from their hiding place one by one only to return them later on? No one was seen in the neighborhood that looked suspicious. I think a neighbor would have noticed someone walking around with petrol cans."

"It was Halloween night. A lot of people were on the street."

"Still a big risk."

"Did someone speak to the homeowner that found them about a time frame?" asked Ryan.

Macy flipped through her notes.

"He hasn't been to the house for about a week but says the fuel cans could have been there longer. He doesn't always work outside."

"I think we're looking for someone who is local to the area," said Ryan.

"We also have to consider the possibility this was a murder-suicide and there's no one else to look for."

"But that doesn't make sense. It was Hannah who wanted to leave Peter. Not the other way around. He was bound and knocked senseless. Stands to reason that if he didn't want Hannah to leave, she'd have been the one with ligature marks, and we've found no evidence of that on the female."

"All sorts of possibilities, but you're right. It does worry me that all we have so far is Jessica's word that she and Hannah were in a serious relationship." Macy held up her hand to get the waitress's attention. "Probably time to have another chat with Cornelia Hart. Did you manage to get any DNA from the blood we found in Peter's office?"

"I was worried it may be degraded but it's a good sample. Now we just need to find a match."

"And the desk chair?"

"Same story, different body fluid. Still waiting for the lab to post results. By the way, the residue on the arm was from packing tape. He had a roll of it in his desk drawer. There were also traces on the other arm in about the same position."

"Could someone have been bound to that chair?"

"It's something to consider. If the urine turns out to be Peter Granger's, that office may be a crime scene after all. Someone cleaned it up well. Hardly a fingerprint in that room."

Thick drops of rain pelted the windshield. The snow that had fallen during the night had already been reduced to a thick gray slush. Macy waited at a stoplight where several smashed pumpkins were slowly turning to pulp in the middle of the intersection. A one-eyed jack-o'-lantern stared up at her. Seconds later she felt it pop beneath her right front tire. She took a left on Paradise Road and continued driving across flat terrain. Strip malls and chain restaurants quickly gave way to open countryside. The nearby foothills were obscured by low clouds. Macy was beginning to think she had the wrong address when she finally spotted a new condominium complex jutting up from what had once been farmland. The parking lot was nearly empty and many of the units appeared to be unoccupied. A woman stood outside the sales office smoking a cigarette while she spoke on a cell phone. She waved as Macy drove by.

Cornelia Hart opened her front door a crack and blinked up at Macy with startled eyes. Her hair was pressed to the side of her head and her expression was slack. Macy once again apologized for disturbing her during such a distressing time.

"May I come in?" asked Macy.

Cornelia opened the door a fraction wider and explained that she'd only just woken up. Macy found herself standing in a nicely furnished living room accented with an intricately woven Persian carpet. A wood-burning stove was blazing in the corner. The sliding glass doors at the far end overlooked the inner courtyard where patches of snow stubbornly stuck to the ground despite the rain that was now falling heavily. Cornelia stood in the middle of the room looking as if she was seeing it for the first time.

Macy started to speak. "Maybe this isn't a good—"

Cornelia held up her hand. She appeared to be counting in her head. Macy waited patiently. Cornelia must have been putting on a brave act when she'd visited Macy at the police station the previous day. She'd deteriorated rapidly over the past twenty-four hours.

"What's happened is only just hitting me. You're the only reason I bothered getting out of bed today. I'll make some coffee," she said, heading into the kitchen.

A collection of Peter Granger's novels took up most of the space on Cornelia's bookshelves. Hannah's paintings covered the walls. There were also several framed photos of Cornelia looking radiant in their company. As far as Macy could see, there weren't any other personal photos. Aside from being her employers, it was becoming apparent that Hannah and Peter were Cornelia's only friends. According to the background information Alisa had gathered so far there didn't seem to be anyone else in Cornelia's life. One of the framed photos started to tip over but Macy caught hold of it before it fell.

There was a small antique frame behind it. Macy picked it up and studied the faded photograph. Cornelia couldn't have been more than twenty. She wore a bathing suit and held a tiny infant in her arms. She smiled broadly and waved at whoever was taking the picture. Macy had thought Cornelia was childless. She checked the room again but there were no other pictures of children. Macy put the frame back where she found it and stepped away from the table. She felt like she was intruding on someone's private grief.

Macy took off her jacket. It was incredibly warm in the condo. She caught sight of her reflection in a mirror. Her face was flushed. A large black cat grazed Macy's leg as it made its way into the kitchen. Its stomach was so bowed it dragged on the floor. Its purring grew in volume until Cornelia relented and opened a can of cat food.

"All this cat does is eat all day. She's getting so fat."

"Maybe she's expecting kittens," said Macy.

"She had the snip years ago, so that would be quite some miracle." Cornelia took a carton of milk from the refrigerator and studied the sell-by date before tipping it into the sink. A sour odor filled the kitchen.

"I haven't been to the supermarket since last week. I hope you don't mind drinking your coffee black."

Cornelia sat on the sofa with her cat, and Macy perched on an ornate gilt-framed chair that looked like it had been taken from the stage set of a costume drama. Not since her high school prom had she felt so regal.

"It was a gift from Peter," said Cornelia. "He liked to call me Queen Cornelia."

"Perhaps you should be sitting here."

Cornelia ignored the suggestion. "Do you have any news? I read that the coroner was finally able to examine the bodies."

"There will be an official announcement tomorrow, but I don't see the harm in telling you now. I'm afraid we've formally identified Peter Granger's remains." Macy let this sink in for a few seconds. "We have reason to believe he was murdered."

"Why would? . . . I don't understand. And Hannah? Is there any news?"

"Identifying the other victim may take some time," said Macy.

Cornelia's eyes widened a fraction. There was a red-wine-colored rash breaking out on her neck.

"Are you telling me that it may not be Hannah who died in that fire?"

"I'd rather not speculate. A few things have come to light over the past forty-eight hours, which is why I need to ask you some follow-up questions. I've been in contact with Jessica Reynolds. In the course of the interview she admitted to being in an ongoing romantic relationship with Hannah. Did you know about this?"

Cornelia nodded. "Hannah told me about it back in January."

"Why didn't you mention this in your initial interview?"

"I didn't think it was relevant."

"The fact that there was a third party in Peter and Hannah's marriage provides us with a possible motive. I'd like to know if there is more that you're not telling me. For instance, was Peter faithful?"

Cornelia folded her hands together on her lap.

"Over the last few years they've had a very open arrangement. I was under the impression that there were other women in Peter's life. I was never told the details and it wasn't my place to ask. It's why I didn't put much weight on Hannah's involvement with Jessica. Neither of them seemed to take things like that too seriously."

Macy pulled out the photocopies of the Polaroids found in Hannah's office and placed them on the coffee table.

Cornelia studied them carefully. "I don't understand what I'm looking at."

"These photos were found in Hannah's office. We want to know if they were taken in the Granger's home. Though we can't see their faces, it does appear from their positioning that they might be unconscious."

Cornelia pointed out the one that had been taken in a bedroom. "I recognize the paisley pattern in that bedspread. I think I was with Hannah when she bought it."

"Are you sure?" asked Macy.

"I've housesat for the Grangers." Cornelia pointed to a photo of a girl sprawled naked across a bed with her arms wide. "I think I've slept in that bed." She held the photograph up to the light. "Although, come to think of it, the bed isn't the same. The one in their guest room has a padded headboard. This one is made of wood."

"It is a five-bedroom house. Are you sure it couldn't have been from another room?"

Cornelia took some time before answering. "I don't believe so. They'd furnished the guest rooms with pieces from the same collection."

"I was hoping you might know who these women might be."

Cornelia couldn't take her eyes off the photos. "There was a constant stream of people coming and going in that house. Parties, dinners, guests from out of town. There were rumors that things were getting a little out of hand. I didn't approve of everything that went on but it wasn't my job to judge."

"Out of hand in what way?" asked Macy.

Cornelia blushed. "Sexually . . . there may have been sex parties."

"That's not something that's been mentioned before."

"I feel like I'm overstepping by saying anything about it. There may not be any truth to it. I certainly wasn't included."

"Hannah was known for breaking boundaries in the art world. Do you think these photos may have been part of her work?"

"I really have no idea," said Cornelia. "Have you asked Jessica? It seems more likely that they would have discussed something like this."

"I'm afraid Jessica is in the hospital. She overdosed on anxiety medication this morning."

"That poor woman."

"Fortunately, the prognosis is good. I'm hoping to speak to her later on today."

"I should have reached out to her. She must be devastated." Cornelia checked the time. "Perhaps I should go see her."

"I'd sit tight for now. It may be awhile before she can have visitors." Macy glanced down at her notes. "I went through Peter's office yesterday. He kept all the manuscripts you annotated. It seems he's been relying on your feedback more and more over the years. Did he ever give you any credit?"

"I never expected any."

"You must have spent a great deal of time reading his work and making notes. I assume there was some financial arrangement."

"You don't understand how honored I was to work with Peter. I wanted to do it for free."

"But surely you'd want some credit in the acknowledgments?"

Cornelia shook her head.

"Did you know he was writing a crime novel?" asked Macy.

"He wasn't proud of it but the publishers had offered him a substantial advance, but only if he published under his real name. Peter was being very secretive about it. I'm surprised you found out."

"I spoke to Richard Nichols at length. He says Peter had said he was going to self-publish under a pen name."

Cornelia made a face. "Richard Nichols, the crime novelist?"

"They have offices in the same building."

"I'm well aware of that. Peter couldn't stand him. He said Nichols was always coming over and poking around while he was trying to work."

"That may be so, but he does appear to know a lot about what Peter's been doing recently," said Macy.

"I guess Peter may have gone to Richard for advice, but I would have cautioned Peter had I known."

"Why is that?"

"For starters, Richard Nichols is a fraud."

"He seems legitimate to me." Macy held up his business card. "It says here that he's an Amazon best-selling author."

"It's a scam. He self-published a three-page e-book in an obscure sub-category. I think it might have been board games but I'd have to look it up again to be sure. He sold ten copies, all of which he probably bought himself, and Amazon listed him as a best-selling author. I imagine he's got the screen shot tattooed to his backside."

"It's that easy?" asked Macy

"Never trust what you read online. I downloaded one of his crime novels to make sure I wasn't being unduly judgmental. It was dreadful. Plot holes you could drive a truck through. God knows how he gets five-star reviews. I assume he must pay a service."

"How was Peter getting on with his crime novel?"

"I know he was struggling to make the transformation from literary fiction to crime. He wanted to write the next *In Cold Blood* but felt the manuscript was falling short of his expectations. He was supposed to send a first draft to his publisher last week."

"Do you know if they received anything from him?"

"I spoke to his editor yesterday. Peter hadn't even sent him a synopsis. They don't have any idea what he was working on and neither do I. To tell you the truth, I think Peter was too embarrassed to go through with it."

"Would it have really been so bad for Peter to admit publicly that he was writing a crime novel?" asked Macy.

"I'm afraid Peter said some very unkind things about crime writers in the past. All of it would have been thrown back in his face."

"He was going to have to eat his words."

"Literally," said Cornelia.

"Sounds like he was going to try to get around that by self-publishing using a pen name."

"The publisher had offered Peter a million-dollar advance. He wasn't in a position to turn it down," said Cornelia.

"We have yet to find his laptop so we have to assume it was destroyed in the fire."

"Thankfully, he backed up everything to his remote server. Has anyone tried to access any of the files stored there?"

"Our tech guys are monitoring the situation carefully. Nothing to report thus far." Macy checked her notes. "I understand the Grangers have another vehicle. A Tundra? It's not parked near the house or on campus. Do you have any idea where it is?"

Cornelia picked at a stray thread on one of the scatter cushions.

"I know they brought it in to be serviced a month ago so I doubt it would be in for repairs. Besides, I arrange that sort of thing and nothing was said to me. I suppose there's a chance they parked it up at their cabin, but I don't see why they'd do such a thing."

Macy thought back on everything she'd been told. No one had ever mentioned a cabin.

"Where is the property?"

"About an hour south of here. I guess you could call it rustic chic. I found it to be a little too isolated for my taste. . . . I imagine the road is inaccessible now. Snow has been falling pretty heavily in that area over the past few days."

"I need the address."

Cornelia shifted the cat from off her lap.

"It's in my address book, but it's better to use the GPS coordinates. I've had to drive out there a couple of times. I would have gotten lost without them."

Ryan Marshall was waiting for Macy in front of what was left of the Granger's home. He wore bright yellow protective gear and held a clipboard under his arm.

"Greeley, you're going to have to suit up if you want to join me inside."

"Your message was pretty vague. Are you going to tell me why I had to drop everything and rush over here? I have to head south toward Yellowstone this afternoon."

"What's down there?"

"I've just learned the Grangers own another property. Cornelia Hart says they may have stored their other car in the garage."

"Wouldn't it be better to send someone else? Surely, Alisa can manage it."

"I really think I should see the property firsthand. So far there hasn't been much to look at that gives me a sense of who they were."

"Well, I think that's about to change."

"What's going on? Did you find something?"

"All in good time, Detective Greeley." Ryan pointed to a tent that had been erected in the middle of the backyard. "The boots you're wearing are fine. You'll find everything else you need in there."

Macy came waddling out in an oversize yellow shell suit and hardhat. "I'm beginning to think that you do this so you can make fun of me."

Ryan held up his camera and took her picture. "I would have set aside a smaller suit, but after all those pancakes you had for breakfast I thought it was best to go large."

"You're such a bastard."

"Correction . . . charming bastard." Ryan checked the photo he'd just taken and laughed. "I think I'll shoot this off to your boyfriend. No doubt Aiden will be amused."

"Don't forget that I have pictures of you plowing through a couple glasses of wine last night. I'm sure your new boyfriend won't be too happy that you're not keeping up your end of the deal."

"I've already confessed. He now thinks you're a bad influence."

Macy held up a hand. "I'm in a hurry and I don't like you very much right now. Tell me what you know or I'm going to shoot you."

"Do I look concerned?" Ryan checked his clipboard. "First, the boring stuff. We are almost certain that a few paintings have been stolen. One was a Basquiat."

Macy whistled. "Christ, if I've actually heard of the artist it must be valuable. How much are we talking?"

"Around eleven million, depending on how the wind is blowing in the art market."

"That certainly changes things. Anything else?"

"A set of prints by Frank Stella."

Macy gave him a blank expression.

"You're such a philistine," he said.

"No reason for name calling. Is that all that's missing?"

"Nope. Prints by David Hockney and Roy Lichtenstein can't be accounted for."

"What about the damage to Hannah's studio? Anything stolen?"

"It turns out the art world got lucky on that count. Most of her work wasn't stored on site and her recent stuff was shipped to her New York gallery a couple of weeks ago. She has a show opening there two weeks from today. Hate to sound morbid but she's going to sell for a lot more money if she's dead."

"Was *any* of her work lost?"

"Definitely, but it's not as bad as we initially thought. Her most recent work wasn't cataloged so there may be more that's been stolen. A little warning, this is just a preliminary finding." He glanced back at the house. "We still have a lot of wreckage to sift through."

Ryan and Macy made their way over to the house. The blackened timber frame groaned as a gust of wind blew through the treetops. Macy had no intention of going inside.

"That's close enough," said Macy. "What is it you wanted me to see?"

"The basement."

Her voice went up an octave. "Is it safe?"

"I hope so. My team is down there."

Ryan pointed to a pair of wooden doors built into a small raised platform that was set down at a slight angle to the home's foundation. The debris that had been blocking the cellar had been removed. Thick power cables dropped into the hole from a generator that hummed next to the entrance.

Macy frowned. "Please tell me you didn't find any more dead bodies."

"No, but I did find a couple more fuel cans. The same make as the ones found at the neighbor's property."

"Any prints?"

"Only Peter Granger's."

"That's interesting."

Macy followed Ryan down a narrow set of wooden steps. The interior was lit up with temporary lighting.

"Careful," he said. "The steps are pretty slippery."

Macy found herself standing in the basement of the Granger's home. Some wooden stairs led up to what she guessed was the kitchen, and a half-dozen storage shelves took up most of the floor space. Water sloshed on the concrete floor and dripped from the ceiling.

"There's no fire damage down here," said Macy.

"We got lucky. This area is pretty sealed off and the fire spread upwards; the water found a way in though. The puddles are pretty deep in some places, so watch your step. The interesting stuff is over here," said Ryan.

Ahead Macy could see a doorway opening onto a brightly lit interior.

"The doorway was hidden behind some shelving," said Ryan. "If it wasn't for one of the engineers the state hired to secure the structure upstairs, we may not have noticed there was a discrepancy between the plans filed with the city and the layout of the basement. The Grangers were keeping secrets."

Macy stood in the threshold of the long rectangular room crowded with crime scene techs. There was a king-size bed with a wooden headboard at one end, a small seating area, and a wet bar. A separate doorway led through to a bathroom. Though there were no windows, the room was well ventilated. Macy recognized one of the chairs and the bed from the photos they'd found in Hannah's office.

"There's soundproofing in the ceiling and the wall separating this room from the rest of the basement. The door is four inches thick," said Ryan. "There's a fan pumping in fresh air, a full bar, Wi-Fi, and satellite television."

"The photographs were taken in this room."

Ryan nodded. "That does appear to be the case. I found a Polaroid camera in the side table next to the bed."

"Any more photos?"

"Nothing so far."

"Do you think they were keeping someone down here?"

"That was my first thought, but the door doesn't lock from the outside. It locks from the inside."

"Cornelia says there were rumors about sex parties."

"Then we may have found the Granger's secret den. The furniture lit up like the Fourth of July when we checked for ejaculate."

"That's disgusting. Anything else?"

Ryan picked up an evidence bag. "A stash of pharmaceuticals, including Rohypnol, the pervert's drug of choice."

"The girls in the photos looked as if they'd been drugged."

"They did indeed." Ryan handed Macy another evidence bag. "Their faces were covered with a mask. I'm pretty sure this is it."

"We'll be able to get DNA?"

"Lots of samples." He held out his arms. "This is going to keep the state forensics lab in Helena busy for some time."

"Missing paintings and sex parties." Macy headed for the stairs. "Things just got a lot more interesting in Bolton."

"Where are you going?"

"I need to call Alisa. She'll have to go check out the Granger's other property on her own."

9

Thursday

Grace stood outside the front entrance to her apartment building and watched as the woman who lived across the hall from her sorted through a pile of mail. Sandra was a talker and Grace, having spent the last few hours in the hospital with Jessica, was in no mood to talk. She thought she might wait in her car until Sandra moved on, but it was too late. Sandra had spotted her. Sandra's brightly manicured fingers fluttered in the air, her version of waving. She was a recent transplant from New York and worked in sales for a local software company. An uncommon sight in Bolton, she was always immaculately turned out and wouldn't be caught dead wearing exercise gear in public. She opened the door for Grace and frowned.

"Grace, I hope you didn't lose your keys. Between you and me, the people in this building are a little slow. How hard is it to keep track of your stuff?"

Grace tried to look friendly.

"Good morning, Sandra. How are you?"

"We need to talk about your dog." She pointed a long fingernail at Grace. "He kept me up half the night. If he's not barking, he's whining at the door. Why do you own a dog if you're not going to take care of it? I had an uncle like that. He ended up getting a fine. When he couldn't pay the fine they threw him in jail. Believe me when I say that you don't want that to happen to you. His wife left him, got full custody of the kids, the house, everything."

Sandra was pretty intense when she was angry. A few weeks earlier she'd had a go at the guy who lived below her because he was always coming home drunk in the middle of the night. He managed to stick up for himself at first but didn't really stand a change once Sandra was in full flow.

Grace braced herself. This wasn't the first time Sandra had complained about the dog.

"I'm so sorry. I promise it won't happen again." Grace quickly moved on to another subject. "Are you on your way to work?"

Sandra looked disappointed that Grace hadn't wanted to spar.

"Yes, Grace. That's what grown-ups do." Sandra gave Grace a once-over. "What is this then? A walk of shame? You don't look like you've slept at all."

"My friend had to go into the hospital. I was there most of the night."

Sandra's expression softened.

"Are they going to be okay?" she asked.

Grace slipped off her hat. She couldn't think about what had happened without revisiting a dimly lit hallway that smelled vaguely of vomit, and she wasn't ready to go back there yet.

"I hope so," said Grace.

Sandra combed her long fingernails through her hair, gave it a little fluff. Her dark roots were showing. She was already slipping. Another year in Bolton and she'd be sorting the mail in her pajamas.

"A guy rang my bell yesterday evening looking for you and then got mad when I wouldn't let him in the building. Figured if he really knew you, he'd know which apartment you lived in."

"Did you get a name?"

"He was gone by the time I came downstairs." Sandra nodded toward a table in the entryway. "He left you a package."

A box covered in floral wrapping paper sat next to a pile of unopened mail. Grace's name was written in capital letters on a yellow Post-it note that was stuck to the top.

"Were you expecting something?" asked Sandra.

"Maybe it's a mistake. I doubt I'm the only woman named Grace who lives around here."

"Oh, honey, this was no mistake. He knew what you looked like. When I wouldn't confirm that you lived here he described you—petite, pale, dark haired, and dresses like she's still living in the fifties. I'd say he nailed it." Sandra touched Grace's sleeve. "Nice coat, by the way; not everyone can get away with wearing that shade of green."

Grace picked up the box. It was lighter in weight than she expected. She gave it a gentle shake.

"Maybe you have a secret admirer," said Sandra. She was standing at Grace's shoulder. The chemical scent of hairspray lingered uncomfortably with her perfume. "Aren't you going to open it?"

Grace peeled away the paper and removed the lid. The shoes she'd lost on Halloween night were wrapped in white tissue paper.

"He gave you shoes?" Sandra looked horrified. "They're not even new. What kind of guy gives a girl an old pair of shoes?"

Grace could hear her dog scratching frantically on the other side of the door. Once safely inside, Grace got down on her knees and buried her face in his black fur. Pound for pound Jack was the best thing in her life.

"Hi baby. Did you miss me?" she asked.

Lara walked into the living room balancing a bowl of cereal and a pile of textbooks. She spoke with her mouth full.

"We both missed you. I was beginning to worry."

Grace dropped her bag on the floor and hung her coat on the back of a dining chair. Jack didn't leave her side.

"I ran into Sandra downstairs. She said Jack was up half the night barking," said Grace.

"Sandra's full of shit. I was home all evening. Jack didn't make so much as a peep." Lara noticed the box. "What's that?"

"It's the shoes I lost on Halloween. Sandra said some guy dropped them off outside the front door yesterday evening."

Lara set aside her bowl of cereal. "Why in the hell would someone do that?"

Grace lifted the lid. "Maybe he mistook me for Cinderella. He even wrapped them in tissue."

"Grace, it's not funny. It's creepy. Is there a card?"

"Nothing quite so romantic as that. Only a yellow Post-it note with my name on it."

"You should call the police."

"I'll think about it."

"There's nothing to think about. You don't need any more craziness in your life right now."

Jack jumped up and curled against Grace's side as soon as she sat down on the sofa. He put his head on her lap and looked up at her expectantly. She scratched behind his ears.

"I'm well aware of that. I'm just too tired to deal with it right now," said Grace.

"Were you in the studio all night?"

"Only until three." Grace leaned across her dog's side. She could hear his heart beating. "Jessica Reynolds was there."

"Did you speak to her? Is there news about Peter and Hannah?"

"Nothing we didn't already know. She'd been drinking." Grace hesitated. "I ended up driving her home."

"So, that's where you were. Did you stay at her house?" asked Lara.

"It didn't feel right to leave her alone. She was in a pretty bad way."

"She shouldn't dump this stuff on you. Doesn't she have any friends her own age?"

"It's so sad. I think Hannah was her entire life." Grace blinked away the tears in her eyes. "She may have tried to kill herself."

"No way."

"I found her passed out in the hallway. She overdosed on Xanax. I don't know if it was intentional."

"Is she all right?"

Grace's chin bobbed up and down. "She's regained consciousness."

"That's got to be a good sign."

Grace noticed the newspaper on the coffee table was open to a story about Peter Granger's writing career.

"How are you holding up?" asked Grace.

"I guess I'm fine."

"I still haven't got ahold of Taylor. Have you heard from her?"

"I'm not exactly her favorite person, so I doubt she'd want to speak to me unless she was desperate," said Lara.

"I have her parent's address in Colorado. Her boyfriend said she was going to see them."

"What are you going to do? Send them a letter?"

"The thought had crossed my mind."

"Grace, if she can't pick up the phone and let you know she's okay that's on her. You've got enough to worry about."

Grace wasn't sure what to do about Taylor. She didn't seem to be the type of person who would run back to her parent's house at the first sign of trouble. Besides, she had a difficult relationship with her mother. On a couple of occasions Grace had overheard them arguing on the phone. It didn't sound like she would be too supportive when she found out her daughter was pregnant. But then again, what did Grace know about mothers? She'd been raised by her aunt.

"Is there a way of getting Taylor's parent's phone number using their name and address?" asked Lara.

"I tried, but their number isn't listed."

Lara's phone buzzed.

"I've got a text from Clare," said Lara.

"I thought you guys weren't speaking."

"We fight all the time. It wasn't a big deal."

"Seemed like a big deal to me."

Lara frowned as she read the message. "An anonymous source in the police department is claiming the remains have been identified."

"And?"

"Just a sec. She sent me a link."

Lara bit into a fingernail that was already shredded. Grace started to say something but stopped. She quietly waited for a memory to pass. Her aunt was forever swatting Grace's fingers away from her mouth but it never worked. The only thing that stopped Grace from chewing her fingernails was leaving home. She stared down at her perfectly manicured hands. Grace wondered what her aunt would say if she could see her now. No doubt she'd comment on her posture. Grace sat up a little straighter.

"Grace?" said Lara.

Grace gave Lara a blank look.

"Sometimes it's like talking to a wall," said Lara. "Did you hear anything I just said?"

Grace tried to focus. "Don't take it personally. I was up half the night."

"They've identified Peter's remains but not Hannah's. Apparently, it's going to take more time."

"Why?"

Lara's face was ashen. She dropped her phone on the cushion.

"It's just some rubbish blog. I don't understand why Clare is taking it so seriously."

Grace put her arms around Lara. It was only a matter of time before her friend cracked. Peter Granger had factored heavily in Lara's dreams of literary success. He couldn't force a publisher to buy her novel but he'd opened a lot of doors for her. Without his patronage it was going to be far more difficult for Lara to get noticed.

"Seriously, Lara, are you okay?" asked Grace.

Lara didn't look sad. She looked angry.

"Truthfully, I'm relieved he's dead."

"It's probably best that you keep that to yourself."

"It doesn't mean that I wished him dead. He could have moved to another country and never had anything to do with us again and that would have been fine too."

Grace hesitated. "He's been playing with your head for the past two years. One day he praised you, the next he treated you like shit. For him it was all a big game."

"Grace, you don't know the half of it."

"Is there something you're not telling me?"

Lara picked up her phone and stared at the screen.

"Let's just say the world is a better place without him in it."

Grace needed to take a shower and walk her dog. She checked the time. She'd already called work to tell them she wouldn't be coming in. As things stood she didn't want to leave the house unless she absolutely had to. Jordan was somewhere out there waiting for her. She stared at the shoes she'd worn on Halloween night. She couldn't remember if she'd left them at the house where she'd eaten the candy or at the tree where she'd found the lost tiara. Not that it mattered. Either way Jordan was clearly crazy.

"Lara," she said. "A guy has been following me around Bolton the last couple of weeks. I'm pretty sure he's the one who dropped off my shoes."

"Why haven't you gone to the police?"

Grace shrugged. "Because I feel like a total idiot every time I walk into the station to report someone. They're always very professional but I get the impression they're a little tired of dealing with me."

"Maybe that's just in your head."

"My uncle was involved in sex trafficking. The police probably think a few stalkers is a small price to pay for my family's sins."

"Grace, your uncle may been guilty, but you were also a victim. And the police know it. They've always looked after you when you've asked for their help. They need to know if this guy is following you."

"He was at K-Bar on Halloween night. I was hoping he hadn't seen me leave but I guess I got that wrong."

"Do you think he followed you when you left?"

"Seems like that's the case."

"Do you know anything about him?"

"He drives a Bronco and his name is Jordan."

Lara raised her voice. "How do you know his name?"

"He's been coming into the café for a while now. I thought he was some lonely guy. All the others have been much older. I didn't think . . ."

"That's crazy. You should have said something."

"I know it was stupid. I was just hoping he'd get bored and leave me in peace. You have no idea how tiring this is."

Lara started to get up. "Come on," she said. "I'll take you to the police station."

"I'm not sure I can do that now."

"Why not?"

"Do you remember that I wrote a letter to Peter telling him what a dick he was for how he treated me?"

"No harm done. You were never going to send it."

"Someone broke into my locker at work. It's gone."

"And you think this guy took it?" asked Lara.

"It's the only thing that makes sense. The break room is right across the hall from the restrooms and a few feet from the employee entrance. It would take some nerve but it's possible. Some shifts are so busy we're stuck at the counter serving for hours at a time. My name is on my locker. The lock isn't exactly state of the art. It could have been picked."

"What's the downside of him having the letter?"

"Some of my language was pretty threatening. I'm pretty sure I wrote something about hoping Peter and Hannah would burn in hell. I may have been more specific."

"How specific?"

"I may have threatened to burn down their house."

"Seriously?"

Grace nodded. "It was just some stupid fantasy, but if this guy gets angry with me and shows the letter to the police, I'm going to be hauled in for questioning. I have a history with the Grangers. It won't look good."

"You were with me on Halloween."

"Not all night. I lost an hour between leaving the K-Bar and seeing you again. If this guy was following me he'll know we didn't leave to-gether. He doesn't even have to show his face. He could leak the letter to the press or mail it to Macy Greeley. Either way I'm screwed."

"What will you do then?"

Grace kicked the box over and the shoes tumbled out onto the floor.

"I guess I'm going to have to find out what this guy wants," said Grace.

"How are you going to do that?"

Grace picked up her phone and scrolled through her recent calls.

"He called me yesterday so I have his number."

"How did he get your number?"

"I assume from off the wall in the break room at the café."

"This keeps on getting worse."

"Tell me about it." Grace buried her face in her hands. "Lara, I wouldn't ask if there was any other way, but I think I need your help. I can't do this on my own."

"We need to come up with a plan. Do you have any idea where he lives?"

"Not a clue."

"You said he always seems to be at the café when you have a shift?"

Grace nodded.

"So, he'll be expecting you to come into work today," said Lara.

"I've already called Steve. I'm not going in."

"Even better. We'll wait for Jordan outside and follow him home when he leaves."

"It won't work," said Grace. "He'll recognize my car."

"Not a problem. We'll take mine."

Grace had done a quick pencil sketch of Jordan so Lara would be able to recognize him when she went into the café to do a reconnaissance while Grace waited in Lara's car. They'd parked opposite the café on Main Street so they'd have a good view. Grace had tried to reel in her friend's expectations, but feared her warnings had been lost in the pop and fizz of Lara's enthusiasm. Grace was understandably wary. Lara didn't seem to appreciate the potential dangers involved. Finding out where Jordan lived was going to be the easy part, but breaking in and searching his house might prove too ambitious a plan. Grace had decided to take a wait-and-see approach. If it was safe, she'd go in alone while Lara kept watch. She may have wanted Lara along for the ride, but there was no way she was going to risk her friend's safety.

Not that Lara had a history of playing it safe. Grace's first road trip with Lara, Taylor, Pippa, and Clare had almost ended in disaster when, instead of walking away, Lara chose to stand up to a man she'd offended. The group had still run as a pack back then. Taylor and Lara were so close they finished each other's sentences, Clare was fearless, and Pippa had all the best lines. Their energy was magnetic. Grace had never met women like them before. Clare's long blond hair hung down past her shoulders. She darted through life, owning every second. Pippa had a comedian's taste for irony and loved a good laugh. Meanwhile, Taylor was this wise and wonderful creature with dark eyes and an insatiable curiosity.

It was high summer and a heat wave was beating down on the state of Montana, fraying nerves and spreading wildfires. They'd been on their way home from a music festival when they convinced Grace to stop in at a bar outside of Missoula. Grace had been nervous from the start, but she was the outnumbered newcomer to the group so she reluctantly agreed when they said it would be fun to have an adventure. They hadn't grown up in the same world as Grace. They'd underestimated the mistrust ingrained in people outside their circle, so they thought they wouldn't be found out. They'd even gone so far as to claim that they were guilty of nothing more than wanting a cold beverage, but Grace knew better and so did every regular sitting in the bar that evening. These women were there to mock them. They'd saddled up onto barstools instead of sitting down quietly in a booth. They'd laughed a little too loudly and whispered a little too often. Grace didn't dare join in, preferring to sit quietly and stare at the sweat gathering on the outside of her water glass. She could feel the tension rise with each of her friends' high-pitched shrieks. They were passing judgment. They found the prominent displays of patriotism and religion hilarious, while the pro-NRA bumper stickers plastered to the wall above the bar were deemed barbaric. They'd read the names beneath the photos of the young local men and women serving in the military with reverence but instead of supporting the cause they were fighting for, they'd questioned America's military aggression a little too loudly.

Grace had met the bartender's gaze. It was a warning. She'd told the others she was leaving with or without them. There must have been something in her tone. They finally noticed what was happening. All the men in the bar were standing, arms folded and openly hostile.

Lara hadn't been frightened. She'd been indignant. She was so used to having right on her side that she couldn't deal with being silenced by all that she felt was wrong with the world. She announced it was a free country and she wasn't going anywhere. A man the size of a mountain threatened to send her home in a body bag if she didn't go quietly. Taylor took hold of Lara's arm and told her to shut the fuck up. Clare and Pippa were already heading toward the door. Grace had wanted to leave too but Lara wasn't backing down. She'd pulled away from Taylor and turned to order another drink.

The man hovered above them. "I told you to leave."

Grace found herself staring into his wide chest. Tattoos ran down the length of his arms and a baseball cap shaded his bearded face. A company name and logo were embroidered into his shirt pocket. Cross Border Trucking had once employed hundreds of men in Montana. The owner had been universally feared. Grace was hoping his name still carried weight. Her voice had cracked.

"Did you work for Arnold Lamm?" she asked.

She had the man's full attention.

"Yeah. Who's asking?"

"His niece."

There'd been a pause. He was clearly deciding whether she was taking the piss.

"Then you know I'm not someone your friends should mess with."

"I'm sorry. I shouldn't have brought them in here. It was disrespectful."

"It's Grace, isn't it?"

"Yes, sir."

"I don't want to see you or your friends around here again."

It was the only time Grace had ever seen Lara back down from a fight. She'd recognized Arnold's name and understood the context. It was how she'd figured out who Grace really was. The group didn't speak again until they were safely loaded back into Grace's truck and driving away. Her friends had been in awe of Grace.

You actually know these people.

Grace checked the early morning traffic moving along Main Street again. There was still no sign of Jordan's Bronco, but Lara had left the café and was standing on the sidewalk waiting for a break in the traffic so she could cross the street. She handed Grace a takeaway cup of coffee and a bagel before settling back down in the driver's seat of her car. She placed the pencil sketch of Jordan on the dashboard.

"I had a good look around the café but I didn't see him," said Lara.

"It's still early."

"Steve really should give you a raise. How many coffee-drinking stalkers does this make so far? Ten?"

"There have only been five. Did you speak to Steve?" asked Grace.

"Yes, I gave him the whole sob story about you having to go to the hospital this morning, so there's no chance you're going to lose your job anytime soon. To his credit, he's really worried about you. By the way, when were you going to tell me you were going on a date with him?"

"He's not your favorite person."

"You still could have told me. It's what friends do."

Grace saw Jordan's Bronco in the side-view mirror. He was pulling into a parking space a few spaces behind them.

"Jordan is behind us," said Grace. "He's in the green Bronco that just pulled in."

Lara squealed. "This is so exciting."

Grace thumped Lara hard on the thigh with her fist.

"What the hell, Grace? That hurt!"

Grace took hold of both of Lara's hands and looked her in the eye. "Calm down or we're going home. We really don't know shit about this guy."

Lara had already forgotten she'd been hit. Her eyes went wide as she looked into the rearview mirror.

"Get down," she said. "He's coming this way."

Seconds later Jordan was walking across the street to the café.

"So, that's what a stalker looks like," said Lara. "Not exactly threatening."

"They don't exactly advertise their intentions, hence the stalking."

"I have an idea," said Lara. She reached for the door handle. "I'll be right back."

"Where are you going?"

"To have a look in his car. It might be unlocked."

"Are you out of your mind? Stay here."

"It will be fine. Beep the horn when he comes out of the café. Better yet," she said, throwing Grace the car keys, "get behind the wheel in case we need to make a quick getaway."

Grace climbed into the driver's seat, accidentally tipping hot coffee all over her pants. She dabbed it up with a napkin. Her hands shook so much she could barely buckle the seatbelt.

Grace adjusted the rearview mirror so she had a good view of Jordan's Bronco. So far Lara was staying out of sight. On the other side of the street things were going along as predicted. Jordan was standing in line at the counter, staring up at the menu board like he was actually thinking of ordering something other than a large filtered coffee, his usual drink. It only took seconds to prepare. This worried Grace.

Grace glanced in the rearview mirror again. She couldn't believe Lara had been crazy enough to get inside Jordan's Bronco. Grace craned her neck to get a better view but there was no sign of her friend. She cursed under her breath.

A delivery truck pulled up next to Lara's car and idled as it waited for the light at the nearby intersection to change. Grace could no longer see inside the café so she had no idea what Jordan was doing. She pressed the car horn several times and checked the mirrors but Lara didn't return as promised. Grace put the key in the ignition and prayed the car would start. She checked the rearview mirror one last time.

Jordan was already at the wheel of the Bronco but Lara was nowhere to be seen.

Grace started the car and put it into gear. When the delivery truck finally moved forward, Jordan pulled in right behind it. Grace's phone beeped. There was a text from Lara on the screen.

I'm still inside his car. Help!

Grace gunned the engine and squeezed Lara's car into the lane without waiting for a break in the traffic. The driver behind her sounded their horn several times, but Grace kept her eyes on the road ahead. Only two cars separated her from the Bronco.

Jordan took a left on Talbot Road seconds before the light changed. Grace was the first in line at the red light. She leaned far forward so she could see down the length of the side road. The Bronco was moving fast. The light changed to green but Grace didn't wait for the intersection to clear before swinging the car out in front of the oncoming traffic. She raced north on Talbot Road. She didn't see Jordan's Bronco again until five blocks later. She took a right on Honey Street and followed him at a safe distance. The residential neighborhood quickly gave way to open countryside. Grace checked how much gas was left in the tank. If this kept up much longer she'd be driving on fumes.

Jordan's Bronco turned onto an isolated dirt road and Grace fell back even farther. Lara's car wasn't built for this type of terrain. It felt like it was losing engine parts every time Grace hit a bump. It was another few miles before Jordan pulled into a driveway in front of a double-wide mobile home. Grace parked next to a tree and waited. There didn't appear to be any vehicles other than a couple junked cars that were parked in front of a shed at the rear of the property. A stand of pine trees flanked the mobile home on its north side and if Grace had her bearings correct, the Gallatin River was probably a little farther along.

The Bronco's driver's side door opened and Jordan stepped out into the sunshine. He seemed relaxed. He held a cup of coffee in one hand and a cell phone in the other. He slowly made his way toward the porch.

Grace's ringtone was loud. She accepted the incoming call without looking at the name of the person on the other end of the line.

"Grace? It's Jordan."

Grace watched him from the car. She nodded.

"Grace, are you there?"

She nodded again. Her voice was weak. "Yes."

"You weren't at work."

Jordan continued to walk across the scrubby lawn. She waited until he'd reached the front door before responding.

"I'm not feeling well," she blurted out.

"I hope it's not serious. Did you get your package?"

"Yes, thank you."

"You don't sound pleased."

"I am. I said thank you."

Jordan stepped inside the mobile home and shut the door behind him. Grace decided the best thing she could do was keep him talking. If he was on the phone she would know what he was doing. The Bronco was parked about twenty feet from the road, but there was a lot of cover under the nearby trees. Lara would be okay as long as she kept out of sight. Grace edged the car forward cautiously. The land was fairly open so there wasn't much in the way of shelter.

"Grace, are you still there?" he said.

"Sorry, there are a lot of people around so it's difficult to talk."

"I thought you said you were sick."

"Sorry, I'm going to put you on hold while I step outside. I'll be right back. Don't go anywhere."

There were eighteen text messages from Lara and two missed calls. Grace didn't have time to read them. She typed quickly.

Lara, get out of the car and go toward the road. I'm just beyond the trees on the right.

Grace hit send and went back to her phone call with Jordan.

"Jordan, are you still there? I'm sorry about that."

"Where are you?"

"I'm surprised you don't know."

"Don't be like that."

"What do you want from me?" asked Grace.

"I just want to talk to you about what happened in Collier. I know there's more to the story."

Grace drove past Jordan's home at a normal speed. Lara's car was a fairly nondescript dusty sedan with over 200,000 miles on it. She was hoping Jordan wouldn't recognize it.

"We're talking now," said Grace.

"I'm not going to hurt you."

"I don't know that."

"You have my word."

"That's not good enough."

"We could meet somewhere—"

Grace hung up on him mid-sentence. She'd reached the stand of trees. She slowed the car down and scanned the dense undergrowth for any sign of her friend. Lara flung the door open before Grace had a chance to come to a full stop. Grace slammed on the breaks and Lara stumbled as she crawled into the car and collapsed onto the passenger seat. Her face was flushed crimson and covered in tears. Great gobs of snot ran down from her nose. She started laughing.

"I found the letter," she said, holding up an envelope like a trophy.

10

Thursday

When Macy and Ryan finally emerged from the Granger's basement it was coming up on seven in the evening and already pitch-dark.

"You'll have to be patient," said Ryan. "The team in Helena will need time to sort all this new evidence out."

"Speaking of Helena, any word on that second body?"

"There should be some news by now. I'll make a quick call."

Macy went into the tent to change out of her protective gear. There were several missed calls from Alisa. She listened to her voice mail. The phone signal wasn't strong, so she could barely make out what Alisa was saying. There was a folding chair next to a small table. Macy sat down heavily and listened to the message again, but it still made no sense. It sounded like Alisa was saying that they'd found Hannah Granger alive. Macy stared off into space for a few seconds. This was unexpected. She tried to return Alisa's phone call but nobody picked up.

"Damn," said Macy.

She looked up. Ryan was standing outside the tent with his phone in his hand.

"Two major developments," he said.

"Let me guess. Hannah Granger didn't die in the fire."

"How did you know?"

"The reception wasn't great on the voice mail Alisa left but I think she said that they found Hannah at the cabin."

"She's been there all this time?" asked Ryan.

"Maybe she was snowed in. According to Cornelia Hart, it's so remote there's no cell phone reception."

"Surely the place has a phone."

Macy shook her head. "No phone. No Wi-Fi. Do we know who died?"

"Nothing so far and there haven't been any missing persons reports made locally. There was a lot of scarring on the torso and arms. Shallow cuts made over the years."

"Self-harm?"

"Looks that way. One of the girls in the Polaroids also had a lot of scarring. The medical examiner is trying to figure out if it's the same person."

"Christ. Anything else?"

Ryan nodded. "She was pregnant. First trimester."

"Was it Peter Granger's baby?"

"Bingo."

"Hannah Granger has a lot of explaining to do."

"She's not the only person who needs to start talking."

Macy tilted her head. "Did they find something else?"

"I assume the name Grace Adams rings a bell."

"What's she got to do with this?"

"We got a match on the bloodstain on the carpet in Peter's office. It was hers."

Alisa and Macy stood side by side watching Hannah Granger through a one-way mirror. It was eight in the evening and Alisa had only just arrived back at the station. Hannah was a compact woman with straw-colored hair that hung loose past her shoulders. The overhead lights cast a shadow across her features, making it difficult to read her expression.

"She insists she's innocent," said Alisa.

"Of course she does," said Macy. "Has she tried to call a lawyer?"

"She thinks she doesn't need one."

"Makes my life easier. Walk me through what happened."

"At least part of her story already checks out. Their road was impassable. Before driving down to the property I arranged for a snowplow to meet us at the turnoff and we followed it up to the house. The driver confirms the track has been blocked since Monday evening, which is the same night of the fire."

"Any sign of anyone coming and going on skis or snow shoes or a snowmobile?"

"We had a good look around but couldn't find any tracks."

"So, you drive up to the house. What happens next?"

"Hannah came outside as the plough was coming up to the driveway. She seemed overjoyed to see us. She also appeared to be genuinely shocked when we told her about the fire."

"What exactly did you tell her?"

"The bare minimum, that her husband's death was a homicide and the remains of a yet-to-be-identified female were found in bed with him."

"Did you tell her that the fire was set intentionally?"

"No, I figured I'd leave that to you."

Macy made some notations. "What explanation did she give for her whereabouts over the past few days?"

"She said she drove up to the cabin on Saturday with the intention of coming back to Bolton on Monday evening, but the Tundra wouldn't start."

"Did you confirm that it wasn't operational?"

"I tried to start it and the engine wouldn't turn over, but I'm not a mechanic so I wouldn't be able to assess whether she'd tampered with it. It snowed all Monday and Tuesday and she says she was cut off. She was hoping Peter would arrange for the snow plough and was becoming increasingly concerned when the road remained blocked."

"So, she left Peter on good terms?"

"That's the impression she gave. I didn't press her for the details."

"The young woman found in the house was in her first trimester of pregnancy. There is evidence she'd been self-harming for some time. She appears to be in her early twenties."

"Like the girl in the Polaroid."

"Exactly what I thought. We need to figure out who she was. The team should look into missing person's reports. Also run through the list of Peter Granger's known associates, narrowing it down by age and gender. Stands to reason that whoever died in that house has been missing since Monday, possibly earlier. You may want to start with his writing workshop."

"I have the contact details for almost everyone."

"There was a name that was crossed out on the latest class list, but references to someone who went by the initials GL in his notes. Did you figure out who that was?"

"No, but we'll find out when we question the other students. I'll make arrangements for them to come in tomorrow."

"Do you remember a case up in Collier a few years back?"

"International sex traffickers and a pedophile ring. Who could forget that?"

"A girl named Grace Adams got caught up in the middle of it but was cleared of any wrongdoing. In fact she was a victim herself. For the past few years she's been using the name Grace Larson to avoid unwanted attention. I think she may be living in Bolton now."

"How is she related to Peter Granger's death?"

"The ME ran the DNA they recovered from that bloodstain in Peter's office through the database and came up with her name."

"So, the GL Peter referred to in his notes might well be Grace Larson?"

"That's what we need to find out."

"I'll look into it. Anything else?"

Macy closed her eyes a second. The coffee in her cup was cold and the hurried meal she'd eaten sat heavily in her gut. She wanted a lot of things, but mostly she wanted to be home where she belonged. It was time to check in with her mother. She studied the woman waiting for her in the interview room. Hannah Granger had her head in her hands. Her shoulders shook. It looked like she was crying.

"I'm going to make a quick phone call before I start the interview," said Macy. "I need to check in at home."

"I'll get you another coffee."

Macy was really beginning to like this girl. "That would be greatly appreciated," she said.

Macy ducked into the office she'd been allocated and shut the door behind her. She was worried she'd waited too long to call home but, thankfully, Ellen had kept Luke up a little later than usual so they could talk. He peered into the camera lens on his grandmother's smartphone and grinned.

"Mommy!"

Macy waved. "Hi, honey, what are you up to?"

He frowned. "Bedtime."

Macy pretended to sleep. "You're lucky. I wish I could go to bed right now."

He giggled.

"Did you have fun at the pool this morning?" asked Macy.

"I jumped off the side."

"Oh, I want to see that. Will you do it again when I get home?"

Luke pressed his face right up to the screen. All Macy could see was a dimpled blur.

"Yes. I jump lots." The phone shook up and down. "Jump. Jump. Jump."

"How was your swimming class?" asked Macy.

Luke backed away from the camera and put his chin in one hand like he was giving his mother's question some serious thought.

"My teacher was mean."

"William is nice. He's a lifeguard. That makes him extra special."

Luke yawned. His voice was lazy and low. "Will was sick. We had a girl."

"And you didn't like her?"

Luke's hair was so long he looked like a spaniel when he shook his head. Macy made a note to herself. She needed to get her son to agree to a haircut. The last time was a disaster.

"Granny's here," said Luke.

Luke disappeared and Ellen picked up the phone.

"Sorry that was so brief," said Ellen. "It's been a long day and he's worn out."

"That's okay. I really appreciate you keeping him up late."

"A little chaos never hurts. How are things in Bolton?"

"We had a bit of a surprise this afternoon. It turns out Hannah Granger is very much alive."

"I assume she's now a suspect."

"That remains to be seen. I'm about to interview her."

Ellen looked over her shoulder. "Luke, go find the hairbrush. It's time we tackled those tangles."

"Remind me to book him another appointment at the hairdresser," said Macy.

"I think I'll let you go on your own this time. I still haven't recovered from our last experience."

"Why do you think he has such an aversion to getting his hair cut?"

"I have no idea. He's far too young to have issues," said Ellen. "And, speaking of issues. Nicole's therapist called this morning."

Nicole was Luke's half sister. Her father, Ray Davidson, was once the head of the state police but was now serving time in Montana State Prison. Nicole hadn't been mentally stable to begin with. Her parent's divorce and her father's conviction pushed her over the edge. Five months earlier she'd tried to abduct Luke from a day care center. Following the incident, Nicole was placed in a psychiatric-care unit for assessment. A final report was pending. As of yet, no charges had been filed.

"What did she want?" asked Macy.

"Apparently, Nicole's mother is suing her for negligence."

"Nicole was showing signs of a full psychotic breakdown. It is a little surprising her therapist missed it."

"I'm in total agreement, but I think there's more to this lawsuit. The family doesn't want Nicole to serve time for trying to take Luke. If they can prove her doctor was negligent they may be able to get a suspended sentence."

"I don't want Nicole to get anywhere near Luke again. That's nonnegotiable," said Macy.

"But that doesn't mean she needs to be locked up in a prison psychiatric ward when it may be a matter of getting the right care. You said it yourself. Nicole is troubled but not dangerous. She saw Luke as the one good thing that came out of all this mess, which, for the record, is pretty much in line with how I feel."

"I'm not heartless. I'm willing to go with the panel's recommendations, but I draw a line when it comes to any further contact. Was the therapist rude to you on the phone? I found the few times we've communicated to be difficult."

"She was polite but firm. She wanted to know what you were going to say if interviewed," said Ellen.

"Why would I be interviewed?"

"The panel wants to know what was said in your phone conversations with the therapist in the lead-up to the incident at the day care center."

"She shouldn't be calling us directly. It borders on harassment," said Macy.

"I pretty much told her that."

"Good."

"So, what are you going to do?" asked Ellen.

"I'm going to wait and see. I'm sure the panel will be in touch sooner or later."

"Have you heard from Aiden?"

"Not a peep. I'm going to call him when I get back to the hotel. Why?"

"Just asking. I better get our boy to bed. We'll talk tomorrow."

"I love you, Mom."

"I love you too."

There was a knock on the door and Alisa stepped inside. She held a cup of coffee in one hand and a Snickers bar in the other. She handed both to Macy.

"Given the number of empty wrappers in your car, I figured this is your favorite," said Alisa.

"It's like you're already reading my mind. Everything ready in the interview room?"

"Yep. Is it okay if I sit in?"

Macy held up the candy bar. "Was this a bribe?"

"That depends on whether it worked."

"Come along then," said Macy. "Let's go see what Hannah Granger has to say for herself."

Hannah Granger's pale blue eyes rarely strayed once they were fixated on someone or something. Macy sat opposite her with the case files stacked neatly next to her coffee cup.

"You already know that I left Bolton on Saturday," said Hannah. She indicated the receipts for gas and groceries on the table next to her cup of tea. "I stopped for gas at a place on Route 191 and bought groceries at a store that is a twenty-minute drive from the cabin. They know me there. They'll remember seeing me come in."

Macy examined the receipts again. "But these receipts only account for Saturday. If you want to be cleared of involvement, we need to confirm where you were on Monday evening when the fire started." Alisa handed Macy a note. "Why was your Tundra's GPS system switched off?" asked Macy.

"I only noticed it wasn't working when I was driving down to the cabin. I assumed it was faulty."

"That's rather convenient. You could have driven back here on Monday and it wouldn't have shown up on the vehicle's tracking device."

"There was a snowstorm on Monday night. I couldn't have set the fire and returned to the cabin before the road closed."

"Arsonists often use timers to delay when a fire starts. Perfect if you need to be somewhere else so you have an alibi."

Hannah crossed her arms. "Have you found any timers?"

"Not yet, but we're still looking."

"If I'd gone to that much trouble to create an alibi, wouldn't it have made more sense for me to have stayed with a friend on Monday night instead of hanging out in a cabin by myself?"

Macy placed the photos of the gas tins found in the basement and in the neighbor's yard on the table. "Do you recognize these?"

Hannah shook her head. "I'm not really sure. Peter may have bought them last summer. He was always worried about running out of gas when we were out at the cabin."

"These two were in your basement and these four were found in a neighbor's yard. We think they were used to start the fire."

Hannah tapped the photo of the gas tins found in the basement. "I thought you said the house was completely destroyed."

"I guess we got lucky. All that happened in the basement was a bit of water damage. So there was plenty to see." She paused. "Tell me about your relationship with your husband. You told my colleague that you left Bolton on good terms. What did you talk about on Saturday morning?"

"A lot of things."

"Can you be more specific?"

Her blue eyes zeroed in on Macy. "I told Peter I was leaving him."

"You call that good terms?"

"It's been a long time coming. He's been living his life and I've been living mine. We've been fairly open about it. He was supportive of my decision."

"Is there anyone who can back you up on that statement?"

"Some of our closer friends knew what was going on in our marriage. I'll give you some names."

"I understand you're in a romantic relationship with Jessica Reynolds."

"She's why I was leaving Peter. On Saturday morning she gave me an ultimatum. If I didn't end my marriage she would end our relationship. I chose to be with Jessica, but that doesn't mean I wasn't upset about divorcing Peter. It's why I went to the cabin for the weekend. Both Peter and I needed the space to process what we'd decided. We've been together a long time."

"Starting late Saturday afternoon and ending Monday at three P.M., he sent you twenty-three text messages. It doesn't sound like he was ready to call it quits."

"I wasn't aware of the messages until this evening. Besides, Peter knew there's no cell phone signal at the cabin so I don't understand why he even tried getting in touch." Hannah nodded at Alisa. "I gave you my phone and password. I assume you've looked at everything. I have nothing to hide."

"Did anything strike you as odd about the texts he sent you?" asked Macy.

Hannah dropped a wadded-up tissue on the table. She seemed to be tiring. She stared into the middle distance when she spoke.

"He wrote as if we'd never agreed to a divorce on Saturday morning."

"How do you mean?"

"He kept asking me to come home so we could talk about how we were going to save our marriage, but that made no sense as it was already agreed that there was nothing left to save . . . he said as much on the morning I left. In the texts he says he's sorry for losing his temper when he'd done nothing of the kind. There was no argument. There was no shouting. We hugged each other good-bye." Hannah pulled a fresh tissue from the box. "He told me he wanted me to be happy."

Macy scrolled through some of the text messages again. Between Saturday afternoon and the time he died, he'd not tried to make contact with anyone else. Macy started to speak but Hannah interrupted her.

"Peter knew where I was. If he was so desperate to speak to me he could have driven out to the cabin," said Hannah.

"We only have your word for that."

"I've never been in trouble with the law. I have no record and no motive. You can look at the GPS on my phone. It will tell you where I've been."

"Your location is confirmed until you switched off your phone on Sunday afternoon."

"I forgot my charger. The battery died."

"You know we're going to check."

"Please do. The sooner we clear this up the better."

"You may not consider infidelity a motive for murder, but many people do. It's plausible that you came home to find your husband in bed with another woman and killed them both."

Hannah didn't respond, so Macy continued.

"The woman found dead in your house was in her early twenties, Caucasian, around five foot six in height with brown hair. Evidence tells us that she was dead before the fire started. We're assuming she'd been in a relationship with your husband for at least two months. Was there someone Peter was seeing regularly?"

"Not to my knowledge. To tell you the truth, I was under the impression Peter wasn't interested in getting involved with anyone exclusively."

"Yet, it turns out he was very involved. The young woman was pregnant with Peter's child."

"Are you sure?"

"She was in her first trimester, somewhere around two months. Do you have any idea who she might be?"

Hannah hesitated for the first time.

"I've had my suspicions about a few young women but couldn't tell you anything for sure," said Hannah.

"From his writing workshop?"

"Yes."

Macy spread the Polaroids out on the table in front of Hannah.

"We found these Polaroids in your office. Do you recognize them?"

"They were given to me. I was keeping them safe while I decided what to do."

"Who gave you the photos?"

"Lara Newcomb. She's a student in Peter's writing workshop, one of the ones who showed a lot of promise. She said she found the photos in Peter's office at the Bridger Cultural Center when she was housesitting for us in August."

"Why did she bring them to you?"

"She wanted me to stop Peter from doing this to anyone else."

"Is Lara Newcomb in any of these photographs?"

Hannah pointed to a girl who was positioned in an armchair. Black curls fell past her shoulders. Her eyes looked black behind the mask. There was a tattoo of a snake on her ankle. Multiple rings on her fingers.

"She thinks Peter drugged her," said Hannah. "She claims she doesn't remember anything."

"How long have these photos been in your possession?"

"A few weeks."

"Did you speak to your husband?"

Hannah looked away for the first time. "I couldn't do it. Peter wasn't just my husband, he was my best friend. I can't accept that he was doing something like this. I'm sure it was consensual."

"So, let me get this straight. A young woman came to you and asked you for help, and you did nothing?" Macy didn't give Hannah chance to respond. She pointed to the bedspread in a couple of the Polaroids. "Do you recognize the bedspread?"

"Maybe, I think we used to own something that looked like that, but it's been years."

"What about the bed and the chairs?"

Hannah stared at the photos. Her confusion was convincing.

"I'm sorry, but I don't know where these photos were taken."

"I have a hard time believing that."

"Well, it's true."

"Hannah, these photos were taken in your house."

"That's not possible."

"We found a room hidden behind some shelving in the basement. Your husband may have been abusing women under your roof and you're saying that you knew nothing about it. Were you hoping that you could make it all go away? Is that why you came back to Bolton on Monday to set the fire?" Macy held up the Polaroid of the woman who died. "Did you get angry when you found out your husband had already moved on? Is that why you killed them both?"

Hannah was crying again. "I swear I didn't do this," she said.

"The room in your basement is bigger than most people's apartments. It has en-suite bathroom, a wet bar and Wi-Fi. It was going on under your roof. How could you be so oblivious?"

"I know what it looks like, but it's the truth. Ask Cornelia. Peter managed most of the restoration work on the house because I was teaching full-time in California. I only came out occasionally."

Alisa spoke for the first time. "That's not what all the magazines say. You've told interviewers that you were involved in every aspect of the building work."

Hannah's voice had lost its edge. "That was all said for PR. We were putting on a united front. It's what was expected from us."

Macy sat down at her desk and opened the video link Alisa had sent her of an interview Peter Granger had done a year earlier. There'd already been over a half-million views on YouTube and hundreds of his fans had left comments. Peter Granger was wearing a sharply cut blue suit with a crisp white shirt that was open at the collar. Though the lines on his face were heavily demarcated, they didn't seem to age him. He was powerful and at ease in front of the large audience and there was both warmth and authority in his voice. The male interviewer who sat with him onstage barely registered. At some point Granger took over the discussion and engaged the audience directly. One after another, predominately female audience members asked him detailed questions about his novels. Microphone in hand, he walked off the stage and into the crowd. A woman was crying about a passage he'd written. She'd wanted him to know that his book had saved her life. He received a standing ovation for giving her his handkerchief.

Macy snapped her laptop shut and slipped it into her bag. If Peter Granger had this sort of effect on an audience full of strangers, she could only imagine what he was like one-on-one. The young women in the Polaroids hadn't really stood a chance.

11

Thursday

Grace drove down the dirt road with one eye on the gas gauge and the other on the rearview mirror.

"Damn, that was fucking scary," said Lara.

Grace was no longer panicked, she was angry. She shot Lara a quick glance.

"That was crazy. You shouldn't have got in his car."

Lara turned sideways in her seat. "I think we got away with it. There's no sign of him."

"It doesn't matter. He'll know it was me who took the letter."

"His car was a mess. He could have just as easily misplaced it." She sniffed her jacket. "God, I stink. It smelled like something died in that car."

"You're lucky it wasn't you."

Lara sat with her knees braced against her chest. Her black jeans were covered in dust.

"I think you should go to the police and report him for harassing you. You've got the letter now so there's nothing he can do."

Grace checked the mirrors again. "I'll go as soon as we're back in Bolton."

Ahead the dirt track ended at a paved road. Grace had no idea where she was. She figured if she kept heading west she'd eventually reach the outskirts of town, but instead the terrain became more and more densely forested.

"We're going to run out of gas soon," said Grace.

Lara patted the dashboard. "My car has never let me down. We've gone a long way on fumes."

"Is there a phone signal?"

Lara checked their phones. "Nada."

Grace took a left onto the paved road and headed south. As least it didn't feel as isolated. With any luck they'd catch a ride with a passing vehicle if they got stranded.

"Do you ever talk about what happened in Collier?" asked Lara.

"Not if I can help it."

"Why did you talk to Peter, then?"

"I guess I was in awe of him. Here was this great writer paying attention to someone like me. You don't come across people like Peter and Hannah where I come from. Thankfully, I didn't tell him everything."

"Why's that?"

Grace suddenly felt very tired of being Grace Adams. Anyone else would do. She did a quick check for Jordan's Bronco in the rearview mirror.

"There are things I don't tell anyone."

"Are you still going to go public at your student art show?"

"I keep changing my mind. Maybe it's not such a good idea."

Grace pumped the gas pedal, but the engine was dead. They were out of gas. They coasted onto the hard shoulder. They'd not seen a single car since they'd left Jordan's home twenty minutes earlier. The weather was relatively mild for November, but it was forecast to rain.

"I'm nervous about walking out in the open," said Lara.

"Do you know if Clare is around today?"

"She said she was going to the library."

"We should have let someone know where we were going," said Grace.

"To be fair, even we didn't know we'd end up here."

They trudged along the hard shoulder with their phones held out in front of them like divining rods.

"Bet you're thankful I bought you that bagel," said Lara.

"I'm surprised Steve made you pay."

"Steve thinks I'm a bitch."

Grace nudged her friend with her shoulder. "He's not wrong."

Lara spread her arms like wings, casting birdlike shadows on the tarmac. "I'm going to write about this," she said.

Grace walked backward so she could watch the road behind them. Sun glinted off the windshield of an approaching vehicle. It slowed down as it came alongside Lara's abandoned car. Grace grabbed Lara by the arm and pulled her toward the trees.

"Run," she said.

"It could be anyone," said Lara. "We could get a ride."

Grace didn't want to argue. The terrain was a mass of broken branches, tufts of silver leafed shrubs, and fallen pine needles. They ducked beneath low-hanging branches and scrambled over rocks. The ruins of an abandoned homestead blended into the forest. They didn't see it until Grace nearly tripped over the remains of the foundation. It was about a quarter mile from the road and at the top of a small rise. Beyond the remains of a back wall, the landscape sloped steeply downward. A thin thread of the Gallatin River was visible through the trees. If they followed its course they would reach Bolton in a couple of hours.

Only one of the homestead's walls was intact. Thankfully, it faced the road. Grace peered through what had once been a window. The glass was green and broken. Jordan's Bronco edged along the road.

"Oh, my God," said Lara. "That's him, isn't it?"

Grace felt sick. "Is there anything in your car that could give us away?"

"Shit, shit, shit."

"What?"

"The sketch you did is still on the dashboard."

Grace dropped to her knees and opened her bag. Her .22-caliber handgun was in the inside pocket.

"Sweet Jesus," said Lara. "You've got a gun."

Grace checked the cartridge and removed the safety. "Keep an eye on that Bronco," she said. "I want to know if he's coming this way."

"He's still sitting in his car."

"We didn't see this building from the road, so I doubt he can either."

Grace rested the gun barrel on the stone window frame and aimed it at Jordan's truck. Her uncle had taught her to shoot when she was little, and she was made to practice until handling a gun was as natural as breathing. Not that it would help them if Jordan brought along something with more firepower. He struck her as someone who would consider a .22 a child's toy. Lara was bouncing from one foot to the other.

"Shouldn't we just keep on going?" she said.

Grace blinked her eyes and tried to focus. He was out of his truck and moving through the trees along the road.

"What is he up to?" said Grace.

Lara grabbed Grace's arm. "I don't know and I don't care. Let's keep moving."

Grace lost sight of Jordan.

"Christ, I can't see him anymore."

Lara made a move. "Please, Grace. We need to go now."

Grace threw her bag over her shoulder and ran after Lara. The clouds thickened overhead and raindrops pelted the forest canopy. Aside from the river there wasn't a familiar landmark in sight.

The descent down to the river was trickier than Grace and Lara had thought it would be. They slid on the thick carpet of pine needles, leaving tracks in the damp soil underneath. The overhead branches protected them from the worst of the rain, but the shoreline was more exposed. They needed to gain some ground on Jordan or he was going to spot them easily. Grace cut across the slope sharply and headed toward a rocky outcrop.

"We'll follow the river but stay out of sight. It will be slower but safer."

"I'm right behind you," said Lara.

Once they were hidden behind the rocks they took a few seconds to get their bearings. The river was farther down the slope, about a hundred yards north. A herd of elk was braving the rain. They crossed over the stony banks in a tight group.

"Do we need to worry about bears?" asked Lara.

"I'd say bears are the least of our worries."

The herd tensed up in unison and took off running. Jordan was also moving down the slope toward the river. He was carrying a hunting rifle and a backpack. Grace covered Lara's mouth and put a finger to her lips. They backed away slowly. The boulders that towered over them were as big as buses. An animal track led them deeper into the forest. Grace doubled back and told Lara to climb up into a tight crevice between the rocks. It was a squeeze for them, which meant it would be impossible for Jordan to follow. Lara was the stronger of the two of them. She pulled Grace through the crevice and they emerged onto a sheltered plateau. Above them a flat boulder balanced precariously across an opening that was about ten feet wide. Grace found a gap in between the rocks. It took her awhile to spot Jordan. He was moving methodically, making a wide sweep of the hillside.

"Not a word," whispered Grace. "Make sure your phone is switched off."

Jordan slowly made his way toward them. The rain was falling harder. It ran down the sides of the boulders, forming a puddle where they sheltered. The temperature may have been mild for November but the water was freezing cold.

Jordan passed out of view as he moved beneath their hiding place. Smoke from his cigarette wafted upward through the crevice. Grace aimed her gun at the opening and prayed.

Overhead, thunder rolled across the valley. Midday quickly descended into night as the sky darkened and a storm barreled across the terrain. There was a flash and lightning split the sky. The puddle beneath their feet grew larger. They pressed themselves to the rock face in an attempt to stay dry.

It no longer smelled of cigarette smoke. From their perch Grace studied the shoreline. The beech trees and cottonwoods bent double in the driving wind.

"I'm freezing," whispered Lara.

Grace threw her a dark look and put a finger to her lips. She'd make Lara wait there all night if she had to. Thunder rumbled closer. Rain gave way to hail. Stones the size of marbles ricocheted off the boulders. The noise was deafening. Overhead the treetops clanged together like church bells. A shudder ran across the river's surface as lightning struck a pine tree on the far shore. The earth shook in the deep crack of it.

Jordan had found shelter in the trees beyond the stony riverbank. He appeared to be watching the hillside. A few seconds later he stepped out into the open. He'd changed into a rain poncho printed with camouflage. The hood was up so his face was obscured in shadow. Grace moved away from the gap between the boulders.

"He's got binoculars," she said.

"Did he see you?" asked Lara. Her face was pale, her lips blue. Rainwater dripped from the loose tendrils of her hair.

"I don't think so."

"What should we do?"

Grace took another peek. Jordan was moving toward them.

"He's coming this way," she whispered.

"Maybe if we keep climbing," said Lara.

"The sides are too slippery. We'd never make it." Grace once again aimed her gun at the opening. "Keep an eye on the hillside," she whispered. "He may be heading back to his car."

"I see him," said Lara. "He's on the far side of the hill again." Grace hunched down next to Lara. Jordan was inspecting the tracks they'd left when they'd hurried toward the river. He eventually shouldered his rifle and headed in the direction of the road.

Overhead the sky settled and the rain lessoned. They waited for it to stop completely before sliding back down through the crevice. It was nearly three o'clock when they emerged stiff and cold. They could see Jordan's heavy boot prints in the damp earth. They found one cigarette butt wedged into a crack in the rocks and another on the path.

They followed the animal track deep into the woods and stayed out of sight until they'd rounded the far bend in the river. The sun broke through the clouds at the same time they stepped out of the trees, but a freezing wind skirted across the valley.

"How far do you think it is?"

In the distance, Grace spotted one of Bolton's many grain silos.

"It's going to take a while to walk along the shore, a couple hours, maybe more. Then we'll have to get a ride the rest of the way. It will be dark by the time we get home."

"Isn't that raft rental place somewhere between here and town?"

"I doubt it's open this time of year," said Grace.

"There's a pay phone."

"I forgot about that. We'll call for a ride when we get there."

Grace checked her cell phone for a signal before striking out along the shore. They were still out of range. Lara and Grace leaned against each other for warmth. Every few minutes Grace turned to see if Jordan was following them. The hunting rifle he was carrying had a spotting scope. That worried Grace now that they were out in the open. If he was a decent shot it would be easy to pick them off from a distance.

The man who'd given them a lift into town offered to drop Grace and Lara off at their apartment, but they said it would be fine for him to leave them anywhere along Main Street. They thanked him again for being so helpful and offered him money for gas. He waved them off.

"Next time you go for a walk in the woods be sure to dress properly," he said.

They'd been hiking along the river's rocky shoreline for nearly two hours when they'd finally come across the little store where they rented rafts during the summer. It was way past the end of the season so they'd been lucky the owner was there. He was doing some necessary repairs to the roof and shuttering all the windows in preparation for winter. He brought them inside and served them coffee next to a wood-burning stove. He was well into his sixties but moved with ease. His long gray beard was flecked with copper. There wasn't much stock left on the shelves, but he'd found them some Cup-a-Soup and boiled water in a kettle on the stove.

He'd asked where they'd run out of gas and shook his head upon hearing their response.

"Another mile up the road and you would have come to a gas station. What on earth possessed you to head through the woods like that?"

There'd been no truth in their answer.

They'd rested near the stove while he'd finished up the work that needed doing. It was dark by the time they squeezed into the cab of his pickup truck and headed for Bolton.

Lara and Grace were both exhausted as they walked along the final stretch of road that would take them home.

"We'll drive out in the morning and pick up your car," said Grace.

"I don't know if that's a good idea. He might be waiting for us. You need to go to the police first."

They stopped about a hundred yards from their apartment building. The overhead trees were thick and lamplight barely touched the pavement for long stretches. A young woman squealed with laughter as a group of teenagers entered the park across the street. Grace and Lara relaxed. There were still people about. They walked down the center of the road. Jordan's Bronco was nowhere to be seen.

Grace took her phone out of her jacket pocket and dialed 911.

"What are you doing?" asked Lara.

Grace had the phone pressed to her ear. "This doesn't feel right. I'm calling the police." She waited to be put through. "26 Spruce Road. A man is threatening us."

They both turned around at the sound of footsteps. Jordan had emerged from between two parked cars. He walked toward them. Grace held the phone in her hand like a threat. She and Lara backed away from Jordan. Grace yelled loud enough for the dispatcher to hear her.

"I've called the police," said Grace. "They're on their way."

Jordan kept coming. "They're going to be too late."

12

Thursday

Macy was beyond tired. Wrapped in a bathrobe monogrammed with the hotel's logo, wet hair secured in a towel, and every muscle aching, she stretched out on the bed and faced a silent television screen. She emptied a miniature bottle of whiskey into a glass half filled with ice. The first taste warmed her lips. The second burned her right down to the core. The third brought on a much-appreciated thaw. She opened a second bottle and tipped more whiskey into the glass.

It had been a long time since Macy last gave Grace Adams much thought. Quite an achievement considering how heavily the young woman once weighed on Macy's personal and professional life. Her mother's murder was linked to the first big case Macy had worked with Ray Davidson. Back then, Macy was a young recruit and Ray already a seasoned investigator. Their subsequent romantic relationship turned out to be one of the biggest mistakes of her life. At the time of Luke's birth, Ray and Macy were no longer a couple, but a snowstorm had trapped Macy in the same town that had brought them together. She'd been alone when she gave birth to their son in Collier County Hospital.

Grace Adams was one of her first visitors. The young woman had also been alone. Wheeled in by a hospital orderly, she'd been left at the foot of Macy's bed with nothing but a sketchbook and a worried smile. Grace hadn't come to apologize, but they both knew that she should have found the courage to tell the truth sooner.

Macy played with the buttons on the television remote, idly scanning the channels. Hannah Granger's surprise return from the dead was all over the news. After the interview she'd been released without being charged but told to remain in Bolton. There were still many unanswered questions. An unidentified woman had died while sharing a bed with her husband and several valuable paintings were missing. No one in Bolton and the surrounding areas had filed a missing person's report, and a search of the Granger's cabin, Jessica Reynolds's home, and the university grounds had yielded nothing in the way of stolen artwork. Macy would interview Cornelia Hart and the students from the writing workshop in the morning. Grace Adams was the first person Macy wanted to speak to.

Macy wondered how much Grace had changed. She'd only had time to skim the thin file Alisa had handed her. Grace Adams had been living under the name Larson and attending Bolton College for the past two and half years. She'd requested assistance from the local police on four separate occasions because she felt she was being followed and feared for her personal safety. The four men had left town without incident after being approached by police officers, so no charges were ever filed. All Macy had in front of her was a list of names. None of the men had criminal records. The most determined of Grace's stalkers had travelled all the way from Eastern Europe. Detective Sergeant Brad Hastings had posted an unofficial note in the file. In July, Grace Adams had been found asleep and presumably drunk on Peter and Hannah's sofa. For some reason Peter Granger and Grace had pretended not to know each other. Macy wanted to know why.

Macy tipped the rest of the second miniature bottle of whiskey into her glass.

"No more after this," she promised herself.

She sipped, she poured, she stirred. She sipped some more.

Her cell phone vibrated angrily on the pillow next to her. She picked it up and scrolled through the missed calls and messages. Her boyfriend, Aiden, was a very understanding man, but if she didn't call him back soon he'd be in his rights to feel neglected.

She closed her eyes and imagined what it would be like to have him by her side. There were times she wanted to leave her job at the justice department and do something else—move to Wilmington Creek and live a quiet life. She'd actively chosen to live a life apart. Her son was in Helena and the man she loved was in Wilmington Creek. Her days were fulfilling but every night she stayed alone in a hotel, far away from them both, felt like an unsuccessful compromise.

Aiden answered on the third ring. He sounded as if he'd been dozing. His voice was full of sleep and a slight growl that could be traced back to a time when he smoked two packs a day. He claimed to have quit completely, but she knew better than to trust him on that score. Their relationship wasn't without its issues. After years of moving through life without firm romantic commitments they both were adjusting to the new boundaries they'd set for themselves. It didn't help that they both had a natural tendency to flirt. She was trying to reel it in and had to trust that he was doing the same. She couldn't call him on it without coming off sounding insecure, so she focused on his illicit cigarettes instead.

"Hey, babe," he said. "I was hoping you'd call."

"I miss you."

"I think I can fix that."

"Please tell me you're in the room next door."

"Not that close, but I am on my way. You have space in that hotel room of yours for one more?"

"You know you don't need to ask. When are you coming down?" asked Macy.

"Tomorrow, early evening if the roads are clear. I have a surprise for you."

"You don't have to bring me anything. Just come."

"How are things? I was watching the news. Hannah Granger looked like a deer caught in the headlights."

"I think we're all feeling that way," said Macy.

"Is she guilty?"

"She seems the obvious choice but I'm not convinced." She hesitated. "You know I'm going to be pretty busy this weekend."

"That won't be a problem. I've got friends in Bolton I'd like to catch up with so I'll see you when I can."

"How's work? Have the new plans for the resort been cleared?" asked Macy.

"It's been tricky but the powers that be finally saw sense."

"I was worried you'd have a long fight on your hands. That stretch of the Flathead River is precious to a lot of people."

"We've been bending over backwards to make the project environmentally sustainable and it looks like our efforts have finally paid off. It also helps that the resort and fishing lodge are going to bring jobs and money into the area."

"When will construction start?"

"Hoping to break ground in the next couple of weeks."

"That's wonderful. Congratulations."

Aiden yawned. "I can't believe it's actually going to happen. I know there will be a fair few hours behind a desk each day, but I'll be on the river as much as possible."

"You'll be able to go fishing for a living. Imagine that."

"Living the dream."

"I'll let you sleep," said Macy.

"Sounds like you need to do the same."

"All tucked up in bed and ready to pass out."

"I love you," said Aiden.

"Love you too."

Macy put her cell phone aside and closed her eyes but, try as she might, she couldn't sleep. A half hour later she was heading out the door with a cup of coffee and Grace Adams's address keyed into her cell phone.

. . .

Macy walked out of the hotel lobby and set off on foot down Main Street. A handful of bars and restaurants were still open but traffic was sparse and few people were about. She walked as far as the K-Bar and stood out front drinking the coffee she'd prepared in the hotel room. Other than a half-dozen bouquets of flowers prominently displayed out front, there was little evidence of the violence that had broken out on the premises four days earlier. Brad Hastings had been downcast when Macy had passed him in the corridor earlier in the evening. Despite hours of interviews, they'd yet to find their missing Elvis.

If the map on Macy's cell phone was correct, Grace Adams's apartment was only a twenty-minute walk away. The most direct route took you within four blocks of the Granger's home, but going there meant doubling back toward Main Street, which made the fact that she'd sought refuge on their sofa following a night out drinking at the bars on Main Street even more suspect.

Macy walked down the quiet sidewalks in the residential neighborhood where the Grangers lived, peering up at windows still flooded with light. The roadblock on Grand Avenue had been cleared and a single patrol car was parked in front of the Granger's house. She showed the officer on duty her badge as he rolled down the window.

Patrol Officer Casey Winn regarded her with hooded eyes.

"You're out late, Detective Greeley."

"I couldn't sleep. All quiet?"

"Thought I saw some lights around back earlier but didn't find anything when I went for a closer look. The kids in the neighborhood have been daring each other to go inside."

"I would have been up to the same sort of crap when I was young, so I can't be too self-righteous."

"Same here. Bolton is pretty boring by most people's standards. This is big news."

"The bars seem to get enough action."

"Yeah, but that doesn't provide the younger folks much in the way of entertainment."

"How often do you have minors trying their luck?"

"More often than is reported. We like to give the bar staff the benefit of the doubt. It's a college town so some nights it's packed. We know they do their best, but these kids are clever and determined. Same for all the underage drinking that goes on at the college parties. We like to take a pragmatic approach."

"Certainly saves on paperwork."

"That it does."

The police radio barked at them from the dashboard. There was a disturbance in front of an apartment building on Spruce.

Casey picked up the radio and let the operator know he was on his way.

"I'm heading that way as well. Do you mind if I ride along?" asked Macy.

Casey told her to hop in.

The modern five-story apartment building was situated across the street from Prospector's Park, a sprawling green space that was riddled with walking trails. Casey slowed the patrol car to a crawl. Three people stood on the sidewalk in front of the building. Macy got out so she could approach on foot.

Two women were in a shouting match with a bearded man.

"I read that letter. Grace threatened to kill him."

The man punched one of the women in the face and grabbed a bag from where it had fallen onto the sidewalk. The other woman tried to stop him but he shoved her out of the way and ran across the road toward the park.

Casey raised his firearm and ordered him to stop but it was too late.

Macy followed him into the park. At first the trail ran parallel to the road and the streetlamps were close enough to cast some light on the densely wooded area. Macy caught a glimpse of the reflective stripes on the man's jacket. He wasn't too far ahead. She quickened her pace. She'd run these paths every day when she was a student at the college.

Up ahead the trail branched off in several directions and entered what the locals liked to call the maze. If she lost him in there she'd have trouble finding him again. Macy heard voices. They weren't the only ones in the park. A girl's high-pitched laughter filtered through the darkness. There was a scuffle and someone crashed through the undergrowth. The girl was no longer laughing.

"What the fuck? Watch where you're going!" she yelled.

Macy came upon a group of kids. One had been knocked to the ground.

"Police," she said. "Which way did he go?"

A girl pointed to a trail that branched out to the right. Macy took off running again. The pathway was completely in shadow. She had to slow down several times. She could hear him moving through the trees on the other side of a narrow creek. It sounded like he was heading into a nearby neighborhood. A security light at the rear of one of the houses went on as he cut through a backyard. Macy slipped on the rocks as she made her way across the creek. One boot ended up in the freezing water. She dragged herself back up onto dry land and kept running.

Several dogs broke into a chorus. Macy followed the noise. He was moving through the backyards, heading east. She took a path between two houses and ran headlong down the sidewalk in the same direction. She turned on Taft Avenue and moved along a high hedge that lined one side of the street. There was no sign of him.

More dogs barked.

He tore through an opening in the hedge and crashed right into her. They both hit the pavement hard. She managed a strangled cry before he put his hand over her mouth. She bit down on his fingers. Instead of letting go he slammed her head back onto the concrete.

"Police," she gasped, smashing the top of her head into his nose.

There was sickening crunch and warm blood poured onto her face. He swung his arms wildly, striking her several times on the head with his open fists. She rocked back and kneed him in the chest. He tried to roll away but Macy grabbed hold of his leg. He shook himself loose and stood over her. His beard was stained red and he was breathing heavily.

He raised his boot and stamped down hard on her stomach. Macy curled up into a ball and gasped for breath. She could hear police sirens, but there was no sign of a patrol car. She watched him run down the darkened street. He was getting away and there was nothing she could do. She couldn't even call for help.

She lay quietly, catching her breath. Her right ear was ringing. Her jaw ached. She pulled a small flashlight out of her jacket pocket and turned it on. Grace's bag was lying open a few feet away. Several items had spilled out onto the pavement. She managed to stand as a patrol car turned the corner. She limped out onto the pavement and waved it down.

By the time Macy returned to the apartment building, both Grace and her friend were gone and the apartment's glass fronted lobby was filled with spectators. Macy got out of the patrol car and went over to speak to Casey Winn. She held up Grace's bag.

"I got her bag back," she said.

"Looks like he put up quite a fight. I hope it was worth it."

"Do you have any idea what happened here?"

"It seems pretty straightforward. The guy tried to rob them as they entered the building. Grace Larson is pretty roughed up so she's gone to the ER, and her friend Lara Newcomb is upstairs in the apartment they share. She'll come into the station tomorrow and make a formal statement."

"There's more to this," said Macy. "I'm pretty sure there's a connection to the fire on Madison. Both the women were Peter Granger's students."

"Could be a coincidence."

"I somehow doubt it."

Patrol Officer Casey continued to scribble notes onto his pad. "I'm just finishing up here. Can I give you a ride to your hotel, or do you want to be dropped off at the hospital?"

Macy nodded. "Appreciate that. The hotel will be fine."

Macy called Ryan while she waited in Casey's patrol car.

"Hey, did I wake you?" asked Macy.

"Never going to happen. What's up?" asked Ryan.

"I'm hoping you're still in Bolton."

"Arrived back here ten minutes ago. Do I need to be somewhere?"

"Meet me in my hotel room in fifteen. Bring your kit."

Macy dropped Grace's bag on her bed and peeled off her clothing. Her hip was heavily bruised and her knees grazed. She stood in front of the bathroom mirror and examined her face. The swelling was minimal but a bruise was forming around her left eye. She gathered a fistful of ice from the bucket next to the bed in a washcloth and gently pressed it to her face. She winced.

There was a quiet knock on the door. Macy wrapped herself in a bathrobe and went to let Ryan in. He threw her a pained expression.

"Jesus, Macy. What in the hell happened to you?"

"I would say, you should see the other guy, but other than teeth marks on his hand I don't think I left much of an impression."

He brushed past her and stood in the middle of her hotel room.

"This isn't funny," he said.

"Do I look like I'm laughing?"

"Let's go into the bathroom where the light is better."

Ryan worked quickly. After collecting evidence from her hair and nails, he had her stand in her bra and underwear so he could photograph her injuries. He measured the boot print on her stomach.

"I'd say he's a size eleven."

"Feels more like a thirteen."

"Where are the clothes you were wearing?"

"In a plastic laundry bag. He had a nosebleed. A real gusher, so there should be plenty of blood."

"Mind if I bag and tag?"

"I need to keep my jacket."

"I'll go over it here then."

He handed her a couple of tablets.

"What's this?" asked Macy.

"I'm afraid it's nothing more exciting than ibuprofen." He winked. "My days as your drug dealer are over."

"I'll put that in my report."

"Any idea who this guy was?"

Macy put the bathrobe back on and sat down on the edge of the bed next to Grace's messenger bag. Though it was in good condition, it had put in some miles.

"I have no idea, but he was very interested in getting his hands on Grace Adams's bag. Apparently, there's a letter inside. I think he said something like 'I saw the letter. Grace threatened to kill him.'"

Ryan tossed her a pair of latex gloves.

"Let's see what that's all about then," said Ryan.

Macy checked the wallet first. Grace's driver's license confirmed it was her bag and the fake ID told Macy she was no longer the young innocent she'd been in Collier. Macy had hoped that she'd learned to live a bit, but maybe that hope was misplaced. It looked like Grace was in trouble again.

"Grace Adams has been living under the name Grace Larson since she moved to Bolton."

She handed Ryan the wallet.

"According to her fake ID, her name is Beth. A good quality fake, by the way. This would have set her back a few bob," he said.

Macy would have raised an eyebrow, but it hurt too much.

"A few bob?" she asked.

"British expression. Think paper."

"Paper as in money?"

"Racks on racks on racks."

"Steady on, Ryan. You're slipping into embarrassing uncle territory." Macy took a pregnancy wand out of the Ziploc bag and held it up to the light. She handed it to Ryan. "Even if someone was overjoyed at the prospect of being a mother, it's an odd thing to carry around."

"The female victim we found in the house was pregnant."

"Could be related, but it's a bit of a leap. By the way, are we any closer to establishing what caused her death?"

"Cardiac arrest but, given she was only in her early twenties and in good health, we have good reason to suspect foul play. The poor condition of the remains makes it difficult to determine with any certainty what happened."

"Any chance it was suicide?"

"A possibility. She had been self-harming for some time. Suicide is often the next step. We're running a tox screen."

Grace's .22-caliber handgun was hidden in an inside pocket. Macy cleared the bullet from the chamber and took out the cartridge before putting everything in an evidence bag.

"Does Grace Adams have a license to carry a concealed weapon?" asked Ryan.

Macy nodded. "She's legal."

"Anything else?"

Macy held up a wrinkled envelope addressed to Peter Granger. "Some light reading material. Looks like it's about eight pages long."

Ryan yawned. "Well, this Hardy Boy is dead tired and in no mood to hear all about some girl's latest crush."

"She's hardly a girl."

He came over to where Macy was sitting and gave her a gentle hug.

"I've become very fond of you," he said. "I'd appreciate it if you tried harder to stay in one piece."

"I'll see you in the morning, Ryan."

He kissed her on the top of her head.

"Breakfast is on me."

Macy was tired, so she skimmed Grace's letter to Peter Granger. It didn't take her long to realize that Grace had every right to be angry with her former mentor. She'd trusted him and he took advantage of that trust. Grace had conveniently written her most explicit threats in capital letters. In one paragraph she wrote that she hoped he'd BURN IN HELL.

Macy stopped reading when she found a passage that was even more specific.

SOMEDAY YOU'LL WAKE UP TO FIND YOUR HOUSE IS ON FIRE. I HOPE YOU DON'T MAKE IT OUT ALIVE.

Macy slipped the letter into an evidence bag. It had been obtained without a warrant so it might not hold up in court. Grace's lawyer would be right to argue that it was his client's way of venting her rage. The letter was never sent. It was for her eyes only. No harm done.

But Macy wasn't going to let Grace off the hook just yet. She'd seen firsthand how unhinged Grace could be and it was possible that Peter Granger's betrayal had pushed her over the edge. This wouldn't have been the first fire Grace Adams had set. Three years earlier she'd burned down the mobile home she'd lived in as a child. It was derelict and empty, so no one got hurt. She'd even admitted to what she'd done. It had been Macy who'd let her get away with it. She'd understood Grace's rage then just as she understood it now. This time was different, though.

Two people had died.

Macy turned off the lights and lay in darkness. Her whole body was throbbing. She dreamed she was running through fire.

Friday

Macy walked into her office and dropped her things on her desk. Ryan was seated in her chair with the newspaper open to the crossword puzzle. He muttered a muted "hello" but didn't look up.

"Don't you have any work to do?" asked Macy.

"I put in some serious overtime last night. How are you feeling?"

"I've had better days."

"Any word on the guy who attacked you?"

Macy was sore all over but doing her best not to let it show. She dropped down into the empty chair and started going through the paperwork that had been left on her desk.

"They spent a few hours combing the area but no luck. I'm interviewing Grace Adams and Lara Newcomb this morning. According to their initial statement they'd never seen him before. I'm fairly sure they're lying."

Alisa walked in looking excited. She held a piece of paper aloft but stopped short of speaking when she saw Macy's face.

"You missed all the action last night," said Ryan. "I suppose you were tucked up in bed watching the Disney Channel."

Alisa didn't miss a beat. "Actually, it was the porn channel."

Macy laughed hard and it hurt. She pointed to her face. "I'll explain this later. What have you got for me?"

Alisa handed Macy the piece of paper.

"Someone has been downloading files from Peter Granger's remote server using a computer at the library. Two of the files were sent to Print Works, a shop that is located here in Bolton. After they were printed out the order was picked up and paid for in cash," said Alisa.

Macy gave the information a quick glance. "Could it have been Peter Granger?"

"The files were transferred yesterday morning."

"Okay, that is suspicious. Are you familiar with the shop?"

"Yeah, it's near campus."

"I want you to head over there and speak to the manager and anyone else who may have worked the day the files were transferred. Hopefully, they may remember who came in. Also check whether they have security cameras."

"Should I go to the library as well?"

"Absolutely. They may keep a log of who uses their computers. Did you manage to get in touch with Cornelia Hart? I have a few follow-up questions."

"She's not answering her phone."

"It's still early, but send a unit out to her place if she doesn't get back to you in the next couple of hours."

13

Friday

Steve had given Grace a dozen pink roses. They were proper ones from a florist, not the grocery store or the gas station forecourt. She rested them on her lap and tried her best to resist the urge to hug them. They were beautiful and she said so. Steve had taken off his hat and was standing as if at attention. Grace had only seen him outside the coffee shop on a few occasions. Despite his height he seemed out of his depth.

"Hospitals make me nervous," he said.

"Maybe you should sit down," said Grace.

Steve pulled up a chair and perched on the edge of the seat like he was ready to bolt.

"It's the time I did in the military," he said, by way of explanation. "Field hospitals in Afghanistan are pretty stressful places."

"I didn't know you were in the military."

"I worked in catering. Not exactly exciting."

"Where I come from you're considered lucky if you survive a trip to the hospital. This is the nicest room I've ever been in." Her eyes drifted to the window. "I mean, look at the view."

Steve looked.

"Good point. That looks nothing like Kandahar. How are you feeling?"

"The doctor says everything is fine but they're still running some more tests." Her mood changed. She was no longer excited. She was anxious. "I guess I'll have to go in to speak to the police at some point this afternoon."

"Did you get a good look at the guy?"

Grace fiddled with the IV tubing sticking out of the back of her left hand. The bandages were making her skin itch. The doctor had told her the IV was just a precaution. Among other things, she was dehydrated.

"It was dark," said Grace. "But, yeah, I think Lara and I gave a good enough description."

Steve glanced over at the side table where a few prescription bottles were lined up in a neat row. "I suppose the hospital has to be extra cautious because of your condition."

Grace had told Steve about her medical history in a moment of weakness that she'd lived to regret. They'd been on their own a lot at the café during the slow period between Christmas and New Year. Steve had just found out his brother was going into surgery to have a tumor removed. One thing led to another and Grace told Steve that she'd had a heart transplant three and half years earlier and was doing fine. She'd wanted to put him at ease, but it had had the opposite effect. Steve was even more anxious. He'd treated her like an invalid until she threatened to quit. Since then he'd been sending her out to the loading bay to collect deliveries and giving her longer shifts.

Grace shook one of the bottles of pills. "These are immunosuppressants. I have to take them for the rest of my life."

"Do you ever think about the man who donated his heart?"

"I don't know much about him."

"Didn't you say that he got shot in a hunting accident?"

"No one knows for sure. He was on his own. There were no witnesses," said Grace.

"Was it suicide?"

"I don't like to think about it."

"That was . . . Sorry. That was insensitive."

Grace changed the subject.

"I can still go to the concert tonight. I mean, I can still go if you still want to take me."

"I'm not sure it's a good idea. You probably need to rest," said Steve.

"I'm not as fragile as people think. I'm just a little tired, that's all. As long as we're sitting down it will be fine."

Steve stood up.

"Are you leaving?" she asked.

"I need to get back to work. I left Matt in charge. He's not good in a crisis. Gets a bit flustered if there's more than four people in line."

Steve kissed her on the top of the head.

"I'll pick you up at seven," he said.

Grace set her cell phone down on the bedside table and closed her eyes. The police officer had been polite on the phone, but Grace couldn't help but feel anxious. They'd recovered her stolen bag and Detective Macy Greeley was on her way to the hospital. Grace had been unable to fake her way through an appropriate response. She'd stuttered, gone silent, and then lied, saying that a nurse had asked her to get off the phone.

It was possible it was a routine interview. Grace had been one of Peter's students. They were probably speaking to everyone who'd had contact with him. Grace was praying this was the case. If Macy read the letter she'd suspect Grace was involved. There was a period of time she couldn't account for on the night of the fire.

Lara arrived carrying an overnight bag. She set it down at the foot of the bed and gave Grace a long hug.

"I was so worried I couldn't sleep," said Lara. "Are you okay?"

Grace wiped the tears from her eyes.

"Better now," she said.

"I thought you might want a change of clothes so I brought you a few things. Will you have to stay much longer?"

"I hope not. The doctors are just running some tests. They're worried I've been under too much stress."

"That's kind of an understatement. Have the police been in touch?"

"They found my bag."

Lara made sure they were alone.

"What about the letter?" asked Lara.

"They didn't say. Macy Greeley is on her way. That can't be good."

"What will you say about Jordan?"

"I'll have to tell the truth."

"Don't be an idiot. Wait and see what she knows first."

"Lara, it doesn't work like that."

There was a light knock at the door. Macy Greeley stood at the threshold watching them. She smiled warmly but there was caution in her eyes.

"Grace, it's good to see that you're still in one piece. Are you feeling well enough to talk?"

Grace felt like she was eighteen years old again and her mother had just died. Different hospital, same detective. Lara squeezed her hand. This time it was going to be okay. Grace had friends. She wasn't alone anymore.

Macy Greeley didn't wait for an invitation. She moved slowly. Her eye was bruised and swollen. There was an angry-looking scrape along her jawbone.

"I had a rough night," said Macy. "But I guess it shows."

"Did he do this to you?" asked Grace.

"He's a dangerous man, but I think you already know that."

Lara spoke up. "Grace doesn't know anything about him."

"That's interesting. I was under the impression you were acquainted." Macy pulled a chair over so it was next to the bed. "The important thing is that everyone is going to be okay, and I got your bag back."

Grace gave Lara a warning look.

"Why am I guessing this isn't the outcome you were hoping for?" asked Macy.

"Did you arrest him?" asked Grace.

"No, but we have DNA and fingerprints. We'll find him soon enough." Macy stared at Grace. "I was hoping you would make it sooner. I need you to tell me what you know about him."

"He came out of nowhere," said Lara. "We don't know—"

"Be very careful what you say from here on out. We found his prints on a letter that belongs to Grace, so we know it was in his possession at some point."

"You read it?" asked Grace.

"It was laying open on the ground so I took the opportunity to have a look. You made it very easy for me to find all the interesting parts. All caps does have some advantages. I guess I should thank you for that."

"Are you going to arrest her?" asked Lara. "'Cause you should know she was with me on Halloween night. We were at the K-Bar together."

"Grace, your friend lying for you is not doing you any favors. We checked the security cameras. Grace left the bar alone at 11:52. Another camera picks her up walking along a street that would have taken her to the neighborhood where the Grangers lived."

"The guy you're looking for is named Jordan," said Grace.

Macy started writing some notes. "No last name?"

"I didn't ask."

"How did you meet him?"

"He showed up at the café where I work about three weeks ago. I think he started following me around Bolton a short time later."

"Why didn't you report this to the police?"

"I was hoping I could deal with it on my own."

Lara spoke up. "He stole that letter out of her locker at work. You can't use it as evidence. My dad is a lawyer. I know things."

Macy stared at Lara. This was the woman who gave Hannah the Polaroids instead of taking them to the police. She had a lot of explaining to do, but it would have to wait.

"Lara, I'm glad you have some basic understanding of the law. It means I won't have to explain what obstruction means and why you could be charged. Yesterday evening you gave a false statement to the police. You should have told the truth. Jordan is a very dangerous man. It's time to drop the bullshit and tell me everything you know."

"He drives an old green Bronco," said Grace.

"Have you had any other contact with him?"

"He followed me home after I left the K-Bar on Halloween night. I had to cut through some backyards to get away from him."

Macy made some more notes. "I'll need details, but that can wait until later. Anything else you want to tell me?"

Grace and Lara remained silent.

"Your paths must have crossed again if you managed to get the letter back from him," said Macy.

"It was in his car," said Lara.

Grace tried to interrupt her but Lara kept talking.

"We waited for Jordan outside the café where Grace works. He comes to all of her shifts." Lara shrugged like it wasn't a big deal. "His car wasn't locked so I decided to have a look inside."

"Where was Jordan all this time?" asked Macy.

"Inside the café."

Macy placed the photos of her injuries on the bed in front of Lara and Grace.

"I want you to see what this guy did to me," said Macy. "Go on, Lara, take a good look. You've got no business climbing into a stranger's car. You're lucky he didn't kill you." Macy lowered her voice. "Now, is there anything else you need to tell me?"

"We know where he lives," said Grace.

"How in the hell do you know that? Did you follow him home?" asked Macy.

"I didn't have a choice," said Grace. "Lara didn't get out of his car in time."

"You're both lucky to be alive. Do you realize that?" Macy held up her pen. "I need to know where he lives."

"I'm not sure of the address, but I can find it on Google maps."

Macy handed Grace her phone.

"Are we going to be arrested?" asked Lara.

"I don't know yet," said Macy. "I want you both to come into the station this afternoon for a formal interview."

"Is this about this guy or the Grangers?" asked Lara.

"You'll have to wait and see." Macy stood with difficulty. "Meanwhile, I'd really appreciate it if you stayed out of trouble for the rest of the day, and don't even think about leaving town."

Grace tried to sneak out of the hospital unseen, but Hannah Granger spotted her as she was making her way toward the elevators. Hannah had been sitting alone in the waiting room, looking rumpled, a newspaper shielding her from curious glances. If she hadn't called out Grace's name she may have gone unnoticed. Their eyes met but Grace kept walking. She was already in enough trouble with Macy Greeley. She was pretty sure the detective would disapprove of any contact between the two women who were probably high on her list of suspects. Besides, Grace had no reason to show Hannah any kindness. Grace stopped at the elevator and pushed the button for the ground floor. The sooner she got home the better. Hannah had other ideas. She stepped between Grace and the opening doors.

"Grace," said Hannah. "Can we talk?"

"I'm not sure that's a good idea."

"There's a chapel at the end of the corridor. We can speak in private."

Grace felt like a schoolgirl trailing behind Hannah. The woman in front of her moved with purpose, her head held high. She waited for Grace at the entrance to the chapel.

"It's perfect. No one here but us," said Hannah.

They sat in a pew near the front. Grace felt a slight pang of guilt. She hadn't been inside a church since her aunt's funeral. More than two and a half years later and she was still trying to find a way to believe in God again.

"How's Jessica?" asked Grace. "I assume she's why you're here."

"She's doing better. We talked a bit this morning."

"She thought you were dead."

"I was snowed in. We have a cabin. . . ."

"Nice story. Is that what you told the police?"

"I know how it looks," said Hannah, "but, I swear to God I didn't kill anyone."

Grace flinched. She may have given up on religion, but saying the Lord's name in vain while sitting in his house wasn't going to fly with her.

"This is a chapel. Show a little respect," said Grace.

Hannah raked her hands through her hair. Her makeup was smudged, her hair greasy. Dark roots blazed a trail down the part.

"I don't care if you believe me. I didn't do it and I have no idea who did."

"Do you know who the woman with Peter was?" asked Grace.

"No, but the police are bound to figure it out soon enough. You should know that they found the Polaroids."

"What Polaroids?"

"Lara said you knew about them. That all of you knew."

"I don't know what you're talking about."

"Lara found a whole box of them when she was snooping in Peter's office while she was housesitting for us in August. He must have been . . . He'd been taking photos of girls for years. I have a feeling drugs may have been involved. The girls are naked. Their faces are covered."

Grace placed a hand to her chest. There was nothing wrong with her heart. It was still beating.

"Are there pictures of me?" she asked.

Hannah's voice sharpened. "That depends. Did you ever sleep with my husband?"

"God, no," said Grace.

"Now who's saying the Lord's name in vain?"

"Fuck you, Hannah."

"That kind of language is uncalled for. You girls threw yourselves at him. Do you know how that made me feel?"

"You just said drugs were involved," said Grace.

"Like you guys didn't do drugs and drink too much whenever you were with him. I've seen you at it with my own eyes. You shouldn't complain when you find out it's not quite as pleasant as you expected."

"How can you continue to defend him?"

Hannah stared at the cross hanging above the altar. "I didn't come in here to argue."

"You could have fooled me."

"Calm down, Grace. I'm not the enemy here."

"Don't tell me to calm down. Peter treated my friends and me like shit and you did nothing. What do you want from me? You sure as hell didn't come in here to face the truth."

Hannah lowered her voice. "You saved Jessica's life. I'm grateful."

Grace stood over Hannah. "Jessica is a nice lady. I just hope she figures out what a bitch you are before it's too late."

Grace found the stack of Polaroids in a box in the back of Lara's closet. She sat on the floor of Lara's ransacked room and stared at the images in front of her. Not daring to touch them, she put on a pair of gloves before bringing them out into the dining room. She turned on the overhead light and studied each photo carefully. She was relieved when she didn't recognize any of the women. She did notice that there were some similarities between them. They all appeared to be very young, for starters.

She didn't look up when Lara came into the apartment. Lara stood at Grace's shoulder, silent and watchful. It sounded like she was holding her breath.

"When were you going to tell me about these photos?" asked Grace.

"I took a few to Hannah. I was hoping she'd do something about it."

"Hannah thinks these women were all consenting adults."

"That's not true. He drugged them."

"How do you know?"

"I know because he did it to me."

"You aren't here."

"I gave those photos to Hannah," said Lara.

"She told me the police have them now."

"They must have found them when they searched her office," said Lara.

"Who were the girls in the photos you gave her?"

"Not you."

"Then who?" asked Grace.

"Me, Clare, Pippa, and Taylor."

"Are you sure there were no photos of me?"

"There were more than this but I checked every single one of them. You weren't there."

"Why didn't you tell any of us about the photos? Clare and Taylor are struggling and Pippa had a nervous breakdown. Her family needs to know what happened to her." Grace sifted through the photos again. "Peter should have been arrested."

"I wanted to do the right thing, but I was worried we wouldn't be able to prove it wasn't consensual. We all partied with him. We all crossed the line."

"I didn't."

"Are you sure about that, Grace? You spent the night at the house a few times. Do you remember everything that happened?"

"Lara, that's irrelevant. You should have let Clare, Taylor, and Pippa decide what to do about these photos. Besides, Hannah has always put Peter first. She was never going to help you." Grace started gathering the photos. If she looked at Lara she would cry. "Lara, I'm really trying to understand why you didn't tell us about these photos but I'm not there yet."

"What happens next?"

"We need to give these to the police."

"I just got a message. They're expecting us at the station in an hour." Grace turned away. "This is going to be hell."

14

Friday

Macy was uncomfortable, cold, and in need of a bathroom. Surrounded by Bolton PD's finest, she was hunkered down on a damp patch of earth thirty yards from a double-wide mobile home. The ground beneath the stand of pine trees was spongy and smelled of decay. Crusted-over snow clung to the shadows and a fierce wind blew through the valley. Overhead, crows cawed angrily as they crashed through the treetops and from somewhere inside the mobile home angry rock music was playing at full volume.

The access roads leading to the property belonging to Jordan Beech's brother were blocked and several officers, who had surrounded the mobile home, were awaiting the signal to move in. Though there'd been no sign of Jordan Beech, his Bronco was parked in the driveway. Brad Hastings stood at Macy's shoulder. They were all nervous. Jordan Beech was a convicted felon who'd served ten years in Oklahoma for assault with a deadly weapon and arson. Macy wasn't sure why he'd fixated on Grace Adams, but the fact that he'd done time for arson had made everyone in the department take notice.

Detective Sergeant Brad Hastings checked his firearm. "Are we absolutely sure this is the property?"

Alisa nodded. "Jordan Beech's brother is away working in the oil fields. Says he had no idea Jordan was staying here. Wanted to make sure we also arrested him for breaking and entering."

"Brotherly love is a beautiful thing," said Macy. She was feeling constricted in her Kevlar vest but that was nothing compared to the other officers, most of whom were decked out in full military gear. "The Bronco is registered in Jordan Beech's name. I pulled his DMV photo. He's definitely the guy from last night."

Alisa tapped Macy on the shoulder.

"Is that him?" asked Alisa.

Jordan stepped out onto the front porch of the double-wide trailer and slammed the screen door shut behind him. He wore a knit cap that was pulled over his ears and a thick fleece jacket and carried a coffee cup. One of his hands was bandaged and the bridge of his nose was swollen and bruised. He opened a packet of cigarettes and held one to his lips. It took a few tries to get it lit.

Macy kept her voice low. "That's him. It would be good if we could take him out in the open."

"Do you hear that?" asked Brad.

"It sounds like a helicopter," said Macy.

Alisa scanned the sky with a pair of binoculars. "It's from a local news channel. I recognize the logo."

"So much for the element of surprise," said Brad.

Jordan stood on his front porch, the cigarette in one hand and the cup of coffee in the other. He wasn't watching the helicopter. He was watching the trees. He flicked his cigarette onto the driveway and made a grab for the screen door, disappearing inside the trailer before the officers could move in. The helicopter came over the trees and circled close enough to make the mobile home's windows rattle.

"Fuck," said Macy. "He's made us."

Brad held up a megaphone. "Let's see if we can reason with him."

The branches above Macy's head splintered as several shots were fired. She grabbed Alisa's arm and pulled her to the ground.

"Was that us or him?" asked Macy.

Brad was standing behind a tree. "Definitely came from inside the trailer."

He spoke into the megaphone. "Jordan Beech, this is Detective Sergeant Brad Hastings. I'm with the Bolton Police Department. Drop your weapon and come outside with your hands up."

Alisa and Macy crawled forward on their stomachs and watched the front of the house. One of the windows was open, its screen broken and twisted outward. Two police officers wearing full protective gear and gas masks positioned themselves at the far end of the mobile home. Two more moved forward from the access road and ducked down behind a junked car. The helicopter swooped in and hovered above the mobile home. Debris whipped around the property. The tree branches clapped together. A cameraman wearing a harness leaned halfway out the helicopter's open door.

"Those idiots are too close. Someone is going to get hurt," said Macy.

More shots were fired. The Bronco's windshield exploded. The car alarm was deafening. Gunfire raked the dirt a few feet in front of the spot where Macy and Alisa had taken cover.

Brad Hastings once again spoke into his megaphone.

"Jordan Beech, the property is surrounded. There is no way out. Come out with your hands up."

The tree next to Brad's head took a direct hit. He ducked down and crawled over to Macy and Alisa. He took out his radio and gave the order for officers to move in.

"That son of a bitch," said Brad. He put his hand to the side of his head. "My ears will be ringing for weeks."

Half a dozen officers in full protective gear gathered near the front of the house. The first in the line kicked open the front door. They all swarmed inside. Several shots were fired before Brad was given the all clear. He tossed the megaphone aside and stomped toward the house, where a couple of officers were waiting for him. He pointed to the news helicopter that had landed in a nearby field. He yelled even though they were standing right in front of him.

"I want you to go over there and find out what the hell those guys in the helicopter thought they were doing. And then I want you to arrest them."

Even with the curtains wide open and the overhead lights turned on, the mobile home felt claustrophobic. Jordan Beech was sprawled out on the floor of the kitchenette. He had a gunshot wound to his right shoulder and was struggling to stay conscious, but that didn't stop him from yelling at the officer who knelt next to him. The emergency sirens of an approaching ambulance and rock music drowned out his words.

Brad's team had found three guns so far—a hunting rifle with a spotting scope, a .38 Special, and a 9mm Glock. None of the weapons were registered to Jordan Beech. There was a laptop on the coffee table. Alisa sat on the sofa staring at the screen.

"He has a taste for some serious porn," she said.

"You're logged in?" asked Macy.

"It was on when I got here."

"Change the settings so we can get access without a password."

Alisa started typing. "Will do."

Brad came into the room and looked over Alisa's shoulder.

"Check what he's got on there about Grace Adams and Peter Granger," said Brad.

"Any of your guys get hurt?" asked Macy.

"Everyone is okay, which is a relief considering how it could have gone down." Brad headed for the door. "I'm going to have a word with the assholes in that helicopter."

Macy wandered into the only bedroom. An officer wearing latex gloves searched the drawers and cabinets while another took photographs.

Another officer found drugs hidden inside the toilet cistern.

He held up a sealed plastic container that was dripping wet. "Looks like we got Oxycontin and fentanyl," he said.

"Any sign of the stolen paintings?" asked Macy.

He shook his head. "Nothing so far, but there are some outbuildings and a crawl space."

"There are also a lot of farm buildings around here. If he has them, he could have hidden them anywhere."

Macy checked the time. She wouldn't get back to the station until 5 o'clock at the earliest. She went into the living room. Brad had already returned and he was fuming.

"I may have said a few things to a reporter I'll regret. Hopefully, they didn't get any of it on tape."

"We found prescription painkillers stashed in the toilet cistern," said Macy. "No sign of the missing artwork yet. Have Alisa check his search history for anything having to do with those paintings. I seriously doubt that this guy knows anything about art."

"Tech guys will take over once we're back at the station. I'm sure they'll be thorough."

"I need to get back to town. Grace Adams is waiting to be interviewed. Could you let me know what the paramedics say? I'll need to question Jordan Beech as soon as possible."

15

Friday

The interview room had a small window overlooking the forested area behind the police department's main building. If not for the security lights strung out along a high chain-link fence, Grace would not have seen the trees. She'd had to call Steve to tell him that she wouldn't be able to make it to the concert after all. Their short conversation had upset her more than she'd thought it would. He'd told her it was okay, but Grace felt the sort of understanding required wasn't humanly possible. Her life was spinning out of control again and nothing she could say or do seemed to make a difference.

The digital recorder sat on the table next to a couple of glasses of water. Grace took a quick glance at the one-way mirror. She wore a green corduroy dress, paisley tights, and red galoshes. Her hair was braided in two bunches that sat on the top of her head. She'd even taken the time to put on makeup, anything to make herself feel more confident. She turned away from the mirror and folded her hands on the table in front of her. It was weird to think that someone was back there behind the mirror, invisible and listening in on the conversation she was having with Macy Greeley, and that others were watching online. She studied the video camera mounted on the wall. Macy had told her to relax but it was impossible.

Macy had also told Grace that she had a right to an attorney. Five minutes into the interview and Grace was already beginning to think she'd made a mistake when she'd declined. She knew she was innocent. She just wasn't sure she could prove it. She looked on as Macy placed Taylor's pregnancy wand on the table between them. It was still in the Ziploc bag Grace had found in a kitchen drawer. Now there was a second bag that looked official. The wand was now evidence.

"Are you pregnant, Grace?" asked Macy.

Grace stared at the wand. Her medical condition made it almost impossible for her to carry a pregnancy to term, but that was more of an answer than Macy Greeley required.

"No, ma'am," said Grace.

"So, who does this belong to?"

"A friend."

"Does this friend have a name?"

"Taylor Moore."

"Why do you have it?"

"I was worried so I went to her house to try to figure out where she's been for the past few days." Grace pointed at the pregnancy wand. "I found it in the trash in the bathroom. I really don't know why I took it."

"How long has Taylor been missing?"

"Since Thursday."

"Why didn't you file a missing person's report with the police?"

"I spoke to her ex-boyfriend and he said Taylor had gone to see her parents in Colorado."

"Ex-boyfriends often don't get told the truth."

"At the time I couldn't see why she would have lied to him."

"I take it you've tried to reach her on her cell phone."

"Yes ma'am, but there's been no reply. I have her parent's address in Denver but their number isn't listed so I couldn't call them." She handed Macy her cell phone. "I've entered it into Taylor's contact details. I'm really worried about her. Could you find out if she's there?"

Macy made a few notes on a blank piece of paper, which she handed to an officer who met her at the door. They spoke in hushed tones. When Macy returned to her seat, she looked a little sad.

"Was Taylor Moore in a sexual relationship with Peter Granger?"

Grace stared at the pregnancy wand. She didn't like where the conversation was going. Hannah was alive, so someone else had to have died. Grace pressed a tissue to her eyes.

"Grace, I need you to answer the question."

Grace spoke softly. "I'm not really sure what was going on. There were rumors, but Taylor had a boyfriend. Until last Thursday she was with Alex."

"I'm not doubting that she was with Alex, but that wouldn't have necessarily stopped her from being with someone else at the same time."

Macy placed four Polaroids on the table. Each one was encased in a separate plastic sleeve. They were similar to the ones Grace had found hidden in Lara's room. All of the women were masked and naked. She felt light-headed. This time she knew who they were.

"Grace, have you ever seen these before?"

"Lara only told me about them today." She looked up at Macy. "There are more."

Macy asked where the rest of the photos were.

"Lara has them. She thought she should be the one to give them to you, to explain herself."

"Your friend has a lot of explaining to do. She should have brought them to the police when she found them."

"She didn't believe Peter was capable of doing something like this. Their relationship was complicated."

"What do you mean by complicated?"

"I think she was in love with him, but then again, I think we all were at one point."

"Had Lara and Peter ever had consensual sex?"

"I honestly don't know. You'll have to ask her that."

Macy made some notes. Grace couldn't help herself. She kept talking. She wanted Macy to understand.

"But just because it may have been consensual in the past doesn't give someone the right to take advantage of someone in the future." Grace's hand hovered over the photo of Lara. "Lara says she was drugged when this photo was taken. She didn't think anyone would believe her. She was hoping Hannah would say something to stop Peter from doing it to anyone else."

"Grace, are you confirming that this photo is of Lara Newcomb?"

"Yes, ma'am."

"I need to know if you recognize the women in these other photos."

"It's not easy to look at them," said Grace.

"I know it's difficult, but it's important that we identify the women. They may need our help."

Clare had started losing her hair six months earlier. It had once been long, blond, and wavy. One of the photos was of a woman lying back on a chair. Her blond hair hung past her shoulders. Grace forced herself to look closer. There were several bracelets looped around her wrists and a silver band around her index finger. Grace closed her eyes for a second.

"It's Clare Stokes," said Grace.

Macy placed the photo facedown next to her and quickly wrote down Clare's name.

Grace picked up to the next image. She was sorely tempted to scream.

"It's Pippa Lomax," said Grace. "She's not well. Her parents need to know that something happened to her."

Macy made some notes in her book. Her hand looked like it was shaking. Her voice caught.

"We've already been in touch with them about the fire. We'll make sure they're informed."

Grace couldn't bring herself to look at the last image properly. Taylor had always been careful to hide the damage she'd done to her body beneath long-sleeve shirts and jeans. She often joked that she was destined to live in a cold climate. Under the harsh light of a camera's flash, the white scars that crisscrossed Taylor's bare skin glowed.

"I think I'm going to be sick," said Grace.

Macy rushed Grace to the women's restroom and waited outside the stall while Grace braced herself over the toilet. She was shivering when she finally emerged. Macy pulled off the sweater she was wearing and wrapped it around Grace's shoulders.

"This shouldn't be happening to you again," said Macy.

"It didn't happen to me this time. There aren't any photos of me."

"Are you sure you don't remember Peter Granger doing anything inappropriate?"

Grace splashed water on her face. "When he drank and took drugs he'd get really physical. I didn't trust him so I learned to steer clear. I should have said something to the others. They're far too trusting."

"Was the woman in the last photo your friend Taylor?"

Grace said a quiet yes. "She's dead, isn't she?"

"I'm afraid it looks that way. The woman who died in the house with Peter was also pregnant."

"Was the baby Peter's?"

Macy nodded. "Some tests will have to be done before everything is confirmed, so I'd like you to keep this to yourself for now."

A policewoman appeared at the bathroom door with a small carton of orange juice. She didn't look much older than Grace. She smiled kindly as she handed the bottle to Grace.

"I thought this might make you feel better."

Grace thanked her.

"I understand if you can't continue with the interview. It's been a long day," said Macy.

Grace turned away from the mirror.

"Are there anymore photos for me to look at?" Grace asked.

"No, we only found these four."

"Are you sure there were none of me?"

"I can't be sure of anything. These are the only ones we had," said Macy. "Do you think something happened?"

"No."

"Then why did you ask whether there was a photo of you?"

Grace didn't have an answer for that. She'd sometimes had disturbing dreams but couldn't be sure where they stemmed from. Her childhood was full of nightmares.

Macy was sitting across the table from Grace again.

"Had Taylor ever spoken to you about suicide?"

Grace looked up at the video camera. "No, never."

"We know she's made attempts in the past."

"I don't know anything about that. I just know what she was like when I was with her."

"Why do you suppose she self-harmed?" asked Macy. "Was there anything in her life that she found particularly upsetting?"

"Her mother was very disapproving. Her father more so. I don't think there was a lot of love in her household. "

"Then why would you think she'd run home to her parents if she was in trouble?"

"I couldn't face the alternative. I've been worried ever since Hannah showed up alive."

"Were you jealous of her relationship with Peter?"

"No, ma'am. By the time she'd started spending more time with Peter I'd gotten over him completely. Ask Clare and Lara. We talked about it. "

"Don't worry, I will be speaking to your friends. We also need to talk about what you said in the letter you addressed to Peter Granger. I—"

Grace interrupted Macy. "The letter was never meant to be seen by anyone but me. It was just some stupid way to get back at him for how he treated me."

"Hannah Granger says you were kicked out of Peter's writing workshop because he felt you were stalking him. There seems to be some truth to that. In early July you were found sleeping on the Granger's sofa. Peter Granger claimed that you'd broken into the house in the middle of the night."

"I admit it was a stupid thing to do, but it happened a month and a half after I was kicked out of his group. Not before."

"Why did you do it?"

"Desperation, I suppose. Peter and Hannah were very important to me. They'd just cut me out of their lives completely. I wasn't coping well."

"Why did you and Peter tell the attending officer that you didn't know each other?" asked Macy.

"I'm not sure. I guess I was following Peter's lead. At the time I thought he did it because he didn't want me to get into trouble with Hannah. If she was there I'm sure she would have asked the police to press charges."

"Do you admit to stalking them?"

"The worst thing I did was crash on their sofa. I didn't set fire to their house. I didn't kill Peter." Grace lowered her voice. "And I could never hurt Taylor."

"Why do you believe Peter Granger kicked you out of his writing workshop?"

"We used to meet twice a week in his office. He'd said that he wanted to tutor me. I'd been flattered when he asked me to join the group but I was struggling with the high standards. After a few sessions it became something else. Looking back I should have asked how he'd figured out my real name, but at the time I was feeling grateful for all he was doing for me. He said he wanted to help me work out the issues I had with my past, but all he really wanted was for me to tell him everything that happened in Collier so he could use it in a book. He'd taped our sessions without my permission and then got angry because I wouldn't sign a release form. I had every right to be upset with him, but he turned it around and made out like I was ungrateful."

"Why did we find your blood on the carpet in his office?"

Grace looked confused. "Blood?"

"It was next to the sofa in the seating area," said Macy.

"I had a nose bleed during the last writing workshop I went to. It was the day after I said I wouldn't sign the release form. He told everyone there my real name." Grace looked down at her hands. "Before that night only Lara knew."

"In this letter you admit to burning down the mobile home you lived in as a child. This would have been three years ago. Is it true?"

Grace raised her voice. "Don't look so surprised. You already knew about that."

"It was never reported."

"That's because nobody cared. It's still there parked next to that truck stop. I doubt anyone will ever bother to clean it up."

"In the letter you threaten to burn down Peter's house in much the same way."

"I was never going to do it."

"You've set fires before when you've been upset. There's precedent."

"There was no one living in my mother's mobile home. It was falling down. I didn't harm anyone. I couldn't harm anyone."

"I can't just take your word for it. Can you account for your movements on the night of the fire?"

"I was with Lara at the K-Bar."

"Just you and Lara?"

"Me, Lara, and hundreds of Elvis impersonators. Clare left earlier. Around eleven, I think."

"Were you together for the rest of the evening?"

"No, I left the bar on my own a little before midnight," said Grace.

"You walked home by yourself even though you knew Jordan Beech had been following you."

"I was drunk. I admit it was a stupid thing to do."

"Did you go straight home?" asked Macy.

"That was the idea, but I passed out on someone's front lawn."

Macy sat back in her chair and stared at Grace for a few seconds without speaking. "You're not exactly looking after yourself these days."

"I was doing better before all this trouble with Peter."

"How long were you asleep?"

"Twenty minutes, maybe less. A passing fire truck woke me up. I'd lost the tiara I was wearing so I had to go back and find it. That's when I saw Jordan's car on the corner of Cedar and Vine. I was so scared I took off running through some backyards."

"Did you happen to run through the Granger's property?"

"No ma'am. I did speak to someone though. He offered to let me inside his house so I could call for help. I couldn't do it though. I decided it was better to face Jordan and find out what he wanted. I'm tired of hiding."

"Did the guy you spoke to give you his name?"

"No."

"What about an address?" asked Macy.

"I'm not sure but I think I could figure it out."

"Okay, we'll work on that later."

Macy pulled Grace's firearm out of the bag.

"Is this yours?"

"I've got a license to carry a concealed weapon."

"Do you always have it with you?"

"Only since Halloween," said Grace.

"You don't seem to catch a break, do you?"

"You have to believe that I wouldn't have done this. I would have never hurt Taylor. She was one of my best friends."

"I want to believe you, but you threatened to burn Peter's house down. You must see how this looks."

"Jordan saw me on the night of the fire. He'll know I was running around Bolton drunk in heels and a prom dress. There's no way I could have set that fire in the state I was in."

"Jordan Beech was wounded when we served a warrant for his arrest. He's still in surgery. I'm hoping to interview him tomorrow," said Macy.

"He saw me. He'll know where I was around the time the fire started."

"I doubt he'll be in the mood to provide you with an alibi."

"I'm innocent. I didn't do this."

"Tell me more about Lara Newcomb. I want to know what her relationship with Peter was like."

"Lara saw Peter as someone who could help her get published and he knew it. He was very manipulative. He'd praise her one minute and put her down the next. Lately she didn't know where she stood."

"To your knowledge, had Lara ever threatened Peter?"

"Lara would have done anything to get published. Harming Peter wouldn't have helped her cause."

"Do you think it's possible that Lara didn't bring the photos to the police because she was worried that her professional relationship with Peter would be destroyed if she did?" asked Macy.

Grace sat at the edge of her seat with her hands folded in her lap. Lara was outside in the waiting room and Clare was on her way to the station. It was only a matter of time before they were sitting in this chair, staring down at those photographs. Lara was strong but Clare wouldn't be able to cope. She would be devastated when she found out what Peter had done to her.

"Lara wouldn't do that. I believe her when she says she gave them to Hannah because she believed the police wouldn't believe it wasn't consensual. Happens all the time."

"Okay, I take your point, but it's one thing to hide this from the police. It's another thing to hide this from three women who are her friends."

"Am I free to go?" asked Grace. She couldn't look at Macy.

"Yes, but you may have to come in to answer more questions. I want you to stay here in Bolton."

"Yes, ma'am."

Macy switched off the digital recorder. She reached across the table and took one of Grace's hands.

"For what it's worth, I believe you," she whispered.

Grace wouldn't be able to breathe properly until she put some distance between herself and the police station. Outside the night air was cold and lamplight puddled on the wet pavement. She felt like running but she kept her cool. The visitor's lot was nearly empty but a couple of patrol officers were loitering near the front entrance, so it was important that she remain calm. Grace waded across the rain-soaked pavement with tears in her eyes. Lara would have to find another way home.

It was like Collier all over again. Grace was still letting people take advantage of her. She was worried that Macy might be right about Lara's reasons for hiding the truth from her friends. This painful realization came into sharp focus when Macy had shown her the Polaroids of Pippa, Clare, and Taylor. The fact that Lara was also a victim didn't matter. If Peter was arrested he wouldn't be able to help her get her precious book published. Grace had always known that Lara was ambitious. She was sure it was Lara who'd dangled Grace's past before Peter like a prize. Grace could only imagine the full extent of Lara's anger when Peter pushed her aside and focused all his energy on his new protégé. There must have been a time when Lara hated Grace.

Now it was Grace's turn to hate Lara.

Grace sat at the wheel of her pickup truck for a few minutes, staring off into space. Her stomach felt raw and hollowed out. The orange-juice chaser couldn't erase the stale taste in her mouth and no amount of denial could ease the sadness she was feeling. She rummaged in the truck's glove compartment, finding some rock-hard gum that had been there since her uncle was still alive. She tossed it aside and backed out of the space. Grace had to prove she didn't have anything to do with the fire. It was time to find the man she'd spoken to on Halloween night.

She cut across town on a secondary road that ran parallel to Main Street. She was careful to signal at every turn and check the mirrors before stopping at each intersection. Anything to avoid drawing further attention. She was halfway home when an oncoming driver flashed their headlights. It turned out she'd been driving blind. She switched on the headlights and decreased her speed further.

On Cedar Street, she stopped briefly in front of the house where she'd fallen asleep on the lawn. The Halloween decorations had been replaced with Christmas lights. An elderly man stood near the bay window holding an infant in his arms. The child was grabbing at his glasses and the man was laughing.

Grace drove along the road until she found an elm tree whose branches hung low over the pavement. Her memories from the night had been disjointed up until the moment Jordan's Bronco had rounded the nearby street corner. Fear had had a sobering effect. She was in no doubt that this was the tree she'd hidden behind as Jordan drove by. Grace stepped out of her truck and used a flashlight to take a closer look at an indentation in the hedge. Branches had snapped clean off where she'd hurled herself through it. She drove to the next block, took a right, and slowly cruised along another quiet street, heading in the direction of Pilot Hill. She stopped in front of the sixth house. It was more ramshackle than the others. The sofa on the front porch was a dead giveaway that university students lived there. The side yard looked like the one she'd passed through on the night of the fire. Madison Road was four blocks farther to the east.

Grace wasn't sure what to do next. The man she'd spoken to on Halloween night had said he was a visitor to the house. She didn't know his name and all she knew of the woman who lived there was a voice. Grace flipped down the mirror on the sun visor and stared up at her pale face.

She was in trouble already.

There really was nothing left to lose.

She went to the door and rang the bell. Now that she was closer she could hear music playing inside. The door swung open and a woman looked down on her from a great height. Already tall, she was wearing six-inch platform shoes, a floral maxi dress, and a long kimono, all of which were vintage. Everything about her was tattooed or pierced.

"Come in," she said. "It's fucking cold outside."

Grace was surprised that the woman didn't ask who Grace was and why she was there. She walked toward the back of the house and Grace followed. A group of about ten people were gathered in the kitchen and dining room. Someone handed Grace an exotic-looking cocktail as she stepped inside. The tattooed woman was at the stove with her back turned to Grace. Grace took a sip of her drink. It tasted strongly of alcohol and berries.

The man who'd handed Grace the drink leaned in. He wore a blazer and a bow tie and carried a pitcher. His beard and mustache were so perfect they looked as if they were molded from plastic.

"I make my own gin. What do you think?" he asked.

"I couldn't judge. I don't have much experience with gin."

"That's about to change. Can I take your coat?" he asked.

Grace gave him a blank look. "I'm sorry," she said. "There's been a misunderstanding." She tilted her head toward the front door. "I rang the bell to ask a question. I don't know anyone here."

"In that case, give me back that drink."

Grace blushed as she tried to hand it over.

He waved her off and laughed. "Don't worry, I'll keep your secret. What should I call you?"

"Grace Adams," she said. She watched his reaction. If he'd made the connection he didn't show it.

He held out a hand. "It's just plain ole Charlie, I'm afraid. What brings you here?"

"It's an odd story."

He held up a hand. "I only want to hear it if it's interesting. Can you promise me that it's interesting?"

Grace had another sip of her drink. She was feeling brave.

"I can definitely promise that it's not something that you've ever heard before."

"I hate being bored."

"You won't be bored." Grace glanced over at the woman at the stove. "Who lives here?"

"A couple of artists, a poet, a documentary filmmaker, some kittens . . . it's a collective of sorts."

"I don't feel like I'm in Montana anymore."

They clinked their glasses together.

"In that case, Dorothy, welcome to Oz."

"I really need to speak to someone who lives here. It's important."

He held a finger to his lips. "It doesn't work like that in our little collective. First you have to tell us your interesting story."

Grace tried to back away. "Us, as in all of you?"

He steered her into the center of the room and relieved her of her coat.

"We're a collective. We share everything. Think Vladimir Lenin and

Kim Kardashian." He poured a bit more booze into her glass and winked. "We even share our homemade gin."

An elderly couple sat on a sofa holding hands. Their eyes darted around the room. The man whispered something in the woman's ear and she put her hand to her mouth to stifle a laugh. A litter of sleeping kittens rested in a wicker basket at their feet. The window behind the sofa looked out onto the garden. An ashtray was balanced on the sill. A door leading out into the back garden was less than ten feet away. This was definitely the right house.

Charlie tapped the side of the pitcher of cocktails with his pipe.

"Grace Adams has just confessed to crashing our little party. Apparently, she has an interesting story to tell us." He stepped away and bowed. "Grace, the floor is yours."

Grace stood in front of the odd assortment of strangers. The floorboards creaked beneath her red galoshes. She wondered if it was too late to click her heels together three times and say there's no place like home. Someone switched off the music.

The tattooed woman stepped away from the stove and wiped her hands on a dish towel. She gazed at Grace with open curiosity.

"You're *the* Grace Adams? From Collier?"

Grace watched her for a few seconds. She was definitely the woman she'd heard on the night of the fire. Grace was keenly aware that everyone was listening now. The color was rising in her cheeks. Her mouth was dry. She took another swallow of gin. It burned in a nice way.

"Yes," said Grace. "That's me."

"What brings—"

Charlie held up a hand. "I've told Grace she has to tell us her story before we tell her what she needs to know. We made a deal."

Grace knocked back the rest of her drink. All that stood between her and proving her innocence was a story. It didn't seem too much to ask.

"I'm afraid I'll have to start at the beginning," said Grace.

16

Friday

Macy needed to calm down before she went into an interview room with Lara Newcomb. Grace had tried to make excuses for Lara's behavior, but Macy couldn't see any reasonable justification for hiding the Polaroids from the police and her closest friends. Witnesses and video footage put Lara at the K-Bar when the fire started, but that didn't stop Macy from thinking that she may have had something to do with it. It was becoming clear to Macy and everyone else involved in the investigation that Lara Newcomb had a complicated relationship with Peter Granger.

The door to the interview room was ajar. Macy could overhear the conversation Lara was having with the officer who was setting up the recording equipment. She wanted to know how everything worked and seemed especially fascinated with the one-way mirror. Macy walked into the room, slammed her folders on the desk, and said nothing for the first few minutes she was seated. She instead went through her notes and checked her messages again. Aiden had arrived and was looking forward to seeing her later. He'd sent her a photo of the pizza he'd just ordered. The table was full of beer glasses so she assumed he was out with a crowd of people. Macy already had enough reasons to be angry with Lara Newcomb, so she put all thoughts of Aiden, beer, and pizza aside. Macy looked up only because Lara spoke. The first thing she asked Macy was if she was free to go.

Lara had been wearing a coat when Macy met her at the hospital but now she wore a loose-fitting sweater. Her shoulder bones poked out from her rounded back and she smelled strongly of tobacco. Macy was once again taken aback by the huskiness of the young woman's voice.

"You're helping with inquiries. We're hoping you'll cooperate willingly," said Macy.

"So, I'm here voluntarily," said Lara.

"For now, but that might change. You've been informed that you have a right to an attorney, which I understand you declined."

"Where's Grace?"

"I assume she's gone home," said Macy.

"Is she a suspect?"

"Lara, this isn't a friendly chat. I'm conducting a formal interview. You've given a preliminary statement to the police." Macy slid the document across the table. "Can you confirm that everything you've written here is correct?"

Lara barely looked at the forms. She sat back in her chair and studied Macy.

"It's all there."

"Tell me about the Polaroids. I want to know why you went searching for them in the first place. Something must have made you suspicious."

"Actually, I was more petulant than suspicious. The woman who was supposed to housesit for Peter and Hannah cancelled at the last minute. Peter implied that I was obligated to do it because of everything he'd done for me. I didn't say anything at the time but his attitude really upset me."

"Why did you housesit for them then? You could have refused."

"Peter was my mentor. He'd helped me get an agent. He was going to help me get a publisher. I was in no position to say no to him."

"But that's not how it's worked out. Thirty-six rejections and count-ing. You must have been feeling pretty desperate."

"At that point I was just feeling grateful. Like I said, he'd done a great deal for me."

"But you did a great deal for him too. Your friend Clare says that you basically handed him Grace Adams on a plate."

"It wasn't like that."

"You're the one who invited him to the poetry evening at the café where Grace worked. You were the one who convinced Grace to read a poem. You're the one who whispered her real name in his ear. You say in your preliminary statement that Grace Adams is your best friend. Why would you do something like that to her?"

"It wasn't meant to go any further than that evening. I was as sur-prised as anyone when he invited her to join the writing workshop."

"But he did even more than that. During May and June they had two private sessions a week in his office. She told him everything about what happened back in Collier. She became a fixture in the Granger's household, staying the night, sharing meals, drinking their wine. I can only imagine how much that pissed you off."

Lara didn't answer. Macy placed photocopies of the four Polaroids they'd found in Hannah's office on the table. For now she'd be leaving in the folder the rest of the Polaroids Lara had given to her colleagues who conducted the preliminary interview. Macy could almost see Lara's justification for keeping them from the police, but Taylor, Clare, and Pippa were her friends.

"Tell me why you were snooping around in Peter Granger's office in the first place."

"I wanted to see if there was anything in Peter's office that related to my manuscript. I was worried he wasn't as confident in my work as he professed to be."

"How did you get in?"

A shrug. "They left all their keys behind. The photos were in a box hidden in the back of a cupboard. There were hundreds of them."

Macy raised her voice. "Of different woman?"

"No, there were half a dozen photos of each woman. I went through them all."

"When did you realize you were looking at photos of yourself and your friends?"

"They were the first ones I found."

"So, let me get this straight. You find these Polaroids and your first thought isn't to go to the police or tell your friends, but to take them to Hannah Granger. Why?"

"I wasn't sure what to do with them. I guess if I actually remembered it happening I'd be more traumatized. In a way I feel very separate from the girl in the photo. She isn't me."

"But she is you." Macy pointed to the other photos. "And this is Clare and this Pippa and this one is of Taylor. Did you ever stop to think that they might see these images in a completely different way? Clare was here earlier. She was devastated when she saw the photos. She trusted you as a friend. She feels that you've betrayed her as well. Your friends had a right to know what happened to them and you tried to take that right away."

"I knew they couldn't handle it."

"But that's my point. They were already suffering. Pippa had a nervous breakdown, Taylor was self-harming, and Clare has pulled out almost all of her hair. They knew something horrible had happened. They just didn't understand what it was. You weren't helping them by hiding the truth."

"When I brought the photos to Hannah I thought she would do something. She has a lot of influence over Peter."

"I have another theory. Would you like to hear it?"

"I'm telling the truth," said Lara.

Macy leaned in. "I think you only gave them to Hannah because the alternative meant going to the police and that wouldn't have suited your needs. Were you trying to get the photos back when you broke into Hannah Granger's office on Tuesday evening?"

Lara looked down at her hands.

"The police found copies of the Granger's house and office keys when your room was searched this evening," said Macy.

"You searched my room?"

"Under the circumstances it was pretty easy to obtain a warrant. Did you break into Hannah Granger's office?"

"I wanted to get the photos back. I didn't want my friends to ever see them. I know you don't believe me, but I did it because they couldn't have coped."

"But you could?"

"I suppose so."

"It doesn't look like you're handling things from this side of the table. When is the last time you ate?"

"That's none of your business."

"Do you want to tell me why there were searches on your Web browser about arson?"

"That was nearly a year ago. I was doing research for a short story I was writing. It was published in an anthology if you want to read it."

"Don't worry. I will. Did you steal Peter's laptop and download files from a remote server?"

"No, never." Lara paused. "Wasn't it destroyed in the fire?"

"Apparently, it wasn't. You had keys to his office and home. That puts you pretty high on my list of people who might have it."

"I didn't do it."

"Where were you Wednesday afternoon between two and three?" asked Macy.

"I was in a lecture."

"Can you prove it?"

"They take attendance."

"You'll have to do better than that."

"I was sitting next to Clare Stokes. She may be angry with me but she wouldn't lie about something like that."

"Let's hope not, for your sake." Macy made some notes. "Clare and Grace told me that you'd always had a difficult relationship with Taylor

Moore and that you'd recently fallen out. They said you were jealous because Peter was giving her all the attention, attention you'd once had."

"They're making a big deal out of nothing and so are you. I didn't have a problem with Taylor, because I knew Peter would move on. She was just his latest project."

"Whereas you were old news."

"He was going to come back."

"Why would he do that? Were you threatening him with blackmail? Is that why you kept the photos instead of going to the police?"

Lara chose to remain silent.

"It troubles me that you had keys to the Granger's home and a difficult relationship with both the victims. . . ."

"I can prove where I was all evening. I'll show you my phone. I have hundreds of photos." Lara placed her cell phone on the table in front of Macy. "I not only took pictures of every single Elvis in the K-Bar, I spoke to them as well. I was nowhere near the Granger's home."

Lara pulled the sleeves of her sweater. Her wrists were birdlike, nothing but veins and sinew. She looked up at the ceiling when she spoke. Her eyes were dry.

"Check my phone. It's all there. I document my entire waking life. I didn't set that fire."

Macy scrolled through the images. It was one Elvis impersonator after another. The images at the end of the night were more chaotic. Macy stopped when she found a video clip.

"Did you realize you shot a video?"

"Possibly. I was pretty drunk."

Macy stopped the interview.

"I need to bring in a colleague to have a look at your phone. I'll be right back."

Brad Hastings hooked up Lara's phone to a monitor and they watched the video footage together. A group of men dressed as Elvis were singing a drunken rendition of "Always On My Mind." Shouting interrupts them and the camera lurches to the left and centers on two men engaged in a shoving match.

"Is that the guy that got stabbed?" asked Macy.

"It's definitely him," said Brad.

Brad continued to move through the footage frame by frame until he found what he was looking for. He zoomed in. The man's face was grainy but clearly recognizable. Macy spoke first.

"Lara, do you remember this guy?"

"We called him Hawaiian Elvis. I think I have a better picture of him somewhere on my camera." Lara hesitated. "Grace is in the picture too, but she doesn't know him any better than I do."

Brad handed Lara her phone. His voice was stiff. "Show me."

Grace was barely recognizable in a wig and tiara. She was wedged between the two men and she didn't look happy about it. One of the men was fat and wore a white satin jumpsuit with a cape, and the other man wore a Hawaiian shirt and lei. Lara pointed at the screen.

"We were just taking photos for a laugh, but when we tried to leave he shoved Grace so hard she fell and hit her head."

"Did they refer to each other by name?" asked Brad.

"No, but the fat one may have worked at the Bakken Oil Fields."

"What makes you think that?"

"Something he said about having so much money he could buy us if he wanted to. No one from around here talks about money like that. I got the impression the other guy was unemployed."

"Why's that?"

"He just seemed a little rough. There was definitely something off about him."

It was coming up to 10:00 in the evening and Macy and Alisa were still at the office.

"Did you manage to pull anything off the security cameras at the shop where Peter Granger's files were printed?" asked Macy.

Alisa turned her laptop around so they could both see the screen.

"It's just like they said in the store. The kid comes in to pick up the order and pays cash. They described him as having shoulder-length red hair; tall and slim, and guessed that he was around fourteen years of age. You can even see his bike leaning against the windows out front."

"If he's on a bike he must be local. Get a decent screenshot and distribute it to the middle schools and high schools. Someone is bound to recognize him."

"I'll also send it to the woman who was working at the library the afternoon the files were downloaded."

"Does the library keep a log of who uses their computers?"

"Yes, but we think whoever downloaded the files piggybacked on someone else's session. According to the log, the terminal was still being used by a woman called Rose Butler."

"How can you be sure she wasn't involved?"

"She's eighty-three, lives in a nursing home, and has just sent her first e-mail. There's no way she downloaded those files from a remote server. We're assuming whoever did this has Peter Granger's laptop, but that may not be the case."

"They would have needed it to get the access codes and passwords for the server. His laptop would be a logical place to look for information like that, especially since he probably was saving to the server automatically. If it's still out there somewhere it's important we get ahold of it. There may be something on the hard drive we can use."

"Such as?"

"Appointments, notes, names . . . anything that would help us build a case."

Macy quickly sorted through the notes on her desk. There was something or someone she was forgetting, but she was too tired to think clearly. She yawned a little too loudly. It was late and Aiden was waiting for her at the hotel. She started to gather her things.

"I'm beat. I'll give you a call in the morning," said Macy.

Alisa was scrolling through her e-mails. "I'm wondering if we should be worried. Cornelia Hart still hasn't answered any of my requests for an another interview."

"That's who I keep forgetting to ask you about. Did you send around a patrol car?" asked Macy.

"Yep, no one was home."

"I'd say we could contact her friends and family but I don't think she has any."

"Hannah Granger might know where she is," said Alisa.

"Give her a call and let me know what she says."

"When will you interview Jordan Beech?"

"He's out of surgery and stable so we're hoping for tomorrow afternoon. Sunday latest."

"Reading his criminal record makes my skin crawl."

Macy reached over and snapped Alisa's laptop shut.

"Alisa, it's Friday night. Find some friends and drink a little too much. Better yet, find a good-looking man and drink a little too much. If you look at this stuff for too long you'll end up jaded and lonely."

"What makes me think you don't follow your own advice?" asked Alisa. "I peg you for someone who works twenty-four-seven."

"As it happens, my boyfriend has come down from Wilmington Creek to see me, so not such a sad case after all."

"It's nice that you have someone. Have you been together long?"

"A little over a year."

"Must be tricky. Most guys don't understand the kind of hours we have to work," said Alisa.

"He used to be in law enforcement, so he gets it."

"I guess that's one way of getting around it. I couldn't date a man in uniform."

Macy laughed. "Don't knock it until you've tried it."

Alisa opened her laptop again.

"I thought I told you to go home," said Macy.

"Once I send out a screenshot of that kid I'm out of here."

Macy headed down the hallway. Most of the offices were dark. On the ground floor a dozen officers were being briefed in a conference room before going on duty. A few people milled around in the waiting room. A young girl was in tears.

Macy stopped in at a twenty-four-hour grocery store on the way back to her hotel. She was hoping a decent bottle of wine would convince Aiden to stay in for the night.

She ran into Brad Hastings in the parking lot. He was coming out and she was going in. It was the first time she'd seen him smile since they'd met.

"Did you find your missing Elvis?" asked Macy.

"Looks like it. Our perp was working on a building site until six months ago so no current address, but we do have a positive ID, a list of family members, and an arrest warrant, so it's just a matter of time."

"Does he have any priors?"

"Minor stuff. Nothing that would make you think he'd pull a knife in a bar."

"It may have been personal. Have you spoken to the victim's family and friends? Maybe there was a dispute," said Macy.

"If there's something there I'm sure it will all come out over the next few days."

Macy noticed he had a bottle of wine under one arm and a box of chocolates under the other. "It looks like you're celebrating," she said.

"I guess you could say that. I've been working twenty-four-seven, so I thought I'd better bring a peace offering home with me." He held up the bottle of wine for her to see. "The wine is for me and the chocolate is for my wife. She's expecting our first child. Gets serious cravings."

"I remember it well," said Macy. "Have a nice evening."

He put his head down and hurried to his car. "You too," he said.

Aiden wasn't alone. He and her son Luke were crashed side by side in the king-size bed. Aiden had insisted that Macy upgrade to a suite with a separate bedroom and sitting room, and now she knew why. The staff had even brought in an extra camp bed for Luke, not that he'd use it. Both Aiden and Luke were lying on their backs with their arms flung out to their sides, complete surrender. Macy knelt down next to her son and tucked the covers around him. He was snoring gently. She kissed him lightly on the forehead. Aiden stirred. She brushed the long strands of blond hair from his face. He opened his blue eyes. They both smiled.

"Hope you weren't expecting a wild Friday night," he said.

"This is better than any wild night," said Macy. "Thank you for bringing Luke with you."

"He was so excited."

"I can only imagine."

"Have you eaten?"

"I'll order something from room service."

"How about a glass of wine?" asked Aiden. "I picked up supplies on the way into town."

"Great minds think alike. I picked up a bottle on the way here."

"I heard a rumor that you got pretty beat up last night. Any truth to it?"

"Where'd you hear that?"

"Pretty much all my friends down here work for the Bolton PD. A bunch of us met for pizza. They all think Luke is very cool, by the way. He was quite entertaining at dinner."

"Hope they think his mom is okay too."

"Not a negative word. Are you going to tell me what happened?"

Macy scooted off the bed and held out her hand.

"Come on," she said. "You pour me a glass of wine and I'll show you my bruises."

"That is some serious sexy talk right there."

"Brace yourself, it's been a long week and I'm just getting started."

Macy was picking at the remains of a cheeseburger she'd ordered from room service. They'd closed the door to the adjoining room and were half dressed and snuggled up on the sofa bed watching a movie. The bottle of wine had gone fast. Macy sipped the last of it. Aiden asked if he should open another.

"Probably not a great idea. I'm hoping to interview Jordan Beech tomorrow. A hangover won't help matters."

Aiden tensed up next to her. She knew he was trying hard not to show how upset he was. He held his lips to her shoulder.

"I worry about you and it drives me a little crazy," he said.

"You know this sort of shit comes with the job. At least we caught the asshole this time."

"I know you can fight your own battles but I'd pay good money to get him alone in a room for ten minutes."

"He's not worth it," said Macy. "I'll heal soon enough."

"Meanwhile all I have to worry about these days is getting a paper cut."

"I always wanted to date a paper pusher."

"You're lying."

"Yeah, I suppose I am. You're not just a manager there though. You'll be out on the river working as a fishing guide all summer."

Aiden held Macy a little tighter and it was her turn to hide how much it hurt.

"I can't wait. If all goes according to plan, we'll be open for business by July," said Aiden.

"That's fast."

"One of the perks of having rich business partners. They're throwing a lot of money at this project."

"Hard to imagine having so much money. Is the highlife rubbing off on you?"

"No, but the pay raise makes it a lot easier to move on from my old job."

"Do you miss being the chief of police?"

"More often than I thought I would. I was in the center of what was going on for a long time. Now I just watch from the sidelines. I'll hear about something that happened and I'll think I would have handled it differently, but I suppose that's normal."

Macy leaned over and kissed Aiden. He tasted like red wine and the cigarettes she knew he was sneaking.

"I've been missing you a lot," she said.

"That makes two of us."

He pulled his T-shirt over his head and helped Macy out of hers. They lay side by side, facing each other, so close there was no space between them.

"You'll have to tell me if it hurts," he said.

She laughed. "I think we'll be okay if I'm on top."

"Not exactly a hardship, but I have a better idea."

Macy wanted to say something funny, to once again make light of what had happened, but she knew Aiden was right to be worried. She'd seen the look in Jordan's eyes. That man had wanted to kill her.

"There was a moment when I thought . . ."

Aiden caught her eye.

"Let it go. You're here and you're okay."

They kissed for a long time, the taste of salty tears on their lips. He kissed her throat, her breasts, and her belly. He rolled her onto her back and parted her thighs. Macy grabbed a fistful of his long hair, closed her eyes, and held on tight.

Saturday

Macy sat in the passenger's seat of Aiden's SUV with one arm dangling over the headrest so she could hold Luke's outstretched hand. Luke was strapped into his car seat, his fat little fist wrapped around Macy's index finger. A waitress at the diner where'd they'd had breakfast had recommended the playground next to the library, claiming it was the best one in all of Montana. Though overcast, the rain wasn't supposed to settle in until the afternoon. At the moment it felt more like a snowstorm might be coming. A cold northerly wind swept through the town. They'd dressed in layers and put some hand warmers in Luke's gloves. Macy was checking her messages regularly. So far there'd been no word from Alisa or the hospital.

Aiden pulled into the parking lot in front of the library. Prospector's

Park was to the right. Beyond the pine trees, Pilot Hill arched up steeply into the low-lying clouds. Macy caught sight of a playground. A young girl flew along a zip line.

"The waitress wasn't telling tales. That playground looks pretty amazing," said Macy.

There were very few spaces available so Aiden had to circle the lot a couple of times.

Luke's excitement had been growing steadily. The blueberry pancakes hadn't helped.

"Don't worry," said Aiden. "We'll work off all that sugar in no time."

"Do you have plans for this afternoon?" asked Macy.

"I booked haircuts for us. One of my friends recommended a salon on Main Street."

"Are you sure you're up for the challenge? The last time I took Luke in for a haircut my mother nearly had a nervous breakdown, and you know how chill she is."

Aiden caught Luke's eye in the rearview mirror. "What do you say, little man? Are you and me going to face the scissors together today?"

Luke kicked his legs out. "Yay!"

"Aside from *little man* Luke hardly understood anything you just said," said Macy.

"Watch and learn, Greeley," said Aiden. "Watch and learn."

Aiden backed into a spot near the library's front doors. A handful of bikes were locked to the racks cemented into the pavement. Macy had been on the lookout for the redheaded boy from the video as they drove through town. So far she'd only seen cyclists decked out in tight-fitting Lycra and helmets. There'd been an all-female cycling team gathered for breakfast at the diner. Aiden had asked them where they were heading. A petite woman with an expanse of freckles had laughed.

"We've already done eighty miles this morning," she'd said. "This is our reward."

Macy's description of the redheaded boy had mostly been met with shrugs, but one of the cyclists had said they might have seen the kid on a couple of occasions. Unfortunately, she couldn't give any more information.

Aiden removed the keys from the ignition and turned to face Macy. "I know you won't relax until you find that kid. Why don't I go ahead to the playground with Luke while you go into the library and have a little poke around."

"And that is why I love you," said Macy, letting herself out of the car. "I promise I'll just be a sec."

The library was a vast modern structure that had been recently built adjacent to the original library, which now served as a historical museum. There was a crowd of teenagers hanging out near an outdoor amphitheater and another smaller group was gathered in a café off the library's central foyer. Most wore baseball caps, making it difficult to judge their hair color at a distance. She scrolled through her e-mails until she found the screenshot that Alisa had sent her.

The library's interior was warm and brightly lit. Macy approached the information desk and introduced herself. The woman's long gray hair was streaked with black strands and her reading glasses hung on the gold chain around her neck. She had to use them to see the image on Macy's phone.

"Oh, that's Chad. He's not in any trouble, is he?"

"We'd just like to speak to him. Any chance you know where to find him?"

She lowered her glasses so they were perched on the tip of her nose and glanced around the library.

"I saw him earlier, so he might still be here somewhere."

"What is Chad like? Is he a good kid?"

"A real helpful boy. Comes in two or three times a week. He loves to read so I have to assume he's perfect."

Macy wrote his name down in her notebook. "Do you have any contact information?"

She frowned. "I don't mean to be difficult but I'm not sure if I'm able to give it to you. His father's name is Ted. He's a builder that works here in town. That should help you track him down."

"Thank you," said Macy. "That's a big help."

"If I see Chad, should I tell him you're looking for him?"

Macy handed the woman her card. "That's probably a good idea. Just make it clear that he's not in any trouble. We only want to speak to him. Do you mind if I have a look around while I'm here?"

The woman told Macy to make herself at home.

Macy found a quiet spot behind a bookshelf and pulled out her cell phone. There were signs everywhere forbidding their use. She kept her voice low.

"Alisa, I'm at the library. I think I've got a name for you," whispered Macy. She read to Alisa from her notes. "Chad's father is named Ted. Apparently he's a builder who works locally."

"I'll get back to you as soon as I have something."

"The kid was seen here earlier today. I'll let you know if I find him."

Macy started at one end of the library and worked her way through the stacks. The upstairs mezzanine overlooked the park and the parking lot. She could see Aiden and Luke. Luke was trying to push Aiden on the swings, laughing hysterically when Aiden wouldn't budge. A couple of teenage boys were walking through the trees. One had a backpack and shoulder-length red hair. They were heading for the bike racks.

Macy took the stairs two at a time and ran headlong across the library's main floor. By the time she reached the exit at the far end of the foyer, the boy and his bike were gone. She watched him pedal out of the parking lot.

She found her phone and called Alisa again.

"I just missed him," said Macy. "He's heading west on Main Street on a bike."

"I'll let dispatch know. Hopefully one of our guys will be able to pick him up."

"I'll be at the park next to the library. Call me if you hear anything."

17

Saturday

Wrapped up in bandages and pale from blood loss, Jordan Beech didn't look particularly menacing lying in his hospital bed. Macy reminded herself of the boot print stamped to her torso. This wasn't a man you messed with. The authorities in Oklahoma believed he'd only been convicted for a fraction of the crimes he'd committed. He was suspected in dozens of unsolved arson attacks and burglaries. They couldn't prove he was involved, but that didn't mean they'd stopped trying.

Grace's letter was sealed in the evidence bag resting on Macy's lap. Contrary to what she'd told Grace and Lara, they hadn't found Jordan Beech's fingerprints on it until after he was arrested. Macy had lied on a hunch and was relieved when it worked. Jordan Beech was in custody. The fingerprints and a statement from an employee at the coffee shop who'd caught him loitering in the break room increased the likelihood that he'd had Grace's letter in his possession before the fire.

"So, why Grace Larson?" asked Macy. "You could have followed any woman around Bolton, yet you chose her."

A shrug.

"Your phone is full of photos of Grace. We know you took them without her knowledge."

"If you say so."

"It wouldn't take much to convince a jury that you were obsessed with her."

Jordan didn't respond.

"Mr. Beech, you're breaking the law just by being in Montana. The terms of your parole forbid you to leave the state of Oklahoma," said Macy. "Why did you risk coming here? Were you looking for Grace?"

"I came to check on my brother's property while he's away working in North Dakota. Come on, now. There's no harm in doing a brother a favor."

"We spoke to your brother. He didn't know you were staying at his place. He told us that he didn't trust you, that we shouldn't trust you."

"Well, he would say that. We don't always get along."

"We found a sizeable quantity of oxycodone and fentanyl in your possession. Way more than you'd need for your own personal use."

"It was at the house when I arrived. Nothing to do with me."

"Are you saying that the drugs belong to your brother?"

"The man has a problem. I was hoping he'd seek help."

"The batch numbers on the packaging give us a timeline. The fingerprints confirm they're yours. We know you picked up the painkillers at a pill mill in Florida within the last two months. It's only a matter of time before we figure out how much you've sold since you started your little road trip. You keep breaking laws at this rate and you can expect to be in prison for a very long time. I, for one, would like to see you stay inside for the rest of your life."

"I didn't know you were a cop."

"Yes, you did. I told you so just before you bashed my head into the pavement."

"I didn't see no badge."

"I would have gladly shown it to you had you given me a chance." Macy took a deep breath. Losing her temper wouldn't help matters. "So, I have a theory, Mr. Beech. Do you want to hear it?"

"Do I have a choice?"

"Not really." Macy held up Grace's letter. "Last Sunday a coffee shop employee saw you loitering near the break room about an hour after Grace's last shift there ended. I think you broke into her locker and stole this letter. "

"Never seen it before."

"It has your fingerprints all over it."

Silence.

Macy continued. "The letter Grace wrote to Peter Granger must have pissed you off. He wasn't treating your girl very nicely."

"Grace Adams isn't my girl."

"So, you have heard of Grace after all?"

"Who hasn't?"

"You've been interested in Grace Adams for a long time. Your Web browser has searches about the murders in Collier that date back years. You've also left numerous posts on a Web site that's dedicated to true crime. In recent posts you bragged about meeting Grace Adams. You even posted photos to prove it." Macy raised an eyebrow at Jordan's reaction. "Don't look so surprised, Mr. Beech. Montana may be rural but our computer technicians are really quite skilled. They'll eventually find every post you've ever made, but let's stick with Grace Adams for now. On one particularly interesting thread you went on and on about how much you loved her and claimed that you would do anything for her. You even mentioned Peter Granger's name on three occasions. Among other choice threats, you described him as a dead man walking. You posted a photo of this letter in that same thread."

Macy let that sink in for a few moments.

"Back in Oklahoma, you attempted to burn down the factory where you worked to cover up an assault of one of your colleagues. She was lucky to get out alive. I hear you were obsessed with her too. Witnesses testified that you were angry because she reported you to management for making inappropriate advances. You were convicted on all charges and served ten years."

"It was her word against mine." Jordan looked Macy in the eye for the first time. "She lied."

"We tracked your cell-phone signal on Halloween night. There were several fires set in Bolton over the course of the evening. We've managed to put you within range of all of the incidences, including the fire at the Granger's house." Macy held up the letter. "Grace threatened to burn down Peter Granger's house. She says it was all a fantasy, but you saw it as an opportunity to impress her. After all, you did say that you'd do anything for Grace. Must have blown your mind when you saw what was hanging on Peter Granger's walls. I wouldn't figure you for a connoisseur of fine art, but you did manage to steal the most valuable paintings in the house."

"I didn't set that fire and I didn't steal no fucking paintings. You said it yourself. Grace Adams made the threats. She did it."

"Given your criminal record, who do you think a jury is going to believe?"

Macy took a look at her notes.

"Grace says you were following her on the night of fire. She'd seen you at the K-Bar and then later when she was a few blocks away from the Granger's home. We know you were in the area because a patrol officer pulled you over for a busted taillight. He didn't have time to issue a citation because he was called away on an emergency."

Jordan sounded smug. "No way you're going to pin that fire on me. I got Grace on video that night. It will prove I wasn't anywhere near the house on Madison Road when the fire started."

"We've already checked your phone. What video are you talking about?"

"I have a dashboard camera in my Bronco. The girl was so drunk she didn't realize I was trailing right behind her. I was doing her a favor keeping an eye on her like that. No one else was looking out for her."

"Mr. Beech, let's be very clear. You weren't looking after Grace Adams, you were stalking her."

Macy picked up her phone and called Brad to tell him what she'd just learned.

"I'll have them go over the Bronco again," said Brad. "If there's a dash cam I'll have them send the footage off it to the station."

Macy told Brad to keep her posted.

"Must be disappointing," said Jordan. "A few minutes ago you thought you had two suspects. Once you see that footage you'll realize you've got nothing on me or Grace."

Macy pulled her hair back so he could see the extent of the bruising around her eye.

"Oh, Mr. Beech, I beg to differ."

Brad apologized several times for missing the dashboard camera. Macy had decided it wasn't worth getting angry, but that didn't stop her from wondering what else the crime scene techs may have overlooked.

"Don't worry," she said. "It happens."

"That may be so, but I've asked them go through everything again just to be sure nothing else was missed."

A video technician was scrolling through the footage on Jordan's dash cam. She leaned in close to the screen and squinted through her quarter-inch thick glasses.

"Mr. Beech isn't very bright," she said. "He's got footage on here that puts him at the sight of two of the smaller fires that were set on Monday evening."

"Anything that puts him at the Granger's house?" asked Macy.

Brad crossed his arms. "Nope."

Macy felt a headache coming on. "What about Grace Adams? We know she leaves the bar at 11:52. Is there anything that proves she wasn't at the Granger's house?"

"He was following her for nearly twelve minutes," said Brad. "We really don't see how she could have managed setting the fire in the little time she had."

Though the image on the screen was grainy, Macy was able to recognize Grace's Halloween costume, so she knew it was her. Grace was stumbling down a suburban street with her arms wide. At one point she started running. She had an awkward gait but that may have been because she was wearing heels. A few minutes later the Bronco pulled up to the curb and she vanished from sight.

"This is when the cop pulls him over for the busted taillight," said the video technician.

"Got called away because of the fires so he didn't have time to issue a citation." Brad pointed to the screen. "After Jordan Beech is pulled over, he continues circling the neighborhood but only gets within a block of the Granger's house. Takes a quick drive to Grace's apartment building and doubles back. Ten minutes later he pulls up to a stop sign at the intersection of Cedar and Vine and then suddenly reverses."

"Grace Adams said she was on Cedar."

Brad nodded. "It looks like that's where Jordan finally catches up with her again."

"It fits what they said in their statements. She says she ran when she saw his car. He denies chasing her."

"Did he say if she was still wearing the prom dress?" asked Brad.

"Same outfit but barefoot."

"That girl is crazy."

"Crazy and incredibly drunk, but not guilty. Grace Adams is making no attempt to hide. She's running through that neighborhood wearing heels and a prom dress. If she was in that state anywhere near the Granger's home someone would have noticed her."

"In that case you're all out of suspects. This video footage proves that Jordan Beech didn't set that fire either," said Brad.

"Thankfully, we've still got plenty we can charge him with."

"Amen to that."

Alisa was once again perched at the edge of Macy's desk, pecking on her laptop. Her ponytail was pulled back so tightly she looked as if she was simulating a facelift.

Macy slumped down in her desk chair. "It doesn't look like Jordan

Beech or Grace Adams set that fire. They weren't anywhere near Madison Road around the time it started."

"There's still a chance they could have done it. They could have used a timer to delay the start of the fire."

"Ryan and his team have found nothing at the scene to indicate that was the case, which gets Hannah Granger off the hook as well. Plus, there's the issue of the missing artwork. Jordan Beech doesn't appear to know anything about art and we've not found any of the missing paintings in his or Grace's possession."

"That house was destroyed. There's a chance that Ryan's team missed something."

"Possibly, but it's all academic if we don't have physical evidence to prove timers were used. Do you have anything more on that kid that picked up that job at the printer?" asked Macy.

Alisa held up a finger. "One second," she said. "I'm just finishing off this last sentence."

Macy started pulling files out of her bag. She put the photocopies of the Polaroids to one side, hopeful that she would never have to look at them again. Now that the Bolton PD had some detectives freed up from the other investigation, it had been decided that they would look into the Polaroids Lara had found in Peter Granger's office. There was a possibility that many of the women in the photographs were unaware of what had happened to them. Macy had mixed feelings about telling them. Clare Stokes's shock at seeing herself naked and masked had been heartbreaking to witness. Brad had insisted on flying out to Wisconsin to inform Pippa Lomax's family of the latest developments and to conduct interviews.

"It's not the type of thing I'm willing to tell someone's parents over the phone," he'd said.

Macy flipped through some of the papers on her desk. She'd been there less than a week and had already colonized the borrowed office. She repositioned a framed photograph of Luke so that it was facing her, opened a Diet Coke, and wrestled a cookie from a box. Luke had been too excited to get upset when Aiden had dropped her off in front of the police station. Aiden was taking him to the dinosaur museum and afterward they were going for haircuts, an event that Aiden was building up to epic proportions. At this point anything short of a rocket firing out of the hairdresser's ass would be seen as a disappointment. She was hopeful Aiden would survive the experience. They'd agreed to meet for an early dinner, which gave Macy a full three hours to fret over the possible outcomes.

Alisa closed her laptop. "Feel like taking a ride? I've got a possible address on Chad."

"I left my car at the hotel. I'm all yours," said Macy.

Winter in southern Montana was proving elusive. The heavy snowfall from earlier in the week had given way to rain. They took Alisa's patrol car. She sat behind the wheel rummaging through her backpack, eventually raising her hands in frustration.

"I left my phone charger at home. Do you mind if we swing by my place on the way?"

Alisa ended up inviting Macy in for a quick coffee. While the kettle came to a boil Alisa went into her bedroom to find her charger. Alisa's apartment was small but nice. There was so much that reminded Macy of when she was younger. She hadn't asked, but she could tell Alisa lived alone. There was a singular type of order that was immediately recognizable.

Macy found a wadded-up tissue in her pocket and blew her nose. There were photos of what she assumed to be family and friends on a shelf and a few artsy prints hanging on the walls. Not surprisingly, the bookshelves were full. Macy pulled out a copy of one of Peter Granger's novels and flipped through it. He'd written a generic note to Alisa.

Very pleased that you came along this evening. With warmest wishes . . .

Macy went into the kitchen. The box of chocolates sat out on the counter in plain sight. It was the same box that Brad had been carrying when she had run into him the night before. Macy nudged open the lid. About half had been eaten.

"Is coffee okay with you?" asked Alisa.

"Coffee would be great," said Macy. She held up a tissue. "Just need to throw this away."

"Trash is under the sink."

Macy opened the cabinet door. There was an empty bottle of wine standing next to the trash can under the sink. Macy turned it so she could see the label. Brad Hastings had lied. He hadn't been on his way home with peace offerings for his wife. He'd been on his way to see Alisa. Macy shut the cabinet door and walked into the living room.

"Do you live alone?" asked Macy.

"Always. I find it easier."

"It does have its advantages."

Alisa went about making coffee—two heaping scoops in a French press followed by boiling water.

"Very low-tech around here," she said.

They sat in the living room. The windows looked out onto a rain-swept parking lot. The sign for the Co-op was just visible in the distance.

"You said you were from around here. Do you still have family in Bolton?" asked Macy.

"Not as such. I have a sister who lives nearby in Lawrence, but we don't get along. Last I heard, my parents were somewhere in Idaho."

"Sounds like you're very much on your own then."

Alisa touched the scars on her throat. "I have my parents to thank for this. Running a meth lab out of a family home is never a good idea."

"How old were you?"

"Fourteen. Went straight from the hospital into foster care."

"That's terrible," said Macy. "No one gets over something like that."

Alisa closed her eyes for a few seconds. "Makes me want to be better than them. I guess that's something."

"All that against you? I'd say you're doing really well."

Macy stared at her cup of coffee but she couldn't bring herself to drink it. She was on the edge of saying something she knew she would regret, so she swallowed back her words. Alisa's personal life was none of her business. None. If she were having an affair with Brad Hastings, nothing Macy could say or do would make any difference. Macy suddenly knew why the apartment had seemed so familiar to her. A great deal of sadness lived here. She could see that Alisa was the type of woman who'd go out of her way to do the right thing, the moral thing. An affair with a married man would slowly take its toll. Alisa was probably beating herself up on a daily basis.

"You're a good cop," said Macy. "I imagine you're going to be a very good detective someday."

Alisa brightened. "Do you really think so?"

"You have all the right instincts. You just have to believe in yourself." Macy hesitated. "If you ever want to talk about how you can move forward or if you're ever considering a move to work for the state, you should let me know. Bolton is nice but it's limited. You don't have any family tying you down here, so it would be easy to move on."

Alisa put her coffee cup down on the table and folded her hands in her lap. She sounded unsure.

"Thank you. It's certainly something to think about."

Macy gulped down some of her coffee. It burned her tongue and throat. She wouldn't say anything against Brad, but that wouldn't stop her from running interference.

"We should go," said Macy. "We're short on suspects. This kid, Chad, is the only promising lead we have at the moment."

Chad Nelson lived in a bungalow south of town. His mother was understandably nervous at seeing two police officers standing on her front porch. Macy tried to reassure her.

"Chad isn't in any trouble, but he may be a witness. We need to speak to him."

"I wish I could help, but Chad is with his father this weekend." A yellow Labrador stuck his snout between the woman's legs. She reached down to give him a reassuring pat on the head. "I'm not even sure whether they're in town. There was talk of going up to Missoula to see Chad's grandparents. Can I ask what this is all about?"

Alisa handed the woman the screenshot of Chad.

"Can you confirm this is your son?" asked Alisa.

The woman's hand was shaking. She nodded.

"Your son picked up an order at a print shop near campus. He paid in cash and left on his bike. Did he say anything to you about this?" asked Macy.

"He sometimes does odd jobs for people around Bolton. Puts up flyers, makes deliveries, babysits—anything to make a few dollars. Do you think he's gotten mixed up in something he shouldn't be doing?"

"It's likely that he's an innocent party," said Macy. "We're only talking about a print job. Only paper. No drugs or anything like that. We'd still like to speak to him as soon as possible. We're hoping he can identify the person he was running errands for. Could we have your ex-husband's phone number?"

"Sure, but don't hold your breath. My ex hates phones so he rarely answers. You should probably send him a text explaining why you need to speak to Chad. I imagine he'll call you back once he reads it."

"Does Chad have a cell phone?" asked Alisa.

The woman hesitated and then started rambling nervously. "Chad is only thirteen, so some people think it's wrong for him to have one but both me and his dad work so sometimes it's the only way we can keep track of him."

"Ma'am, there's no need to apologize," said Macy. "We're sure Chad is a great kid."

Macy copied out the phone numbers in her notebook and shook the woman's hand.

"Can you tell me anything more about what this is about?" she asked.

"Not at the moment, but we'll be in touch soon," said Macy.

Alisa spoke under her breath as they made their way back to the car. "We can track Chad's movements the day he picked up the order using his phone number. May give us an idea of who we're dealing with."

"Let's try calling them first. Dad may not be keen on cell phones, but I can almost guarantee that Chad will have his within reach wherever he is."

Macy was wrong. Neither Chad nor his father answered their phones. Macy sent the father a text while Alisa drove them to Cornelia Hart's condominium.

Rainwater cascaded down from the condominium's rooftop and pooled on the wide concrete walkways and front porch. There were few cars parked in the lots. Most of the condo interiors were dark and the sales office was closed for the day. Macy rang Cornelia Hart's bell several times and waited in the driving rain. The drumming was so loud she could barely hear the bell's chime inside Cornelia's home. Alisa stood next to Macy, but she was facing away from the door.

"I'm pretty sure that's Cornelia Hart's car parked out front," said Alisa.

There was nowhere to go on this end of town unless you were planning on taking a long walk, and Cornelia didn't strike Macy as someone who went for walks. She certainly wasn't going to go out in this weather. Her front curtains were drawn shut, but the gate leading to the backyard stood ajar. Macy led the way. A cold blast of wet wind shot down the narrow alleyway. For a couple of seconds Macy was walking blind. They hopped a low brick wall and stood on a small covered courtyard that could be accessed from Cornelia's back door. A common area dotted with newly planted trees was boxed in by a dozen condominiums. Despite the overhead cover it felt very exposed.

"This place is soulless," said Alisa.

Macy didn't disagree.

Cornelia's cat peered out at them through the open sliding glass door. The curtains fluttered inward, brushing the fur back on the cat's head. There was broken glass all over the wooden flooring. Macy drew her firearm and told Alisa to call for backup and an ambulance.

Macy stood to the right of the door and pounded on the wooden doorframe hard with the butt of her gun.

"Cornelia Hart!" she shouted. "This is the police. Please answer if you can hear me!"

The cat scampered away and the curtains fell flat.

Macy called out again.

"Police! We're coming in."

Macy pushed the sliding glass door open completely and quickly stepped out of the way. The curtains billowed inward. Loose papers fluttered across the floor. A glass vase that had once been filled with artificial flowers lay splintered into hundreds of shards. They reflected off the overhead light. There was a wide smear of what looked like blood trailing across the wood floor. Macy pulled the curtain open completely.

"The carpet that was here is gone," said Macy. "Looks like it was rolled up and dragged across the floor."

Alisa's eyes were wide and searching. "Do you think there was a body inside?"

"Follow in my footsteps as closely as you can," said Macy.

They skirted around the edges of the room with their weapons drawn. Broken glass cracked underfoot.

"There's more blood on the kitchen floor. Shoe prints too. They look too large to be a women's shoe," said Alisa.

"Cornelia Hart!" yelled Macy. "Are you in here?"

The cat headed for the stairs. Macy followed.

"The bedrooms should be upstairs," said Macy.

There was no sign of Cornelia Hart in the home office or bedroom, but everything had been pulled out of the drawers and cupboards. Other than a couple bloody shoe prints at the base of the stairs, there was no sign of a struggle outside of the kitchen and living room. The smear of blood went from the back door to the front door, then disappeared.

"She's not here," said Macy.

Alisa was studying the front door.

"No signs of forced entry anywhere," said Alisa. "She may have known her attacker."

Macy and Alisa carefully retraced their steps back through the apartment and took shelter under the covered porch. The rain had lessened. It was falling in a thin veil, silent rain that softened the light and left everything a muddled gray. Emergency sirens were approaching from the east.

"There would have been a lot of noise," said Alisa. "I'm surprised one of the neighbors didn't call the police."

"What neighbors? Most of the units are empty."

Macy knelt down to take a closer look at the bloodstains. They appeared to be completely dry.

"I interviewed Cornelia Hart on Thursday morning. Has anyone spoken to her since then?" asked Macy.

"No, ma'am. I've been trying to reach her since we found Hannah Granger on Thursday evening."

"Did the patrol unit that you sent out report seeing anything unusual?"

"Nothing out of the ordinary. They've come out a couple of times. Hannah said she'd been trying to reach her as well." Alisa pointed to the floor. "Does that seem like a lot of blood to you?"

The complex was isolated. No one would have heard Cornelia's cries for help. The perpetrator could have cut across the common area and entered through the sliding glass doors. The front door had been chained and locked when Macy came to see Cornelia. She wasn't like other people in Bolton. She was from New York. She locked her doors. Macy had a horrible feeling she'd missed something and Cornelia Hart had paid the price.

"It's not a lot of blood but there may be more on the rug. If they dragged it outside there should be glass and fibers out front in the parking lot, but the rain would have washed away other evidence." Macy stood up. "Until DNA proves otherwise we're going to assume the victim is Cornelia Hart. When I came here on Thursday the front door was double locked and the security chain attached. It isn't now."

"Maybe her attacker left that way."

"They would have had to wait until it was dark to move the body."

"We're assuming she's dead?"

"If this is her blood I'm afraid we're going to have to assume the worst.

We would have heard if Cornelia Hart was dropped off at a local hospital."

"Why would they risk taking her body with them? It's not like they could disguise that a crime took place."

"Hard to say. They may have been thinking no body, no murder charge, or there could be physical evidence on the body. Something that could be used to identify the killer. I didn't see anything that looked like a murder weapon either."

Macy's eyes darted from the bookshelves to the walls. She was pretty sure a couple of paintings were missing, but harder to explain was the methodical search of the entire condominium. Someone had taken their time going through every drawer and cupboard. They were confident that no one was going to come visit Cornelia.

"What in the hell were they looking for?"

"The missing artwork?" asked Alisa.

"They weren't going to find it in a kitchen drawer."

"Money then?"

"Fuck." Macy closed her eyes for a second. She needed to think. Ted Nelson and his son still hadn't returned their calls. "Give Missoula PD a call. They need to send a patrol unit to Chad Nelson's grandparents' house right away. I'm worried about that boy."

Macy pulled her phone from her pocket and scrolled down until she found Aiden's phone number. He didn't answer so she left him a message. She was going to be working late again. He and Luke would have to have dinner on their own.

The television blinked in the darkened hotel room. Luke and Aiden were asleep on the sofa bed this time. Aiden was propped up on the pillows with Luke tucked beneath one of his arms. Macy turned on the light in the adjoining room and left the door ajar. She sat on the edge of the sofa bed and watched as their features slowly came into focus. She smiled, then shook with laughter, covering her mouth so she wouldn't wake them. Aiden opened one eye, then another. He cracked a smile.

"You're not supposed to laugh," he said.

Macy rubbed her hand over his hair. It was less than a quarter inch in length and felt like the quills on a hedgehog.

"What possessed you to get buzz cuts?" she asked.

"Luke insisted."

"He's not even three. You didn't have to listen."

"Figured I'd take one for the team. You can go with him next time."

"You still look good."

He ran his fingers through his nonexistent hair.

"It's going to take some getting used to. Feels cold, for one. Just think of the money we'll save on shampoo."

She rubbed his ear lobe between her thumb and forefinger.

"It's a good thing you have nice ears," she said.

"A little warning. Luke's do stick out a fair bit."

"So do mine. It's a Greeley trait." Macy snuggled in next to Aiden and closed her eyes. "It has been a long evening. What did you guys get up to?" she asked.

"We had dinner with Brad Hastings and his wife, so I'm all caught up on the case. Heard you've got another missing person on your hands."

"It's worse than that. We may be looking for a body." She hesitated. "How well do you know Brad?"

"We go way back. Invited him up to Wilmington Creek, but they've got the baby on the way so who knows if he'll be able to make it. Funny. I could never imagine he'd get married and now he's going to be a father."

"Why's that?"

Aiden yawned. "He was a bit of a player, that's all."

"A bit like you were then?"

"No, this was different. He always seemed to have a girlfriend. He just never seemed to care."

"I don't think he's changed."

Aiden held his lips to her forehead.

"Why do you say that? Did he hit on you?"

"No, but I'm pretty sure he's seeing Alisa on the side."

"That ain't good. How sure are you?" he asked.

"Fairly. I ran into Brad coming out of the supermarket late last night with a bottle of wine and a box of chocolates. He said he was on his way home, but the next day the same bottle of wine and box of chocolates were in Alisa's apartment."

"Maybe he had good reason to be there. He could have stopped by and forgot them."

"The bottle was empty and the box had been opened. I'm not imagining things."

"Do you think I should say something?"

"I don't know," said Macy. "Alisa reminds me a lot of myself when I first started out on the force. I think she has promise. News of their relationship gets out and we both know who's going to get blamed."

Aiden shifted Luke and tucked the covers around him. He sat up and stretched.

"Let's move to the other bed," he said. "Last night just about killed my back."

Macy switched off the television and they leaned against each other in the dark hotel room. She was crying and she wasn't sure why.

"You'd tell me if you weren't happy," she said.

He kissed her for a long time.

"What's this all about?" asked Aiden. "You know I'd let you know if we weren't okay. I'm not shy about bitching."

"But I'm always working."

"There's nothing wrong with missing the person you love. It's what makes you love them even more."

18

Sunday

Grace had driven past Bolton's only Episcopal church on a number of occasions and had always liked the look of it, but this was the first time she'd ventured inside. She'd woken up at 7:00 A.M to walk her dog, but still had to rush in order to make it in time to attend the earliest service. She quietly slipped inside and stood near the doors. It was much as she'd expected. Most of the parishioners were elderly. Grace picked up an order of service from a table near the entrance before taking a seat in the second pew from the back.

Clare had called her late Friday night. Her interview with Macy Greeley had gone on for over an hour. Clare had insisted it was a misunderstanding until she'd seen the Polaroids for herself. Nothing could have prepared her for seeing herself like that. Clare's parents had arrived in time to pick her up at the police station. They were all staying at a hotel on the outskirts of town. Clare couldn't stop crying.

At least my parents now know that all the problems I've been having are real. It's not all in my head.

Grace hadn't known how to comfort Clare. Her friend's memory was full of blind spots. She didn't remember being photographed and, with

Peter dead, there was no way of finding out exactly what took place in that room.

I don't even know how upset I should be. Should I assume the worst or hope for the best?

Grace sank back in the pew and stared into the middle distance. She was confident God would forgive her recent lapses in church attendance. The only thing that mattered was that she had returned. She wasn't raised in the Episcopal Church, but everything from the vicar to the altar to the stained-glass windows to the smell of wood polish was familiar. It was like coming home.

Taylor Moore was special by anyone's standards. Her quiet confidence stood in contrast to Lara's showmanship. She was incredibly curious and took the time to listen, but there was also something about her that was intangible, something you couldn't touch. Peter had never wanted to help Taylor become a better writer. He'd only wanted to contain her. He wanted to pin her down to a page like a dark-winged moth. Try as she might, Grace couldn't picture them as a couple. Taylor was too clever. She should have seen right through Peter's lies.

Grace opened the *Book of Common Prayer* to Psalm 39. She kept her eyes on the page even though she knew the verses by heart. Common prayer was like meditation. She found the rise and fall of voices soothing. She tipped down the padded bar and knelt with the rest of the congregation.

Grace wanted to focus on Taylor as she was in life but her mind refused to settle on something beautiful. All she could see was the woman Peter had left behind. Pinned down on a Polaroid, Taylor's scarred body had been laid bare. Her head was tipped back and her arms sprawled out to the sides. She'd looked like she was asleep.

This one comfort was tiny but Grace clung to it.

Taylor probably had no idea it was happening.

The police didn't know how Taylor had died or why she'd been in the same bed as Peter. All they knew for sure was that she hadn't died in the fire. Grace had lied when Macy asked if Taylor had ever talked about committing suicide. Taylor spoke of death like other people spoke of the weather. There'd been at least two failed attempts that Grace knew of. This time she may have succeeded. Grace certainly wasn't going to blame her for taking Peter Granger with her.

Grace wiped away the tears in her eyes. She hadn't realized she was crying. Everyone was standing, but she was still on her knees. They'd moved on to a hymn. Grace was confused. She'd never heard it before.

Grace snuck her dog into the art department's back door for the second day in a row. She should have taken him home but didn't want to risk going back to the apartment for fear of running into Lara. It had been a day and half since Lara had waved at her from the waiting room at the police station. There'd been several missed calls and a few dozen texts since then. Over the last thirty-six hours their tone had gone from upset to bewildered to angry. Lara had yet to say she was anything close to sorry, so Grace had left the calls unanswered.

After some coaxing Jack curled up into a ball on a blanket she'd tucked beneath her worktable. There were two other students working in the far side of the studio. They hadn't said anything about the dog the previous day so Grace figured she was okay. She found a blank canvas in her cupboard and set it out on the easel next to a sketch she'd done the day before. A man was trying to walk across a wide river that was covered with thin ice.

Grace sharpened a pencil and put on her headphones. Chopin's nocturnes filled her head. If she focused on her work everything else in her life always disappeared. She was praying this was still the case as she touched pencil to canvas. In the beginning she was always tentative. The lines were faint, but with time concrete shapes started to emerge. The man had a narrow face and high cheekbones. His long hair was in disarray. A wide river grew out of the mist. A thick pine forest covered the hillside on the opposite shore. The river ice buckled and broke. Great fissures cracked open beneath the man's feet.

Jack stood up and let out a low growl. Grace held a hand down to quiet him.

"Shhh, Jack. I'm here."

Jack continued to grumble. He was staring at something out of Grace's sightline. The fur on his back rose and he barked loudly. Grace pulled off her headphones and turned around.

Jessica stood ten feet away. She was bundled up in a coat and hat. She'd worn makeup to disguise the puffiness around her eyes, but the color she'd applied to her cheeks and lips couldn't hide her weariness.

She asked if Grace felt like going for a walk.

Forsaking the more popular spots, they drove to a lonely trailhead near where the river slipped slow and wide across the open land. A cold wind swept across the rocky shores and wide valley. Grace parked her car in the empty lot and stepped out onto the gravel. Other than commenting on the weather and asking Grace about how her preparations for the art show were going, Jessica had barely said a word during the ride from campus. Grace filled in the silence as best she could, prattling on about how she'd spent all of the previous day and most of the night in the art studio. Grace hadn't felt it necessary to admit that she'd been too afraid to go home. Facing Lara was still something she was hoping to avoid. Short of moving into the art studio, she wasn't sure how she was going to manage getting away with it for much longer. It seemed a confrontation was inevitable.

Jack shot off toward the river as soon as Grace opened the back door. It was his second walk of the day and it seemed he wasn't going to waste it.

"I'm sorry I caught you in the middle of working," said Jessica. "I imagine it's been difficult to find time to get anything done."

Grace lied. "It's okay. I needed a break."

They walked across the uneven river stones, their arms held wide like puppeteers. Jack was running up and down the shoreline barking at a herd of elk that had gathered under the trees on the opposite bank. They eyed him with thorny impatience.

"I want to apologize," said Jessica. "I can only imagine how awful that night was for you. It's not like me to do things like that. I've always been so steady."

"You were in a bad way. It's lucky I was there."

"I still shouldn't have put you through that. You must think I don't have anyone I can go to."

"Jessica, I don't regret being there," said Grace.

Jessica was too upset to speak so she only nodded.

"Why did Hannah stay away for so long without calling you?" asked Grace.

They jumped a narrow tributary and continued eastward along the river's banks. All that was visible of Jack was his long tail. It stuck up through the tall tawny grass like a periscope. He was digging for something. Red earth pelted the air.

"Hannah was snowed in up at the cabin. It's isolated and has no phone or Wi-Fi. Under normal circumstances I wouldn't have thought anything if she was out of touch for a few days." Jessica saw the look on Grace's face. "The police have cleared her of any involvement. She didn't set that fire."

"It just seems odd that you're so close but she doesn't get in touch for days."

"There have always been long gaps. She is, or rather was, married."

"I just feel that if you're a couple you should stick together."

"We don't really work like that," said Jessica.

"Has she spoken to you at all about what happened?"

"A little. It's difficult for her. She's lost everything." Jessica hesitated. "I'm hoping we can build something new together."

"You don't seem very confident."

"We've never been a proper couple before. I'm not sure how she'll manage being out in the open. Sometimes I felt she hid me away because she wasn't sure about being with a woman."

Grace threw a rock into the churning water. "Did you know about the Polaroids?"

Jessica was looking up at the sky. "It's not going to rain again. This feels like snow."

Grace repeated the question.

"Hannah only mentioned them in passing," said Jessica. "She said the police had found some photos that belonged to Peter."

"He'd been taking photos of naked women."

Jessica picked up a handful of stones and sifted through them, dropping the ones that weren't flat.

"He really was an asshole."

Grace started crying. "Some of the women were my friends. They don't remember anything. Lara brought the photos to Hannah a month ago. She did nothing."

"Are you sure?"

"Hannah told the police that she couldn't believe Peter would do something like that, but I don't trust her. I think she was worried about her and Peter's reputations. She only cares about herself."

Jessica sat down on a fallen tree. "She didn't tell me any of this."

"There are dozens of women in the photos. The police said they were taken in a basement room at the house."

Jessica had lowered her voice so much that Grace had to lean in to hear her.

"She's being interviewed by the police again today," said Jessica.

"About the photos?"

"No, I don't think so. Something has happened to Cornelia Hart. It sounded bad."

"Who is Cornelia Hart?"

"Their personal assistant. She's missing. They think she's been harmed."

"Are you going to say something to Hannah about the photos?"

"That and other stuff. It's going to be a difficult conversation."

"I was hoping I'd be gone before you got home," said Lara.

Jack sat in front of Lara and wagged his tail while Grace tried to look anywhere but directly at Lara. The entrance to their apartment building was crowded with Lara's stuff. Hastily packed, her life spilled out of bags and boxes. If Grace had stayed at the studio another hour she could have missed this final encounter entirely.

"I'm going home for a while," said Lara. "My parents are picking me up."

"I'm surprised the police are letting you leave town."

"I haven't asked them."

"That's just like you."

"I haven't done anything wrong," said Lara.

Grace looked over Lara's shoulder. All she could see of their neighbor Sandra was a pair of high-heeled boots. She was standing on the stairs, no doubt listening to every word. Grace raised her voice.

"Taylor is dead because of you," said Grace.

"Don't blame that on me. It wasn't my fault."

"She had a right to know about those photos. She may have handled things differently with Peter if she knew what happened. She could have gotten help."

"We don't know what went on in that house on the night of the fire."

"We can make a good guess. We know what Taylor was capable of."

"You think Taylor killed herself and Peter? Where are the stolen paintings then? She couldn't have done both."

Grace didn't have an answer.

"What's wrong?" asked Lara. "Haven't you worked that out yet?"

"When were you going to tell Pippa that she wasn't crazy?" asked Grace. "She's been in Wisconsin all this time knowing, but not being able to prove, that something horrible happened to her."

"It happened to me too, Grace."

"Yes, it did, and it's great that you decided to deal with it your own way but there were other people involved."

"I didn't think anyone would believe us."

"You found photos of thirty-two different women. You know damn well that the police would have believed you. You just couldn't risk letting the world know that Peter Granger was a monster. All you cared about was your own ambitions. You're just like Hannah. No wonder you loved the same man."

Lara was clear-eyed but Grace was in tears.

"You just don't give a shit, do you?" asked Grace.

"I didn't love him."

"Is that really all you're taking from what I just said?"

"I know you're angry right now but I hope you can forgive me someday."

"How can I ever forgive you when you're not sorry?"

Lara crossed her arms. "Clare is devastated. Do you really think it was better that she saw the photo?"

"Yes, I do. She said as much. She now knows her problems weren't all in her head."

"Why is everyone so keen on being a victim? You all just wallow in it." Lara pointed at Grace. "You pretend you've moved on from your past but anytime you can't cope with something you blame it on shit that happened years ago in Collier."

"I was coping just fine until you told Peter who I was."

"He could have helped you if you let him."

"How was his next bestseller going to help me?" asked Grace.

"He would have given you a voice."

"I already have a voice. I don't need some man giving me one. Especially not a man like that."

"Your little paintings aren't going to make a difference. Peter would have taken your story to the world. Everyone would have known what you went through."

"Why would that be a good thing?" Grace placed a hand to her chest. "These are *my* issues. I get to choose how to deal with them."

"Then make a choice and get on with your life."

"Give me your keys?" said Grace.

"I may come back."

Grace held out her hand. "You won't come back here. Give me the keys."

Lara handed Grace the keys to the apartment. "I'll make sure the rent is paid until you find someone else."

"That's the least you can do."

Lara softened her tone. "Grace, your friendship is important to me so I'm going to walk away but that doesn't mean I'm giving up. I'll do whatever it takes to prove that I meant right by Clare, Pippa, and Taylor."

A phone rang and they both turned to the stairs. Sandra wasn't alone. Three other tenants had joined her. Grace held tight to Jack's leash and walked toward them. They moved to the side. Sandra touched her arm as she passed by.

19

Sunday

Chad Nelson had the most beautiful copper-colored hair Macy had ever seen. She was tempted to say something but stopped. He was a teenager, not a child. He didn't need a woman in her mid-thirties telling him his hair was pretty. He stood next to his father in the police department's waiting room. They both shook Macy's hand when she came to greet them. Chad's handshake was firm and he wasn't afraid to look her in the eye. Both were good signs.

"I'm sorry for dragging you away from a weekend with your grand-parents, but this really couldn't wait," said Macy.

Chad's father was understandably wary. "The officers that came to see us yesterday evening didn't seem to know what this was all about. My ex-wife said it had to do with an errand Chad ran."

"That is correct," she said. "The officers should have also told you that I would have been happy to meet with you in Missoula, but I guess they didn't get that message. Anyway, I do appreciate you coming back to Bolton on such short notice."

Macy led them into a conference room and offered them coffee and juice. She was grateful someone had thought to pick up some pastries as well. At the moment she was running on an empty stomach and five hours of sleep. She'd left Luke and Aiden the same way she'd found them the night before, sleeping soundly. Aiden had stirred, mumbled something about getting up for a quick breakfast with her, and immediately dozed off again. She'd tucked the covers around her son and her boyfriend and kissed them both good-bye. Outside, frost covered the rooftops and the previous night's puddles were frozen solid. Macy's breath had been thick in the air.

Alisa came into the conference room and stood close to Macy so she wouldn't be overheard.

"Just got a call from Helena. They've confirmed it was Cornelia Hart's blood," she said.

Macy kept her expression in check. The last thing she needed was for Chad to get any more anxious than he was already. The news was troubling, but she made it sound as if Alisa had just told her she'd won the lottery.

"That's great news. Thank you for letting me know," said Macy. "Alisa, why don't you join us as well. It will save me from having to brief you afterwards."

Macy smiled up at Chad and Ted Nelson. They were both taller than her and Chad didn't appear to be anywhere near his full height. He was also physically awkward. She asked them to please have a seat and watched as Chad struggled to fold himself into the chair.

"Chad, I want to assure you that you're not in any trouble. I'm going to show you a video and once you've seen it, I want you to tell me whether it is you in the video."

Macy turned her laptop so Chad and his father could watch the security-camera footage from the print shop.

"On Thursday a teenage boy fitting your description went into Print Works on Woodstock Road and picked up a job that had been ordered online. He paid cash and left on a bicycle. Can you confirm this is you in the video?"

A blush crept up Chad's neck. "Yes, ma'am."

Macy turned off the video and moved the laptop to the side. She folded her hands on the table in front of her.

"Have you ever heard of a man named Peter Granger?"

Chad's father blanched and Macy threw him a warning look. "I really need Chad to answer."

"He's the writer they're talking about on the news," said Chad.

"Have you ever met him?"

"No, ma'am."

"I understand people hire you for odd jobs. Is that what's going on in this video? Did someone pay you to pick up an order at Print Works?"

"Yes, ma'am." He gave his father a worried glance.

His father reassured him. "It's okay, Chad. You haven't done anything wrong."

"Why don't you walk me through what happened?" said Macy.

"I was at the library putting up flyers on the bulletin board for a concert. I guess he must have seen me. He came to talk to me when I was getting my bike."

"Did he give you his name?"

"He told me to call him Mark. He said his car was broken down and asked how much I would charge to pick up something at Print Works for him."

"Do you think you can describe him for us?"

Chad hesitated for the first time.

"How about I ask you some questions to get you started," said Macy. "Was he white or black?"

"Oh, he was white."

"What about his height and build?"

"He was tall and thin."

"You're quite tall. Was he taller than you?"

"Yes." His face lit up like he suddenly remembered everything clearly. "He had a thin face. He had on sunglasses and a baseball cap so I can't tell you much more."

"What about clothing? What was he wearing?"

He raised his voice slightly. "It was a Chicago White Sox hat and a black jacket. Does that help?"

"It certainly does. Did he have an accent?"

Chad shrugged. "Nothing weird like that. He actually seemed really nice."

"What happened after you went to Print Works? Did he tell you where you were to meet afterwards?"

"No, he gave me his phone number and some cash and told me to call him when I was finished and he'd tell me where to meet him. But right after I picked it up there was already a text from him telling me to go to 18 Addison Road."

"Do you still have his number?"

Chad pulled his phone out of his jacket pocket and scrolled through his recent calls.

"It's this one," he said.

Macy reached for his phone.

"Do you mind? I need to write it down," said Macy.

Macy handed a sheet of paper to Alisa and told her to run a trace on the number and find out what she could about the residence.

"What happened when you went to Addison Road?" asked Macy.

"He wasn't there, but he'd left a note on the door asking me to leave the printouts on the porch behind some plants and said my money was in an envelope under the matt."

"Did you see him again?"

"No, ma'am."

"Did you keep the envelope?"

Chad made a face. He touched his chin. "Actually, it might be . . ." He shook his head. "No, I'm pretty sure I threw it away."

"What about the money?"

"I put it in the bank."

"May I ask how much it was?"

"Twenty dollars."

"Chad, do you know what a police sketch artist does?"

"Yes, ma'am."

"Good. Robert should be here soon. He's going to sit with you for a little while. Hopefully, the two of you can put together a good likeness of the man who hired you."

"Cool."

She turned and addressed Chad's father. "I'm sorry to have inconvenienced you, but your son has been a huge help."

"Do we have any reason to be worried?"

"We're going to take some precautions just to be on the safe side, but I really don't think there is anything to worry about. A patrol car will be parked outside your residence and your wife's residence for the next few days."

"That sounds serious. Can you tell us what's going on?"

"I can tell you a little. Someone accessed Peter Granger's remote server using a computer at the library and sent files to Print Works, which were later deleted from the server. We believe this same person hired your son to pick up the order. We've since learned that the files were manuscripts that Mr. Granger was working on at the time of his death."

"Do you think this guy was involved in the fire that killed Peter Granger?"

"It's a possibility, which is why we're so thankful you and your son came in today."

Macy paced the covered sidewalk outside the restaurant where she was having a quick meal with Aiden and Luke. She tapped on the window and waved. Their meal had arrived. They'd tucked in, but her food was growing cold on the plate. She had her cell phone glued to her ear. Eighteen Addison Road had proved to be a dead end. The owner had been out of state for nearly three weeks.

"Alisa, I'll be back in the office in half an hour. In the meantime, see if there is any connection between the house where we found the fuel cans and the one at 18 Addison Road."

"What are you thinking?" asked Alisa.

"Both properties were unoccupied. Maybe the owners are employed by the same company or belong to the same gym . . . anyplace that would be able to access their details and know if they're away. There may be something they have in common with whoever downloaded those files."

"Okay, I'll get on it."

"Has the sketch artist finished?"

"Just a sec. I'll check."

Macy headed for the restaurant's entrance. There was a strict no-cell-phone policy. The waitress working at the front desk glared at Macy. Macy hovered near the doors and lowered her voice. She'd left her jacket inside and didn't think she could handle the dropping temperatures a moment longer.

"Macy, are you still there?"

"Yep."

"The sketch artist was late getting here. He's going to be another hour."

Macy felt so guilty. She'd been sitting down laughing with her son and boyfriend while Chad and his father were stuck in the police station.

"Please, make sure Chad and his father are comfortable. Offer to get them something at the Co-op. They've been very patient. I'll be back at my desk as soon as possible."

Macy scrolled through the case notes on her computer looking for Cornelia Hart's ex-husband's contact details. They'd been married for twenty-five years, so Macy was hoping they still communicated on occasion. John Hart continued to live in Manhattan but had retired from his law practice. Macy was surprised to hear how distressed he was about Cornelia's disappearance. She'd been under the impression that their divorce had been acrimonious, but perhaps that wasn't the case. He'd not remarried.

Macy didn't think it was right to give Cornelia's ex-husband false

hope. "We have reason to believe she's been the victim of a violent assault. She didn't leave her home on her own steam. She was carried out."

"Oh, my God. Is there anything I can do?"

"I was hoping you could tell me a little more about her. She doesn't
seem to have any friends other than her employers, and you're the closest thing she had to family."

"I'd hoped the move to Montana might do her some good, but it
seems she simply fell into long-established patterns."

"Has she always been a loner?"

"We lost a child to illness in 1978. Cornelia was only twenty-one at
the time. She took it hard. We both did. Daisy was our world. . . . I guess
the one good outcome is that it gave Cornelia a sense of purpose. She
studied to become a nurse with the intention of working in a children's
ward, but that proved too emotional for her. She worked in a critical-
care unit instead."

"I saw a photo of Cornelia and Daisy in her home. It looked like it
was taken on a beach."

"I still remember that day. Cornelia couldn't bear the thought of
burying Daisy so she kept her ashes in a cookie jar that she'd had especially made. I've been trying for years to get her to agree to a burial so
that we would both have access to Daisy's final resting place, but Cornelia refused to cooperate with the legal settlement set out in the
divorce papers. I'll of course go through the necessary legal channels,
but it's important to me that Daisy's remains are looked after."

"Yes, of course," said Macy. "I'll make a note of it."

"That would be appreciated. I'm not heartless. My hope is that Cornelia is okay, but I'm afraid I may be burying both her and my daughter
together."

"I promise we're doing everything we can to find her. Had Cornelia
been in touch recently?"

"Sadly, no. I tried to reach out a few times with no success. I haven't
spoken to Cornelia since that last meeting with the lawyers. I guess it's
been fifteen years. I know she still visits Tess, but she must be nearly
ninety-five by now so I doubt she'd be able to help you."

Macy flipped through her notes. There was no mention of anyone named Tess.

"Tess?"

"Tess Madden. She's in a nursing home in Bolton. Cornelia had her moved there a few years ago so she could be closer. She was like a second mother to Cornelia. They're very devoted to each other."

"Do you know the name of the nursing home?"

"One second. Tess is kind enough to send me a Christmas card every year so she's in my address book."

Alisa stepped into the office just as Macy was hanging up the phone.

"That was Cornelia Hart's ex-husband," said Macy. "He seemed genuinely upset, which was surprising as I was under the impression that the split was acrimonious. For some reason I assumed he'd had an affair."

"You can never tell what's going on in a marriage," said Alisa.

"This is true. As I recall, Cornelia provided an alibi for the night of the fire. She was at Norwood Pines Home for the Elderly until late?"

"Yes, she was there for several hours on Sunday as well. She volunteers a few times a week. We checked. Why? Do you think someone at the home is involved in her abduction?"

Macy shook her head. "No, nothing like that. Her friend Tess Madden is a resident there. Cornelia had said she didn't have any family or friends in Bolton, so I'm a little surprised she didn't mention it."

"Perhaps she passed away?"

"She's nearly ninety-five, so it's a definite possibility, but if Tess is still there she may have heard from Cornelia in the last couple of days so we'd better follow up. Any news on the home where Chad dropped off the printout? Any ties with the house where we found the fuel cans?"

"Nothing so far." Alisa handed Macy a sheet of paper. "Here's what we've found out about the two owners. We can't find any overlap."

Macy thought she recognized the name of the woman who owned

the house on Addison Road. Macy turned her laptop back on and scrolled through the scanned documents she'd collected.

"There might be a link to Peter Granger after all," said Macy. "Remember that letter of complaint filed against him by a group of tenants at the Bridger Cultural Center? The woman who owns the Addison Road house is one of the signatories."

"There was nothing in her records that indicated she has offices there. According to her Web site, she works out of her home."

"She may not have updated her Web site recently. Happens all the time."

"Nice catch," said Alisa.

"Any word from the sketch artist? I wanted a likeness, not a Rembrandt."

"Apparently, Chad Nelson is very thorough. I'll go check."

Macy stood at the interview room's only window and stared out into the driving snow. A fast-moving weather front had forced Aiden and Luke to return to Helena a little earlier than planned. They'd come by the station to say good-bye. It was Sunday, so very few staff members were there to see Luke run laps around the empty desks. His buzz cut made him look like a madman. Macy had pressed her hand against the window glass when Luke gave her one last wave from where he was safely strapped up inside the cab of Aiden's SUV. Now they were heading north along Highway 287. Macy looked up at the restless sky and reminded herself that she could trust Aiden with Luke.

Chad Nelson and the sketch artist may not have produced a Rembrandt but, as far as Macy was concerned, the drawing was priceless. Alisa and Macy had both recognized Richard Nichols's likeness immediately.

Mr. Nichols had been sitting down with his wife and children for a late lunch when police officers burst into his house with one warrant for his arrest and another to search the premises. Investigators found Peter Granger's laptop and the printouts Chad had picked up at Print

Works along with Nichols's work computer and two other computers that were used by the family. Computer technicians and detectives were pouring over the hard drives and his cell phone.

Macy had said it was okay for the attending officer to remove Richard Nichols's handcuffs. He may have been guilty of a crime, but he was far from dangerous. He'd been in Minneapolis from Saturday evening until midday on Tuesday. He couldn't have murdered Peter Granger and Taylor Moore.

"Have you checked with the hotel and airline yet?" he asked. "I was nowhere near Bolton when that fire started."

Macy turned away from the window. He'd hindered the investigation and may have been indirectly responsible for the deaths of at least two individuals. The swagger that he'd thrown about when they'd first met in Peter Granger's office was gone. Richard Nichols made his living writing crime novels so he knew enough about the law to realize he was in a lot of trouble. The man who sat in front of her was scared. Macy pulled her chair out a little harder than was strictly necessary just to see him flinch.

"So much depends on how helpful you are, so I suggest you cooperate," said Macy.

He unfolded his hands, then folded them again. They were shaking.

"Of course. Anything," he said.

"Walk me through what happened on Saturday. I want to know how Peter Granger's laptop came to be in your possession," said Macy.

"Well, I'd had a late start—"

She held up a hand. "You've already wasted enough of my time. Please skip to the good part."

"I needed a few things for my trip so I stopped by the office at two o'clock on Saturday afternoon. It's on the way to the airport."

Macy felt a headache coming on. She reached for her Diet Coke.

"I know where your office is already," said Macy.

"Yes, sorry. Um . . . As I was passing by Peter's door I overheard a heated argument between himself and a woman."

"What was the argument about?"

"She was yelling something about all that she'd done for him. Said that he'd taken advantage of her once too many times."

"Did you recognize the voice?"

"I'm sorry, but no."

"Could it have been Peter Granger's wife?"

He shrugged. "I've never met her so I have no idea what she sounds like."

"Was the voice high in pitch or husky?" asked Macy.

"Definitely high in pitch. I got the impression she was very agitated."

"Older or younger female?"

"I couldn't say."

"Did you overhear anything that could help us identify who it was?" asked Macy.

"My phone rang while I was standing outside the door. They must have heard because it went quiet in the room after that. I slipped into my office down the hall and didn't think about it again until I was on my way out."

"Go on."

"I knocked on Peter's door as I was leaving, but it wasn't closed properly so it swung inward. I called Peter's name a couple of times and received no answer. The room was empty."

"Other than it being empty, was there anything else that struck you as odd?"

"He'd left his laptop out in plain sight, which was strange because the door wasn't properly locked."

"What about the state of the room?"

"It was a bit of a mess. The cabinet doors were open and a bunch of files were spread out on the floor. There was some packing tape wadded up on the desk. I think the roll might have been on the floor. The chair wasn't at the desk where it should have been."

"Did you clean it up?"

"Aside from the laptop, I left everything where it was."

Macy pulled a photocopy from a file. Investigators had found a list of Peter Granger's accounts, usernames, and passwords in Richard's house. It was all anybody needed to break into Granger's computer and steal everything on the hard drive, on his remote servers, and in his bank accounts.

"That's not quite true. Do you recognize this list?" asked Macy.

"I'm sorry. Yes. I did remove that from the desk. It was in a file labeled ACCOUNTS AND PASSWORDS. It was almost too easy." He closed his eyes. "I know it was the stupidest thing I've ever done in my life, but I was just so curious about the crime novel he was writing. I couldn't help myself. I actually believed I'd gotten away with it."

"Not even close," said Macy. "So far you're one of the few people in this mess we can definitely charge with a crime."

"I didn't kill anyone."

"Maybe not, but if you'd reported what you saw in Peter's office to the police he might still be alive today." Macy paused. "You're a crime writer so I suppose you're always imagining what a crime scene looks like, and yet you failed to recognize one when you walked into Peter Granger's office."

"I couldn't have known."

"At the time perhaps not, but you must have known Peter Granger's laptop was valuable to the investigation. Instead of turning it in you had the audacity to download files from Peter Granger's server."

"I'm sorry."

"Were you going to try to pass off his work as your own?"

"No, absolutely not. I'd never do that."

"Are you absolutely sure you've told me everything you know?"

Richard Nichols nodded slowly. He was in tears. "I really am sorry."

"So am I," said Macy. "So am I."

Richard Nichols was escorted to a jail cell, leaving Macy alone for the first time since Friday morning. She sat down at the table where she'd conducted his interview and made a few notes. In her head she was ticking off a roster of possible suspects one by one. So far no one on her list was anywhere near Peter Granger's office when Richard Nichols over-heard him having an argument with a woman.

Hannah Granger had been over a hundred miles away buying gro-ceries at a supermarket near her cabin. The store's clerk and a receipt proved her innocence. Jessica Reynolds was cycling with a team she trained with on Saturdays. Grace Adams, Lara Newcomb, and Clare Stokes were attending a roller derby match between the Bolton Bandits and the Runaway Brides. Pictures of the trio were all over their social media accounts.

That left Taylor Moore. Contrary to what she'd told her boyfriend, she was at home in Bolton Thursday and Friday night, but at some point on Saturday she'd made her way to Peter Granger's house. The police had since found her car parked around the corner. Whether she'd gone to the Bridger Cultural Center was anyone's guess. It was a Saturday, so not many people were in the building when the meeting took place. Police would be interviewing tenants, but that would take time.

The computer techs had been able to hack into Taylor's online e-mail account. She'd sent her last e-mail on Saturday morning. It was to a company in Chicago that had offered her a job six months earlier. She'd wanted them to reconsider her application. Taylor didn't sound desper-ate. She was someone who was making plans for her future.

And then there were the missing paintings. They didn't just walk away. Someone stole them. Taylor couldn't have done that. The coroner figured she died as early as Saturday evening.

Macy put her head on the table's clammy surface and stared at the video camera. A few rooms away, several detectives were going through the Polaroids. There were a lot of women who had good reason to hate Peter Granger, but it might take years to track them all down and Macy needed answers now. Cornelia Hart was missing and Macy had no idea where to begin her search.

Macy went in search of the computer techs. They'd had Peter Grang-er's laptop for two hours. She was hoping they'd found something.

20

Sunday

Peter Granger only had one appointment on the Saturday he'd dropped out of sight. He was meeting with Cornelia Hart in his office at one o'clock. He'd made a few helpful notes in his calendar. One referred to the confidentiality clause in her employment contract. He would need to remind her that the clause wasn't only restricted to the time she was employed. The other note he'd made was in regard to a severance payment. He'd put down a range of offers. He'd start with the lowest and work from there. He also reminded himself to be firm, noting that *she was going to take it hard*.

Macy thanked the computer technician and picked up her phone. Hannah Granger answered on the first ring.

"Mrs. Granger," she said. "I need to ask you a few questions about Cornelia Hart. Is this a good time?"

"Have you found her?"

"We haven't been able to locate her, but we've released her photo to the press and a statewide alert has been issued. Believe me, we are looking."

Macy waved Ryan into her office. She'd gotten hold of him just as a waitress was serving him his dinner. He dropped a takeout box on Macy's desk before slumping down in the only other chair, from where he'd kept a steady glare going through the duration of her phone call.

"I'm actually calling about some information we found on your husband's laptop," said Macy.

"I thought it was destroyed in the fire. Where was it all this time?"

"In turns out a fellow tenant at the Bridger Cultural Center stole it. He's since been cleared of involvement in your husband's murder but will be charged with theft and obstruction. Your husband had an appointment with Cornelia listed in his calendar for this past Saturday. He was planning on terminating her employment. Did you know anything about this?"

"Sort of. I'd been pressing him to let her go for the past year but he'd always resisted."

"Why did you want to fire her?"

"It wasn't just that she was expensive, she'd also become a little too familiar. Don't get me wrong; Cornelia has been a brilliant personal assistant. I'd recommend her to anyone, but she'd begun to act like one of the family. It was kind of like having a mother-in-law come to stay. She meddled."

"Did your husband mention the meeting he was having with her?" asked Macy.

"No, not a thing. To tell you the truth, I'm a little surprised. The last time we discussed it he was adamant that she stay on."

"Maybe your conversation with him on Saturday morning changed his mind. A divorce was going to be expensive."

Snow was falling heavily. Visibility was poor so Macy had to slow down several times on the drive over to Cornelia's apartment complex. She sliced through the crime-scene tape sealing Cornelia's front door and unlocked a newly installed dead bolt. She and Ryan shook off the snow that had accumulated on their hats and jackets before going inside. They trailed through the condominium, turning on the lights as they went. The entire place had been dusted for fingerprints. So far they'd only been able to find Cornelia's.

"Okay, you've dragged me back here. What do you need to know?" asked Ryan.

"I have a theory about what went on here. I need you to tell me if it's possible," said Macy.

Macy went over to the table where Cornelia's framed photos had all been so carefully arranged the day Macy had come to interview her. Everything that wasn't bagged as evidence was left the way it was found. She sifted through the overturned frames. She looked under the table and sofa.

Ryan was hovering near the sliding glass doors. He was being so quiet she almost forgot he was there. His voice made her jump.

"It would help if you told me what you are looking for," said Ryan.

"A small oval-shaped silver frame with a photo of Cornelia holding her daughter."

"I don't think anything like that was bagged as evidence. It should be here."

Macy said, "I can't find it. It's not where it was last Thursday when I came to interview Cornelia."

"It's a two-bedroom condo. She could have moved it. What's so special about it?"

"Cornelia's daughter died when she was two. According to her ex-husband, Cornelia had a difficult time parting with anything that reminded her of Daisy."

"I guess that explains the ceramic cookie jar she's using as an urn."

"You found it?"

"It's upstairs in the bedroom."

"Did you check whether there were ashes inside?" asked Macy

"Of course I checked."

"Is it possible to tell if they're not human?"

"Is this the part where you tell me your theory and I start counting the holes?" asked Ryan.

256

"We're getting there. Tell me if it's possible."

"Absolutely. Cremated human remains have unique elemental compositions."

Macy stood in front of the wood-burning stove. There'd been a hot fire blazing the day she'd come to speak to Cornelia. Macy opened the glass door and peeked inside. Macy was pretty sure Cornelia Hart had been burning books. Something told her that Peter Granger was probably the man who had written them.

"I think we should have a look at what's inside that cookie jar. I need to know if they're really Daisy's ashes."

"I'm not doing anything until you tell me about this theory of yours."

"Cornelia may have faked her assault and abduction. I'm certain she was the person Richard Nichols overheard arguing with Peter on Saturday. She was yelling about how he'd taken advantage of her one too many times, which fits what I know about their relationship. She must have been livid when she found out she was being fired. I'm guessing that she pulled a gun on him at some point, which is how she could control him. She's not a registered owner, but getting one illegally isn't all that difficult."

"Okay," he said. "Go on."

"Evidence suggests that he'd been taped to his chair. Perhaps he'd urinated he was so frightened. Things have gotten out of hand and she's suddenly in a hurry. She bundles him off to her car, thinking she'll come back to clean up later. She accidentally leaves the door ajar."

"Enter Richard Nichols."

"Precisely. Cornelia takes Peter to his house on Madison Road and at some point Taylor Moore stumbles in on them. Cornelia kills her and makes arrangements to set the fire, but she hesitates. If she wants to get away with this she really needs to get rid of Hannah as well, which is why she sends the texts from Peter's phone. Maybe Cornelia assumes Hannah knows that Peter was going to fire her, or that it was Hannah's idea in the first place. Either way her plans are on hold. Halloween provides an opportunity she doesn't feel she can pass on. Someone is setting fires around Bolton so she acts fast. The paintings have already been removed from the house and Peter and Taylor are both dead. She douses the house, stashes the fuel cans, lights the match, and leaves."

"I thought you said earlier that Cornelia had an alibi for Monday evening."

"Her alibi is a ninety-five-year-old woman named Tess Madden," said Macy.

"I have a ninety-five-year-old uncle who smokes a pack a day and cheats at golf. Your problem is?"

"Tess is Cornelia's much-loved friend. Someone she saw as a second mother. Tess is absolutely devoted to Cornelia. She may have lied to protect her."

"There's devotion and then there's perjury. It's a big jump."

"Cornelia has been looking after Tess for years. Plus she's ninety-five. She had nothing to lose by lying to the police when they checked Cornelia's alibi."

"And what about the crime scene we're standing in right now? Something happened here."

"Cornelia was a critical care nurse for twenty years. A sixteen-gauge needle and some tubing and she'd have enough blood to stage this. All we have is what appears to have seeped through a carpet as she was dragged away—a half a pint would have been more than enough."

"The shoe prints are a size eleven."

"She puts on some men's shoes and walks around the condo a bit. Not exactly sophisticated. You didn't find any trace in the footprints, which means they could have been straight out of the box. The thing I keep going back to is when Cornelia's body could have actually been moved. A patrol officer stopped by the apartment on Saturday morning. He went around the side just like I did, but the back door was shut and the curtains were closed, which means that if this really was a serious assault, Cornelia would have had to have been dragged out of here in broad daylight on Saturday. That would have taken some nerve. The sales office was open and is only five hundred yards away."

"Did they see anything?"

"Apparently there was a minivan parked nearby for most of Friday and Saturday. She only noticed it when it drove into the complex on Friday because she thought it was a potential buyer and sales have been slow. She couldn't make out who the driver was."

"Let's have a look at that cookie jar," said Ryan. "If you're right about that, I'll believe everything you're saying."

"Won't that take time?"

"Give me five minutes to do a preliminary examination here. The answer may be very obvious. If it's paper there should be visible fibers, while cremated remains normally have the consistency of coarse sand."

Ryan had positioned one of the spotlights the crime-scene techs had left in the house so it was shining directly onto the dining room table, where he'd placed some sterile plastic sheeting and a petri dish. He carefully removed the cookie jar's lid.

"This feels wrong," said Macy.

"Do you want answers or not?"

"You're not just going to dump them out on the table?"

"No, I'm going to scoop out a small sample. I'll use a magnifying lens to look at it. I've got a microscope in my van if we need to take a closer look."

"Shouldn't we say a prayer or something?"

Ryan ignored her. He placed the cookie jar's lid to the side and turned on his headlamp. Ryan used a spatula to scoop some of the contents into the petri dish. He peered at it with his magnifying glass for a few seconds. He switched off his headlamp.

"These aren't human remains," said Ryan.

"Are you absolutely sure?"

Ryan handed Macy the magnifying glass. "Have a look for yourself."

"Fuck, I can actually see bits of lettering."

"Still feel like praying?" asked Ryan.

"Cornelia Hart fooled everyone."

"Not quite everyone. You figured it out."

"She could be anywhere by now." Macy checked the time. It was coming up on nine o'clock. "I need to get over to the nursing home where her friend is a patient. I'm pretty sure it's on this end of town."

"You'd better get going. The roads may not be passable for much longer."

The receptionist at the Norwood Pines Home for the Elderly was pacing the small area behind her desk with a telephone pressed to her ear. She took a long look at Macy's detective badge before returning her attention to the person she'd been speaking to.

"That was fast. A police officer has already arrived." The receptionist pulled her hair back from her face. Beads of perspiration had formed along the bridge of her nose. "It's a Detective Macy Greeley," she said. "Yes, she's standing—"

Macy interrupted her. "I'm here to see Tess Manning. I know it's late but it's important I speak to her immediately."

The receptionist put her hand over the phone's mouthpiece.

"Tess Manning was found dead in her room. Isn't that why you're here?"

They stared at each other.

"When did this happen?" asked Macy.

"Just now. Someone broke in. There's glass . . ."

A heavyset nurse came barreling down the hallway waving her arms. She was red-faced and breathing hard. According to the nametag, her name was JOYCE.

"I just saw a car driving out of the parking lot. It was Cornelia . . ."

Macy held up her detective badge.

"Joyce," said Macy. "This is important. What did the car look like?"

Joyce took a big gulp of air. "It was minivan. Dark color. Blue I think."

Macy's cell phone rang. Brad had just got word that she was already at the care home. Macy spoke as she ran from the building.

"Brad, we've got to move fast. Cornelia Hart was just spotted driving away from Norwood Pines in a dark blue minivan. I'm heading after her. You need to set up roadblocks on Route 90."

The weather had worsened. It was difficult to see anything through the heavily falling snow. Macy walked a few paces in each direction before finally stopping so she could get her bearings. She took out her car keys and pressed the fob that unlocked the SUV's doors. She ran toward the flashing headlights.

"That doesn't make any sense," said Brad. "Cornelia Hart is missing, presumed dead."

"She staged the whole thing and if we don't move fast she's going to get away."

Macy climbed behind the steering wheel and started the car. The big engine rumbled to life.

"I'll arrange the roadblocks and send assistance. Anything else?"

Macy almost laughed. "Don't suppose you can do something about the weather," she said.

"Sorry, you're on your own on that front."

Macy tucked the phone in her pocket and turned on the sirens. Cornelia had a head start but the road back down to Route 90 was steep and had several hairpin turns. Snow was falling heavily throughout the valley. In this weather there were only a handful of roads out of Bolton that would be passable in a minivan and Route 90 was one of them. If the police set up roadblocks in time they might be able to keep Cornelia Hart from leaving town.

Snowflakes glowed like paper lanterns in the glare of Macy's headlights. The town of Bolton was no longer visible in the distance. The powder-dry snow swirled in eddies across the slick surface as sixty-mile-an-hour gusts of wind smacked hard against Macy's big-four by-four SUV. Keeping it on the road was proving to be a struggle.

Macy sat as far forward in the driver's seat as she dared and peered over the steering wheel. Another vehicle had left faint impressions in the freshly fallen snow. She was hoping it was the minivan. She took the first switchback a little too fast and her vehicle's back end started to go into a slide. She turned into the direction of the skid and slowed down. She was no good to anyone if she ended up in a ditch.

After the third switchback the road straightened out. It was now a five-mile stretch of relatively flat terrain before the road intersected Route 90. Nothing was visible outside of the headlight's arc. She pressed her foot down on the accelerator and drove as fast as she dared.

At first the twin pinpricks of red taillights were barely visible, but it wasn't long before Macy caught up with the minivan. She flashed her high beams several times but Cornelia wouldn't pull over to the side.

Macy risked a quick glance at the speedometer. They were travelling at nearly seventy miles an hour. The minivan was starting to fishtail on its narrow wheels and soft suspension. It soon lost traction and went into a skid, its back end whipping around until it was sideways in the middle of the road. Macy veered to the right to avoid broadsiding it but clipped its front bumper as she hurdled past. There was a loud crunch, then silence. In the rearview mirror Macy watched as the minivan spun out of sight.

Macy came to a stop and reversed until she was parallel to where the minivan had crashed into a tree that overlooked a shallow drainage ditch. Macy looked toward the southeast. The emergency lights on the horizon were growing brighter. She put a call into dispatch and requested an ambulance before stepping out into the storm.

Macy struggled to stay upright on the icy surface and ended up sliding down the side of the shallow drainage ditch on her bottom. She shined a flashlight into the minivan's dark interior. Cornelia Hart was staring straight ahead with her hands gripping tight to the steering wheel. A fallen tree branch blocked the door so Macy couldn't get it open. She knocked on the window with the butt of her gun.

"Cornelia, are you okay in there?"

Cornelia started sobbing. She rested her head against the steering wheel. Macy removed her firearm from its holster.

"I want you to roll down the window," said Macy. "No sudden movements."

Cornelia did as directed.

"Keep your hands back on the steering wheel where I can see them," ordered Macy. "You got a firearm in there?"

Cornelia took one hand off the steering wheel and gestured to the glove compartment.

"I told you to keep your hands on the steering wheel," said Macy.

"There's a handgun in the glove compartment," said Cornelia.

Macy removed a pair of handcuffs from her belt. "Anything else?"

"No, ma'am."

Macy reached in and secured Cornelia's wrists with the handcuffs before pulling the key from the ignition. Two patrol cars drove up just as she started to inform Cornelia of her rights.

It was freezing in Tess Manning's room. A bitter wind lifted the drapes and rattled the sliding glass doors. The elderly woman appeared to be sleeping. Ryan stepped away from her body.

"She hasn't been dead long. A little over an hour, tops."

"There's a pillow on the floor. Do you think she was asphyxiated?" asked Macy.

"I believe that is the case, but we will have to do tests to be absolutely sure. According to staff, Tess has been despondent since Thursday afternoon. She was refusing to eat."

"I bet Cornelia told her she was leaving."

"I imagine Cornelia was getting a little jumpy. Hiding twenty million dollars' worth of paintings in a minivan is a tall order for anyone," he said.

"She also knew someone out there had stolen Peter's laptop. She had no choice but to run."

Macy checked her phone but there wasn't anything new from the team at the accident site. In the morning, they'd interview Cornelia Hart formally, but as far as Macy was concerned she'd already gotten a confession. The whole story came out while they'd waited for rescue workers to remove Cornelia from the vehicle.

"Cornelia murdered someone she saw as her mother. How could she do that?" asked Macy.

Ryan was pouring over Tess Manning's medical records.

"You'll have to ask Cornelia to be sure, but my best guess is that it was a last act of mercy. According to these charts, Tess Manning was in the final stages of bone cancer. She would have been in a lot of pain."

Macy inspected the sliding glass doors. The glass was broken from the outside and the lock forced. Fresh snow was thick on the ground. Any tracks Cornelia may have left were gone.

"Coming back to Bolton was very risky. Until this evening Cornelia had a good head start on us."

Ryan handed Macy an evidence bag containing a cell phone. "I found this earlier. It looks like they were keeping in touch."

The last message Tess received was still on the screen.

**DON'T WORRY. I'M COMING BACK FOR YOU.
I WON'T LET YOU DOWN THIS TIME.**

Macy checked the timing on the message. It had been sent six hours earlier. All the other texts had been erased.

"Tess lied when she said Cornelia was here on the night of the fire. These sliding glass doors open out onto a common area and the parking lot is what? Another hundred yards away? It was late. Cornelia could have come and gone without anyone noticing."

"How come we didn't know Tess Manning and Cornelia Hart were close?" asked Ryan.

"Cornelia isn't listed as Tess Manning's next of kin, and though Cornelia is down as an emergency contact for Tess, she's also the emergency contact for several other patients here. It was only by chance that Cornelia's ex-husband mentioned Tess by name."

"Cornelia almost got away with it."

"She's the type of woman who would have blended in most anywhere. We would have struggled to find her." Macy had been going over all her past interactions with Cornelia, but there'd never been anything suspicious in the woman's behavior. "I never once suspected her," she said.

"Did she tell you what happened at Peter's house?"

"Not in great detail, but I think I got the gist of it. She'd only meant to make him listen but he wouldn't even look her in the eye. At some point she lost it and pulled a gun. Once that happened, things quickly spiraled out of control."

"Why did she have a gun with her in the first place?"

"She says it was in her car. Instead of going home after the meeting she came back to his office, held him at gunpoint, and taped him to the chair so he'd listen to her."

"I guess that's one approach to mindfulness. Doesn't explain how his and Taylor Moore's bodies ended up in the same bed," said Ryan.

"I admit there are still a few holes in the story. I still don't know how she managed to move Peter from his office to the house on Madison without being seen. She claims he tried to get away and she hit him on the head with a cast-iron frying pan," said Macy.

"That would explain why his skull was caved in. And Taylor?"

"She showed up when Cornelia was trying to drag his body upstairs. There was a struggle and Taylor fell from the first-floor landing."

"It's like something out of a dark comedy," said Ryan.

"Except nobody is laughing."

"A lot of people will see Cornelia as a hero once the truth about Peter Granger comes out."

Macy suppressed a yawn. "She's not a hero, she's a murderer. I have no patience and even less sympathy."

He checked the time. "It's ten thirty and my team is stuck in a snowdrift somewhere. Do you want to help me process this mess so we can go get a drink?"

She held up her gloved hands. "I'm all yours. Tell me where to start."

21

Tuesday

The snowbound campus sparkled beneath late-afternoon sunshine that filtered through the gallery's north-facing windows. The turn-out for the student art show was unusually high. For the most part the crowd was comprised of faculty members, parents, and students, but several of Grace's friends had shown up, including her colleagues from the café. Steve was noticeably absent but he'd called to wish her luck. The strange group of artists she'd met a few nights earlier was also in attendance. The man with the beard and mustache had reintroduced himself and the rest of the group before handing her a silver flask.

"It's gin," he'd explained. "You may need it for later."

There'd been a note attached.

Congratulations from your new best friend. Love, Charlie

Grace was too preoccupied to enjoy the praise her work was receiving. Macy Greeley was standing a few feet away and her presence in the gallery was making Grace nervous. Each time Macy took a step forward, Grace took a step back. It was as if they were having a secret dance, but then the music stopped and the detective remained rooted

to one spot. The painting that caught Macy's eye was of a man crucified in the tree branches arching above the Flathead River.

"There is a sketch of this same scene hanging in Peter Granger's office," said Macy.

Macy's voice seemed to come out of nowhere. For a second Grace
thought she might have been imagining things. She felt obliged to check.
They faced each other for the first time.

"Pardon?" said Grace.

Macy kept her voice low. "There is a sketch of this same scene hanging in Peter Granger's office."

"I never gave . . ." Grace stopped speaking when she realized what
must have happened. She felt as if she might be sick. Her voice faded.
"It must have been Lara."

Macy reached out and touched Grace's sleeve. "Why am I not surprised? Have you heard from her?"

"Not since she left on Sunday."

"It's probably for the best. She took advantage of you."

"Only because I let her. Nothing will change unless I do," said Grace.

"I'm sorry if this sounds harsh, but you don't get points for realizing
you have an issue. You've got to do the hard work now. It's up to you to
make sure it doesn't happen again."

"That may be so, but I'm not giving up on Lara yet completely. She
told me she was going to work hard to regain my trust. I want to believe
it's true."

"Just promise me you'll be careful," said Macy.

Grace felt oddly exposed when she was in Macy's company. Everyone else in her life would happily settle for a quick reinvention, but Macy
had seen the raw material. She was the only one left who really knew
how far Grace still had to go.

"A year ago I wouldn't have lasted in a situation like this for more
than five minutes, so I guess that's something." Grace closed her eyes
for a few seconds. "That's one good thing Lara did. She showed me how
to be brave."

"Grace, you were always brave." Macy focused in on the next painting.

"This is a beautiful portrait of your aunt. She would have been proud of you."

Grace looked down at the floor. She'd promised herself that she wouldn't cry. Macy was speaking so softly Grace had to lean in.

"I had a look at the book Peter was writing about you. It will never see the light of day, but I still think you should read it."

"That man stole so much from me."

Macy looked confused. "Are you still talking about the sketch?" she asked.

"No, I'm talking about something far more intangible . . . like my soul. He pinned it down in a book just like he pinned all those girls down in photographs."

"They weren't girls, they were women."

Grace shook her head. "He'd stripped them of their clothing, identity, and voice. They couldn't be women on those terms. Women would have been too much of a challenge for him. Peter Granger, Jordan Beech, and those men back in Collier . . . they're all the same. They're cowards."

"I'd like to think there are good men out there too," said Macy.

"You don't sound so sure. Are you trying to convince yourself or me?"

"Both of us. It's been a long time, but I'm starting to feel hopeful."

Macy stood in front of the last painting. A mother and her newborn baby were propped up in a hospital bed. Grace held her breath the entire time Macy stared at it. Macy read the title aloud.

"*Madonna and Child.*"

"I hope you're not angry," said Grace.

"Far from it. I'm actually flattered, but I think you may have me all wrong. I'm many things, but a mother figure isn't one of them."

"I saw how you were with your son."

"When was this?"

"In the park last Saturday. I was walking my dog."

"A couple hours a weekend doesn't count. I'm away all the time for work. Luke is young now, but someday he's going to want to know why I wasn't around more."

"I grew up without a mother. In my eyes Luke is spoiled."

Macy half smiled. "When the day comes, I'll be sure to tell him that."

"Detective Greeley, why are you really here?"

Macy was quiet for a long while. When she spoke she sounded a little sad.

"I suppose I needed to see that you're going to be okay, that something good came out of that mess that happened in Collier. When I interviewed you the other day I got the impression that you were struggling, yet here you are. As I've walked around I've overheard what people are saying about your work and about you and it's all good. You've made this amazing new life for yourself. I don't get to see many positive outcomes in my line of work. I guess I needed to feel hopeful."

Macy held out her hand and Grace took hold of it.

"Grace, you're incredibly talented. You should feel very proud of yourself."

Grace didn't know what to say. She felt Macy's fingers slip away. Macy was leaving. There was a tap on her shoulder and Grace turned to see Clare. She wasn't wearing a hat. Her head was clean-shaven. They held each other for a long time. When Grace looked again Macy was gone.

22

Macy sat on a barstool, scrolling through her messages. The Gallatin Bar & Grill was getting noisier as the evening went on. Any local who could get the time off work had been skiing in powder for the past three days, so there was a lot goodwill in the air. It was Macy's last night in Bolton. In the morning she'd be returning to Helena. She looked up from her phone and scanned the crowd. Alisa was almost unrecognizable out of uniform, and it wasn't just the high-heeled boots and miniskirt. Her hair and makeup were done on a level Macy hadn't expected. Alisa moved through the room completely unaware of the attention she was receiving. Macy removed her bag from the barstool she'd been saving and smiled.

"Wow. You look gorgeous," said Macy.

Alisa touched her hair gently. "It's going to take some getting used to. My girlfriends were fed up with me dressing like a boy so they staged an intervention."

"It's quite a transformation." Macy waved the bartender over. "I'm having a glass of red. What can I get you?"

Alisa removed her wallet from her handbag but Macy shook her head.

"Tonight is on me. Pick your poison."

"You don't have to . . ."

"I insist. Just don't order the Dom Perignon."

Alisa gave her a blank look. "I don't know even know what that is."

The bartender approached to take Alisa's order but then suggested a full bottle when Alisa also said she was drinking red wine. Macy asked to see the wine menu.

"I thought Ryan was joining us," said Alisa.

"He had to get back to Helena. He has a court appearance in the morning."

"You guys never seem to stop working."

"Sometimes it seems that way. Cornelia Hart has confessed to all charges, which makes all our lives a lot easier. Not that it matters. I'm sure the state will find another way for me to spend my time."

"Cornelia Hart is the world's most unlikely villain."

"It really goes to show that all it takes is one bad decision for your life to spiral out of control," said Macy.

"She's not very physically fit. I'm surprised she managed."

"I imagine desperation played a big part."

"If Hannah Granger hadn't been stuck at the cabin, she'd be dead too," said Alisa.

"Small mercies. Cornelia only came back to Bolton because Tess begged her."

"I'm not sure I believe that."

"It's true. We have the messages Tess sent to Cornelia's phone. She wanted to die. It was the deal they made when Tess provided an alibi, but Cornelia left town without honoring her end of the bargain."

"That's crazy."

Macy took a long drink of wine before turning her attention to the wine menu that had been placed in front of her.

"I had a good look at Peter Granger's so-called crime novel. It's nearly one-hundred-twenty-thousand-words long and he couldn't have published it without Grace's permission, yet he kept on writing. Also crazy," said Macy.

"Maybe he was confident she'd change her mind."

"That confidence was misplaced. Grace was never going to agree to it."

"I don't know what to do with his books. It feels wrong to destroy them, but I can't give them to charity either."

"Good thing I just have the one then," said Macy.

Macy sat up a little taller in the barstool. Her lower back was killing her. They had a table reserved for eight o'clock. She checked the time. It was only half past seven.

"It will be interesting to see how many women we're able to identify in those Polaroids. Brad told me they were going to appeal directly to the public," said Alisa.

"I'm not sure I agree with that strategy. You're going to get an avalanche of phone calls, most of them useless."

"Maybe he should . . ."

Alisa stopped speaking. She craned her neck. Macy followed her gaze. Brad Hastings and a woman Macy assumed was his wife were approaching the bar. They were arm in arm and laughing. He pulled his wife close and kissed her on the cheek. He spotted Macy and Alisa and his smile faded for the briefest of moments. He rearranged his features. The smile was back, but there was caution in his eyes. His wife placed her hands protectively across her belly. It looked like she was in her second trimester of pregnancy. The silence went on for a few beats too long. Macy took charge of the introductions.

"Brad, this is a wonderful surprise. This must be your wife."

Brad's wife held out a hand. It was warm and powder dry. "Sasha," she said. "It's a real pleasure to meet you. We met your son Luke when we had dinner with Aiden on Saturday. Such a sweetheart." Sasha looked at Alisa properly for the first time. There was the slightest hesitation before she smiled. "Alisa, I'm so used to seeing you in uniform I almost didn't recognize you."

Macy couldn't keep her eyes off Brad. His eyes were darting from Alisa to his wife. If he kept it up he'd go cross-eyed.

Alisa blushed. "You're looking well. . . . Pregnancy suits you."

Sasha's hands had migrated back to her bump. "We couldn't be happier."

Brad cleared his throat. "I should go see about our table."

Sasha put a hand on his arm. "Don't be silly. Our reservation isn't until eight. Let's stay and chat for a while. Another month and I won't be able to stand in a bar without people giving me the evil eye."

Macy checked the time. "Actually, we're the ones that need to make a move. We have a table booked at the North Street Bistro."

Sasha nodded approvingly. "You're so lucky to get a reservation there. I hear the food is wonderful."

The bartender came over to take Macy's order. She leaned in close so she could talk to him without the others overhearing. Macy slipped off her barstool and grabbed her coat. Alisa was already bundled up and ready to bolt. She, Brad, and Sasha were trying but failing to make small talk.

Macy wished Brad and his wife a good evening before taking Alisa by the arm and steering her to the door. It was a clear evening and the wind was still. The temperatures outside had plummeted.

"Come on," said Macy. "If I remember correctly, there's a really good Chinese restaurant near campus."

Alisa stopped in her tracks. "How did you know about me and Brad?"

"I saw him leaving the grocery store on Friday night. I assume the wine and chocolates were for you."

"I feel so ashamed."

"I've done pretty much the same thing so I'm in no position to judge, but other people will. You might think you're being careful, but it will come out eventually and we both know who will get the blame." Macy pointed to the restaurant they'd just left. "I'm pretty sure Sasha knows something is going on. She just doesn't have any proof yet. This is only going to get worse."

"I don't know what to do."

"You're going to have to end it."

"But I love him."

"It doesn't matter. You saw how they were together. He isn't going to leave his wife for you." Macy tilted her head so she could look Alisa in the eye. "I've been exactly where you're standing, but I wasn't lucky enough to have someone throw me a lifeline. You can either drag this out for years or you can cut it off now. A few weeks of pain and you'll be over him. I promise."

"I don't see how that's possible when I see him every day."

"Which is why you're requesting an immediate transfer to the department of justice."

"Brad won't like that," said Alisa.

"Don't worry about what Brad likes or doesn't like. He lost all authority over you the second he crossed the line. This is your life, Alisa. I just need to know if you're willing to make a change. You've got good instincts and I'm in no doubt you'll be a brilliant investigator someday, but if you stay here in Bolton, you'll be miserable. If you want this to happen, I'll take care of the details. If necessary I'll even have a quiet word with Brad."

Alisa looked back at the restaurant again. She wasn't crying yet but she looked like she might.

"Alisa, you really have nothing to lose."

"I think I need a drink," said Alisa.

"Is that your way of saying yes?"

"It is."

Macy took Alisa by the arm again.

"Is that dive bar on Temple still in business?" asked Macy.

"The owner keeps threatening to close it down but his regular customers won't let him."

"Sounds perfect, we'll start there."